THE BOOK
OF SKULLS

Robert Silverberg

The right of Robert Silverberg to be identified as
the author of this work has been
asserted by him in accordance with the
Copyright, Designs and Patents Act 1988.

This edition published in Great Britain in 1999 by
Millennium
An imprint of Victor Gollancz
Orion House, 5 Upper St Martin's Lane,
London WC2H 9EA

Second impression 2000

A CIP catalogue record for this book
is available from the British Library

ISBN 1 85798 914 7

Printed in Great Britain by
The Guernsey Press Co. Ltd, Guernsey, C.I.

THE BOOK
OF SKULLS

Also by Robert Silverberg

for Saul Diskin

one
elí

Coming into New York City from the north, off the New England Thruway, Oliver driving as usual. Tireless, relaxed, his window half open, long blond hair whipping in the chilly breeze. Timothy slouched beside him, asleep. The second day of our Easter vacation; the trees still bare, ugly driblets of blackened snow banked in dirty heaps by the roadside. In Arizona there wouldn't be any dead snow around. Ned sat next to me in the back seat, scribbling notes, filling up page after page of his ragged spiral-bound book with his left-handed scrawl. Demonic glitter in his dark little eyes. Our penny-ante pansy Dostoevsky. A truck roared up behind us in the left-hand lane, passed us, abruptly cut across into our lane. Hardly any clearance at all. We nearly got racked up. Oliver hit the brakes, cursing, really made them screech; we jolted forward in our seats. A moment later he swung us into the empty right-hand lane to avoid getting smashed by a car to our rear. Timothy woke up. "What the crap," he said. "Can't you let a guy get some sleep?"

"We almost got killed just then," Ned told him fiercely, leaning forward, spitting the words into Timothy's big pink ear. "How would that be for irony, eh? Four sterling young men heading west to win eternal life, wiped out by a truck driver on the New England Thruway. Our lithe young limbs scattered all over the embankment."

"Eternal life," Timothy said. Belching. Oliver laughed.

"It's a fifty-fifty chance," I observed, not for the first time. "An existential gamble. Two to live forever, two to die."

"Existential shit," Timothy said. "Man, you amaze me, Eli. How you do that existential number with a straight face. You really *believe*, don't you?"

"Don't you?"

"In the Book of Skulls? In your Arizona Shangrila?"

"If you don't believe, why are you going with us?"

"Because it's warm in Arizona in March." Using on me the airy, casual, John-O'Hara-country-club-*goy* tone that he handled so well, that I despised so much. Eight generations of the best blue chips standing behind him. "I can use a change of scenery, man."

"That's all?" I asked. "That's the entire depth of your philosophical and emotional commitment to this trip, Timothy? You're putting me on. God knows why you feel you have to act blasé and cool even when something like this is involved. That Main Line drawl of yours. The aristocratic implication that commitment, any sort of commitment, is somehow grubby and unseemly, that it—"

"Please don't harangue me now," Timothy said. "I'm not in the mood for ethnic analysis. Rather weary, in fact." He said it politely, disengaging from the conversation with the tiresomely intense Jewboy in his most amiably Waspish way. I hated Timothy worst of all when he started flaunting his genes at me, telling me with his easy upper-class inflections that his ancestors had founded this great country while mine were digging for potatoes in the forests of Lithuania. He said, "I'm going to go back to sleep." To Oliver he said, "Watch the fucking road a little better, will you? And wake me up when we get to Sixty-seventh Street." A subtle change in his voice now that he was no longer talking to me—to that complex and irritating member of an alien, repugnant, but perhaps superior species. Now he was the country squire addressing the simple farm boy, a relationship free of intricacies. Not that Oliver was all that simple, of course. But that was Timothy's existential image of him, and the image functioned to define their relationship regardless of the realities. Timothy yawned and flaked out again. Oliver stomped the gas hard and sent us shooting forward to catch up with the truck that had caused the trouble. He passed it, changed lanes, and took up a position just in front of it, daring the truckie to play games a second time. Uneasily I glanced back; the truck, a red and green monster, was nibbling at our rear bumper. High above us loomed the face of the driver, glowering, sullen, rigid: jowly stubbled cheeks, cold slitted eyes, clamped lips. He'd run us off the road if he could. Vibrations of hatred rolling out of him. Hating us for being young, for being good-looking (me! good-looking!), for having the leisure and *gelt* to go to college and have useless things stuffed into our skulls. The know-nothing perched up there, the flag-waver. Flat head under his greasy cloth cap. More patriotic, more moral, than us, a hardworking American. Feeling sorry for himself because he was stuck behind four kids on a lark. I wanted to ask Oliver to move over before he rammed us. But Oliver hung in the lane, keeping the needle at fifty, penning the truck. Oliver could be very stubborn.

We were entering New York City now, via some highway that cut across the Bronx. Unfamiliar territory for me. I am a Manhattan boy; I know only the subways. Can't even drive a car. Highways, autos, gas stations, toll-booths—artifacts out of a civilization with which I've had only the most peripheral contact. In high school, watching the kids from the suburbs pouring into the city on week-end dates, all of them driving, with golden-haired *shikses* next to them on the seat: not my world, not my world at all. Yet they were only sixteen, seventeen years old, the same as I. They seemed like demigods to me. They cruised the Strip from nine o'clock to half past one, then drove back to Larchmont, to Lawrence, to Upper Montclair, parking on some tranquil leafy street, scrambling with their dates into the back seat, white thighs flashing in the moonlight, the panties coming down, the zipper opening, the quick thrust, the grunts and groans. Whereas I was riding the subways, West Side I.R.T. That makes a difference in your sexual development. You can't ball a girl in the subway. What about doing it standing up in an elevator, rising to the fifteenth floor on Riverside Drive? What about making it on the tarry roof of an apartment house, 250 feet above West End Avenue, bulling your way to climax while pigeons strut around you, criticizing your technique and clucking about the pimple on your ass? It's another kind of life, growing up in Manhattan. Full of shortcomings and inconveniences that wreck your adolescence. Whereas the lanky lads with the cars can frolic in four-wheeled motels. Of course, we who put up with the urban drawbacks develop compensating complexities. We have richer, more interesting souls, force-fed by adversity. I always separate the drivers from the nondrivers in drawing up my categories of people. The Olivers and the Timothys on the one hand, the Elis on the other. By rights Ned belongs with me, among the nondrivers, the thinkers, the bookish introverted tormented deprived subway riders. But he has a driver's license. Yet one more example of his perverted nature.

Anyway, I was glad to be back in New York, even just passing through as we were, en route to the Golden West. This was my turf. Would be, once we got past the unfamiliar Bronx into Manhattan. The paperback bookstores, the frankfurter-and-papaya-juice stands, the museums, the art movies (we don't call them art movies in New York, but *they* do), the crowds. The texture, the density. Welcome to Kosher Country. A warming sight after months in captivity in the pastoral wilds of New England, stately trees, broad avenues, white Congregationalist churches, blue-eyed people. How good it was to escape from the Ivy League simplicities of our campus and breathe foul air again. A night in Manhattan; then westward. Toward the desert. Into the clutches of the Keepers of the Skulls. I thought of that embellished page in the old manuscript, the archaic lettering, the ornamental border with the eight grinning skulls (seven missing their lower jaws, yet they manage to grin), each in its little columned cubicle. Life eternal we offer thee. How unreal the whole immortality thing seemed to me now, with the jeweled cables of the George Washington Bridge gleaming far to the southwest, and the soaring bourgeois towers of Riverdale hemming us on the right, and the garlicky realities of Manhattan straight ahead. A moment of sudden doubt. This crazy hegira. We're fools to take it seriously, fools to invest so much as a dime of psychological capital in a freaky fantasy. Let's skip Arizona and drive to Florida instead, Fort Lauderdale, Daytona Beach. Think of all the willing suntanned nookie waiting there for the sophisticated northern lads to harvest. And, as had happened on other occasions, Ned seemed to be reading my thoughts. He threw me a sharp quizzical look and said softly, "Never to die. Far out! But can there be anything at all to it, really?"

two

#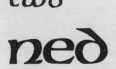

The fascinating part, the challenging part, what is for me the esthetically rewarding part, is that two of us must perish if the other two are to be exempted from mortality. Such are the terms offered by the Keepers of the Skulls, always assuming, first, that Eli's translation of the manuscript is accurate, and, second, that there's any substance to what he's told us. I think the translation must be correct—he's terribly precise in philological matters—but one must always allow for the possibility of a hoax, perhaps engineered by Eli himself. Or that it is all nonsense. Is Eli playing some baroque game with us? He's capable of anything, of course, a wily Hebrew, full of tricky ghetto lore, concocting an elaborate fiction so that he might inveigle three hapless *goyim* to their dooms, a ritual bloodbath in the desert. *Do the skinny one first, the gay one, thrust the blazing sword up his ungodly asshole!* More probably I'm giving Eli credit for more deviousness than he has, projecting into him some of my own feverish warped androgynous instability. He seems sincere, a nice Jewish boy. In any group of four candidates who present themselves for the Trial, one must submit voluntarily to death, and one must become the victim of the surviving two. *Sic dixit liber calvariarum.* The Book of Skulls so tells us. See, me spikka da Caesarish too! Two die, two live; a lovely balance, a four-cornered mandala. I tremble in the terrible tension between extinction and infinity. For Eli the philosopher this adventure is a dark version of Pascal's gamble, an existentialist all-or-nothing trip. For Ned the would-be artist it is an esthetic matter, a problem of form and fulfillment. Which of us shall meet what fate? Oliver with his ferocious midwestern hunger for life: he'll snatch at the flask of eternity, he'll *have* to, never for an instant admitting the possibility that he might be among the ones who must exit so that the others may live. And Timothy, naturally, will come out of Arizona intact and undying, cheerfully waving his platinum spoon. His kind is bred to prevail. How can he let himself die when he has his trust fund to look forward to? Imagine, interest compounding at 6 percent per annum for, say, 18 million years. He'll own the universe! Far out! So those two are our obvious candidates for immortality. Eli and I therefore must yield, willingly or otherwise. Quickly the remaining roles designate their players. Eli will be the one they kill, of course; the Jew is always the victim, isn't he? They'll honey him along, grateful to him for having found the gateway to life everlasting lying in the musty archives, and at the proper ritual moment, wham, they seize him and give it to him, a quick whiff of Cyklon-B. The final solution to the Eli problem. That leaves me to be the one who volunteers for self-immolation. The decision, says Eli, citing appropriate chapter and verse from the Book of Skulls, must be genuinely voluntary, arising out of a pure wish for self-sacrifice, or it will not release the proper vibrations. Very well, gentlemen, I'm at your service. Say the word and I'll do my far, far better thing. A pure wish, perhaps the first one I've ever had. Two conditions, however, two strings are attached. Timothy, you must dip into your Wall Street millions and subsidize a decent edition of my poems, nicely bound, good paper, with a critical foreword by someone who knows his stuff, Trilling, Auden, Lowell, someone of that caliber. If I die for you, Timothy, if I shed my blood that you may live forever, will you do that? And Oliver: I require a service from you as well, sir. The quid pro quo is a sine qua non, as Eli would say. On the last day of life I would have an hour in private with you, my dear and handsome friend. I wish to plough your virgin soil. Be mine at last, beloved Ol! I promise to be generous with the Vaseline. Your smooth glowing almost hairless body, your taut athletic buttocks, your sweet unviolated rosebud. For me, Oliver. For me, for me, for me, all for me. I'll give my life for you if you'll lend me your bum a single afternoon. Am I not romantic? Is your dilemma not a delicious one? Come across, Oliver, or else no deal. You will, too. You aren't any puritan, and you're a practical man, a me-firster. You'll see the advantages of surrender. You'd better. Humor the little faggot, Oliver. Or else no deal.

three
timothy

Eli takes all this much more seriously than the rest of us. I suppose that's fair; he was the one who found out about it and organized the whole operation. And anyway he's got the half-mystic quality, that smouldering Eastern European wildness, that permits a man to get worked up really big over something that in the last analysis you know is imaginary. I suppose it's a Jewish trait, tied in with the kabbala and whatnot. At least I think of it as a Jewish trait, along with high intelligence, physical cowardice, and a love of making money, but what the crap do I know about Jews, anyway? Look at us in this car. Oliver's got the highest intelligence, no doubt about that. Ned's the physical coward; you just look at him and he cringes. I'm the one with the money, although Christ knows I had nothing to do with the making of it. There are your so-called Jewish traits. And the mysticism? Is Eli a mystic? Maybe he just doesn't want to die. Is there anything so mystic about that?

No, not about that. But when it comes to *believing* that there's this cult of exiled Babylonian or Egyptian or whatever immortals living in the desert, *believing* that if you go to them and say the right words they'll confer the privilege of immortality on you—oh, lordy! Who could buy that? Eli can. Oliver too, maybe. Ned? No, not Ned. Ned doesn't believe in anything, not even himself. And not me. You bet your ass, not me.

Why am I going, then?

Like I told Eli: it's warmer in Arizona this time of year. And I like to travel. Also I think it might be an amusing experience, watching all this unfold, watching my roommates scrabbling around looking for their destiny on the mesas. Why go to college at all if not to have interesting experiences and increase your knowledge of human nature, along with having a good time? I didn't go there to learn astronomy and geology. But to watch other human beings making pricks of themselves—now, there's education, there's entertainment! As my father said when he sent me off as a freshman, after reminding me that I represented the eighth generation of male Winchesters to attend our grand old school, "Never forget one thing, Timothy: the proper study of mankind is man. Socrates said that three thousand years ago, and it's never lost its eternal truth." As a matter of fact it was Pope who said it in the eighteenth century, as I discovered in sophomore English, but let that pass. You learn by watching others, especially if you've forfeited your own chance to build character through adversity by having picked your great-great-great-grandparents a little too well. The old man should see me now, driving around with a queer, a Jew, and a farm boy. I suppose he'd approve, so long as I remember I'm better than they are.

Ned was the first one Eli told. I saw them huddling and whispering a lot. Ned was laughing. "Don't put me on, man," he kept saying, and Eli got red in the face. Ned and Eli are very close, I suppose because they're both scrawny and weak and belong to oppressed minorities. It's been clear from the beginning that in any grouping of the four of us, it's the two of them against Oliver and me. The two intellectuals versus the two jocks, to put it in the crudest way. The two queers against the two—well, no, Eli isn't queer, despite Uncle Clark who insists that *all* Jews are fundamentally homosexual whether they know it or not. But Eli *seems* queer, with his lisp and his way of walking. Seems queerer than Ned, as a matter of fact. Does Eli chase girls so hard because he wants to camouflage something? Anyway, Eli and Ned, shuffling papers and whispering. And then they brought Oliver into it. "Do you mind telling me," I asked, "what the crap you're discussing among yourselves?" I think they enjoyed excluding me, giving me a taste of what it's like to be a second-class citizen. Or maybe they just figured I'd laugh in their faces. But at last they broke it to me. Oliver serving as their ambassador. "What are you doing over Easter?" he asked.

"Bermuda, maybe. Florida. Nassau." Actually I hadn't thought about it much.

"What about Arizona?" he asked.

"What's there?"

He took a deep breath. "Eli was examining some rare manuscripts in the library," he said, looking sheepish and uneasy, "and came upon something called the Book of Skulls, which apparently has been here for fifty years and nobody's translated it, and he's done some further research now and he thinks—"

That the Keepers of the Skulls actually exist and will let us in on what they've got. Eli and Ned and Oliver are willing to go out there and look around, anyway. And I'm invited. Why? For my money? For my charm? Well, matter of fact, it's because candidates are accepted only in groups of four, and since we're all roommates anyway, it seemed logical that—

And so on. I said I would, for the hell of it. When Dad was my age, he went searching for uranium mines in the Belgian Congo. Didn't find them, but he had a ball. I'm entitled to some wild geese too. I'll go, I said. And put the whole matter out of my mind until after exams. It wasn't until later on that Eli filled me in on some of the rules of the game. Out of every four candidates, two at best get to live forever, and two have to die. A neat little touch of melodrama. He looked me straight in the eyes. "Now that you know the risks," he said, "you can back out if you like." Putting me on the spot, searching for the yellow streaks in the blue blood. I laughed at him. "Those aren't bad odds," I said.

four

ned

Quick impressions, before this trip changes us forever, for it will change us. Wednesday night the ? of March, approaching New York City.

TIMOTHY. Pink and gold. A two-inch layer of firm fat coating thick slabs of muscle. Big, massive, a fullback if he'd bothered to try. Blue Episcopalian eyes, always laughing at you. He puts you down with a friendly smile. The mannerisms of the American aristocracy. He wears a crew cut in *this* era: by way of telling the world that he's his own man. Goes out of his way to seem lazy and coarse. A big cat, a sleepy lion. Watch out. Lions are smarter than they look, and faster on their feet than their victims tend to think.

ELI. Black and white. Slender, fragile. Beady eyes. An inch taller than I am, but still short. Thin sensual lips, strong chin, curling mop of Assyrian ringlets. The skin so white, so white: he's never been in the sun. An hour after he's shaved he needs a shave. Dense mat of hair on chest and thighs; he'd look virile if he weren't so flimsy. He has bad luck with girls. I could get somewhere with him but he's not my type—too much like me. A general impression of vulnerability. Quick, clever mind, not as deep as he thinks it is, but no fool. Basically a medieval scholastic.

ME. Yellow and green. Agile little fairy with a core of clumsiness within his agility. Soft tangled golden brown hair standing up like a halo. Forehead high and getting higher all the time, damn it. You look like a figure out of Fra Angelico, two different girls said to me in a single week; I guess they're in the same art appreciation class. I have a definitely priestly look. So my mother always said; she envisaged me as a gentle monsignor comforting the heartsore. Sorry, Ma. The pope won't want my sort. Girls do; they know intuitively I'm gay and offer themselves anyway, I suppose for the challenge of it. A pity, a waste. I am a fair poet and a feeble short-story writer. If I had the balls for it I'd try a novel. I expect to die young. I feel that romanticism demands it of me. For consistency of pose I must constantly contemplate suicide.

OLIVER. Pink and gold, like Timothy, but otherwise how different! Timothy is a solid, brutal pillar; Oliver tapers. Improbable movie-star body and face: six foot three, wide shoulders, slim hips. Perfect proportions. Strong, silent type. Beautiful and knows it and doesn't give a damn. Kansas farm boy, features open and guileless. Long hair so blond it's almost white. From the back he looks like a huge girl, except that the waist is wrong. His muscles don't bulge like Timothy's, they're flat and long. Oliver deceives no one with his hayseed stolidity. Behind the bland, cool blue eyes a hungry spirit. He lives in a seething New York City of the mind, hatching ambitious plans. Yet a kind of noble radiance comes from him. If I could only cleanse myself in that brilliant glow. If I could only.

OUR AGES. Timothy, 22 last month. Me, 21½. Oliver, 21 in January. Eli, 20½.

Timothy: Aquarius

Me: Scorpio

Oliver: Capricorn

Eli: Virgo

five

OLIVER

I'd rather drive than be driven. I've held the wheel ten and
twelve hours at a stretch. The way I see it, I'm safer when
I'm driving than when somebody else is, because nobody
else is quite as interested in preserving my life as I am.
Some drivers, I think, actually court death—for the thrill
of it, or, as Ned might say, for the esthetics of it. To hell
with that. There's nothing more sacred to me in all the
universe than the life of Oliver Marshall, and I want as
much control over life-or-death situations as I can get. So I
intend to do most of the driving. Thus far this trip I've
done all of it, though it's Timothy's car. Timothy's the
opposite; he'd rather be driven than drive. I suppose it's a
manifestation of class consciousness. Eli doesn't know how
to drive. So it comes down to me and Ned. Ned and me, all
the way to Arizona, with Timothy taking a turn once in a
while. Frankly, the thought of entrusting my neck to Ned
terrifies me. Suppose I just stay where I am, foot on the
gas, driving on and on through the night? We could be in
Chicago by tomorrow afternoon. St. Louis late tomorrow
night. Arizona the day after next. And start hunting for
Eli's skull house. I want to volunteer for immortality. I'm
ready; I'm fully psyched up; I believe Eli implicitly. God, I
believe! I *want* to believe. The whole future opens before
me. I'll see the stars. I'll zoom from world to world.
Captain Future from Kansas. And these bonzos want to
stop in New York first for a night on the town, a night in
the singles bars! Eternity is waiting, and they can't pass up
Maxwell's Plum. I'd like to tell them what hicks I think

they are. But I have to be patient. I don't want them to laugh at me. I don't want them to think I'm losing my cool over Arizona and the skulls. First Avenue, here we come.

síx

eli

We went to a place on Sixty-seventh that had opened last Christmas; one of Timothy's fraternity brothers had been there and had reported the action was groovy, so Timothy insisted on going. We humored him. The name of the place was The Raunch House, which tells you the whole dull story in three syllables. The decor was Early Jockstrap and the clientele ran heavily toward suburban high school football players, with girls outnumbered approximately three to one. High noise level, much moronic laughter. The four of us entered as a phalanx, but our formation shattered the moment we were past the entrance. Timothy, all eager, went plunging toward the bar like a musk-ox in rut, his burly body slowing as he realized by his fifth step that the ambiance wasn't what he was looking for. Oliver, who in some ways is the most fastidious of us all, never even went in; he sensed at once that the place was inadequate and planted himself just inside the doorway to wait for us to leave. I ventured halfway into the room, was hit by a blast of raucousness that jangled every nerve, and, totally turned off, retreated to the relative tranquility of the checkroom alcove. Ned made straight for the washroom. I was naive enough to think he was simply in a hurry to take a piss. A moment later Timothy came up to me, a bumper of beer in his hand, and said, "Let's get the crap out of here. Where's Ned?"

"In the john," I told him.

"For crap's sake." Timothy went off to fetch him. Emerging a moment later with a sulky Ned, Ned accompanied by a six-foot-six version of Oliver, maybe sixteen years old, a young Apollo with shoulder-length tresses and a lavender headband. A quick worker, Ned. Five seconds to size things up, thirty seconds more to locate the head and scout up a little rough trade. Timothy now cramping his style, ruining dreams of an exquisite beating in some East Village pad. Of course we had no time now to let Ned indulge his whims. Timothy said something curt to Ned's find and Ned said something sourly to Timothy; the Apollo went hulking off and we four cleared out. Up the block to supposedly more reliable haunts, The Plastic Cave, where Timothy had gone with Oliver several times last year. Futuristic decor, undulating sheets of thick, shimmering gray plastic all over, waiters togged out in garish science-fiction costumes, periodic outbursts of strobe lights, every ten minutes or so a numbing hammering blare of hard rock smashing out of fifty speakers. More of a discotheque than a singles bar, really, but functioning as both. Much favored by Columbia and Barnard swingers, also utilized by girls from Hunter; high-schoolies are made to feel unwanted. To me it was an alien environment. I have no sense of contemporary chic; I'd rather sit around coffeehouses, swill cappuccino, and talk Big Thinks than do the singles/discotheque number. Rilke instead of rock, Plotinus instead of plastic. "Man, you're straight out of 1957!" Timothy once told me. Timothy with the Republican brush-fuzz haircut.

The main project for tonight was to find a place to sleep, that is, to acquire girls with a flat capable of accommodating four male guests. Timothy would take care of that, and if he found the pickings slim we could always unleash Oliver. This was their kind of world. I would feel

less out of place at high mass at St. Patrick's. This was
Zanzibar to me, and I suppose Timbuctoo to Ned, although with his chameleon adaptability he was able to fit
right in. Thwarted in his natural desires by Timothy, he
now chose to fly the hetero flag, and in his usual perverse
fashion he had picked out the ugliest girl in sight, a
pasty-faced heavy with sprawling cannonball breasts under
a sagging red sweater. He was giving her the high-voltage
seduction treatment, most likely coming on like a gay
Raskolnikov looking to her to save him from a tormented
life of buggery. As he purred in her ear she kept moisten-
ing her lips and blushing, and batting her eyes, and fingering the crucifix, yes, the *crucifix*, that hung between her
jumbo bazooms. Some Sally McNally fresh out of Mother
Cabrini High and not long parted from her cherry, and
what a job *that* was getting rid of it, and now, praise all the
saints, someone was actually trying to make her! Doubtless
Ned was going into the spoiled-priest routine, the failed-
Jesuit number, donning his aura of decadence and romantic Catholic angst. Would he really follow through? Yes, he
would. As a poet in quest of Experience he frequently
went slumming in the other sex, seducing always the dogs
and creeps, the debris of the gender, a one-armed girl, a girl
with half a jawbone, a stork twice his height, etc., etc.
Ned's idea of black humor. In truth he got laid more often
than I did, gay as he was, though his conquests were no
prizes except booby prizes. He claimed to take no pleasure
in the act, only in the cruel game of the chase itself. See,
he said, tonight you will not let me have Alcibiades,
therefore I choose Xantippe. He mocked the whole
straight world with his pursuit of the deformed and the
undesired.

I studied his technique awhile. I spend too much
time watching things. I should have been out and prowling
instead. If intensity and intellectualism were currently
fashionable commodities here, why did I not peddle mine
for a little tail? Are you above the merely physical, Eli?
Come off it; you're just clumsy with girls. I bought myself
a whiskey sour (creeping 1957ism again! Who drinks

mixed drinks now?) and turned away from the bar.
Clumsy is as clumsy does. I collided with a short, dark-
haired girl and spilled half my drink. "Oh, I'm terribly
sorry," we both said at once. She looked terrified, a
frightened fawn. Slender, bird-boned, hardly five feet tall,
shining solemn eyes, a prominent nose *(shayneh maideleh!*
A member of the tribe!). A turquoise semi-see-through
blouse revealing a pink brassiere beneath, indicating some
ambivalence about contemporary mores. Our shynesses
kindled a spark; I felt heat at my crotch, heat in my
cheeks, and picked up from her the bright warmth of
reciprocal combustion. Sometimes it hits you so unmistakably that you wonder why everyone around doesn't
start to cheer. We found a minuscule table and mumbled
husky introductions. Mickey Bernstein, meet Eli Steinfeld.
Eli, Mickey. What's a nice girl like you doing in a place like
this?

She was a Hunter sophomore, government major,
family from Kew Gardens; she shared an apartment with
four other girls at Third and Seventieth. I thought I had
found us our lodgings for the night—imagine, Eli the
schmendrick scoring a crash!—but quickly I got the impression that the apartment was really two bedrooms and a
kitchenette and wasn't set up for that much company. She
was quick to tell me that she didn't often go to singles
places, in fact almost never, but her roommate had dragged
her out tonight to celebrate the beginning of the Easter
recess—indicating the roommate, tall skinny acne-pocked
gawk conferring earnestly with a gangling shaggy-bearded
type dressed in 1968 floral mod—and so here she was, ill at
ease, deafened by the noise, and would I please get her a
cherry Coke? Suave man-of-the-world Steinfeld nailed a
passing Martian and placed the order. One buck, please.
Ouch. Mickey asked me what I was studying. Trapped. All
right, pedant, reveal yourself. "Early medieval philology,"
I said. "The disintegration of Latin into the Romance
languages. I could sing you obscene ballads in Provençal, if
I could sing." She laughed, too loudly. "Oh, I have a
terrible voice, too!" she cried. "But you can recite one, if

you like." Shyly taking my hand, since I had been too scholarly to think of taking hers. I said, half shouting the words into the din,

> Can vei la luzeta mover
> De joi sas alas contral rai,
> Que s.oblid.es laissa chazer
> Per la doussor c.al cor li vai—

And so forth. Utterly snowed her. "Was that awfully dirty?" she asked at the end.

"Not at all. It's a tender love song, Bernart de Ventadorn, twelfth century."

"You recited it so beautifully." I translated it and felt the waves of adulation coming at me. Take me, do me, she was telepathing. I calculated that she had had sexual intercourse nine times with two different men and was still nervously searching for her first orgasm, while worrying a good deal about whether she was becoming too promiscuous too soon. I was willing to do my best, blowing in her ear and whispering little treasures from the Provençal. But how could we get out of here? Where could we go? Wildly I looked around. Timothy had his arm around a frighteningly beautiful girl with sweeping cascades of glossy auburn hair. Oliver had snared two birds, brunette and blonde: the old farmboy charm at work. Ned still courted his pudgy paramour. Perhaps one of them would come up with something, a nearby apartment, bedrooms for everybody. I turned back to Mickey and she said, "We're having a little party Saturday night. A few really groovy musicians are coming over, I mean, classical, and perhaps if you're free you might—"

"By Saturday night I'll be in Arizona."

"Arizona! Is that where you're from?"

"I'm from Manhattan."

"Then why—I mean, I never heard of going to Arizona for Easter. Is it something new?" A sheepish flicker of a smile. "I'm sorry. You have a girl out there?"

"Nothing like that."

She wriggled, not wanting to pry but not knowing how to halt the inquisition. The inevitable sentence tumbled out: "Why are you going, then?" And I was stopped. What could I say? For fifteen minutes I had been playing a conventional role, horny college senior on the prowl, East Side singles bar, timid but available girl, hype her with a little esoteric poetry, the eyes meeting across the table, when can I see you again, a quick Easter romance, thank you for everything, good-bye. The familiar collegiate waltz. But her question opened a trapdoor beneath me and dropped me into that other, darker world, the fantasy world, the dreamworld, where solemn young men speculated on the possibility of being reprieved forever from death, where fledgling scholars noodled themselves into believing that they had come upon arcane manuscripts revealing the secrets of ancient mystic cults. Yes, I could say, we're going on a quest for the secret headquarters of the Brotherhood of the Skulls, do you see, we hope to persuade the Keepers that we are worthy candidates for the Trial, and of course if we are accepted, one of us must give his life gladly for the others and one is going to have to be murdered, but we're prepared to face those eventualities because the two lucky ones will never die. Thank you, H. Rider Haggard: exactly. Again I felt the sense of harsh incongruity, of dislocation, as I contemplated the juxtaposition of our up-to-the-minute Manhattan surroundings and my implausible Arizona dream. Look, I could say, it's necessary to make an act of faith, of mystic acceptance, to tell yourself that life isn't entirely made up of discotheques and subways and boutiques and classrooms. You must believe that inexplicable forces exist. Are you into astrology? Of course you are; and you know what *The New York Times* thinks of *that.* So carry your acceptance a little further, as we have done. Put aside your self-conscious oh-so-very-modern rejection of the improbable and allow the possibility that there *could* be a Brotherhood, there *could* be a Trial, there *could* be life everlasting. How can you deny without first investigating? Can you afford to take the risk of being wrong? And so we're going to Arizona, the four of us, the big beefy one with the crew cut and the Greek god over there and the intense-looking fellow talking to the fat girl and me, and although some of us have more faith than others there isn't one of us who doesn't believe at least fractionally in the Book of Skulls. Pascal chose to have faith because the odds were stacked against the unbeliever, who might be tossing away Paradise through his refusal to submit to the Church; so too with us, who are willing to look foolish for a week because we have at least the hope of gaining something beyond all price and can at worst lose nothing more than the cost of gasoline. But I said none of this to Mickey Bernstein. The music was too loud, and, anyway, the four of us had sworn a terrible sophomoric oath to reveal nothing to nobody. Instead I said, "Why Arizona? I guess because we're cactus freaks. And it's warm there in March."

"It's warm in Florida, too."

"No cactus," I said.

seven

timothy

It took me an hour to find the right girl and arrange things. Her name was Bess; she was a busty kid from Oregon; she and four other Barnard juniors shared an immense apartment on Riverside Drive. Three of the four girls had gone home for the holiday; the fourth was sitting in the corner, letting a sideburned twenty-fivish advertising-man type make his pitch. Perfect. I explained that I and my three roommates were passing through the city tonight en route to Arizona and hoped to crash someplace groovy. "We should be able to manage it," she said. Perfect. Now I just had to get it together. Oliver was talking in a bored way with a skinny, too-bright-eyed chick in a black jumpsuit, maybe a speedhead; I pried him loose, spelled out the scene, and turned him on to Bess's roommate Judy. A Nebraska lass, no less; quickly the Mad Ave delegate was in the can and Judy and Oliver were discussing the price of hogfeed, or whatever. Next I rounded up Ned. The freaky little fucker had picked up a *girl,* of all strange objects; he does shticks like that occasionally, I suppose for the sake of thumbing his nose at the straights. This one was a downer—giant nostrils, giant tits, a mound of meat. "We're splitting," I told him. "Bring her along, if you like. " Then I found Eli. This must have been National Heterosexuality Week; even Eli was scoring. Thin, dark sort, no flesh on her, a quick nervous smile. She was flabbergasted to discover that her Eli was rooming with a galumphing *shegitz* like me. "There's room at the inn," I said to him. "Come on." He almost kissed my boots.

The eight of us piled into my car—nine, counting Ned's catch as the double she was. I drove. Introductions went on forever. Judy, Mickey, Mary, Bess; Eli, Timothy, Oliver, Ned; Judy, Timothy; Mickey, Ned; Mary, Oliver; Bess, Eli; Mickey, Judy; Mary, Bess; Oliver, Judy; Eli, Mary—oh, Jesus. It began to rain, a cold drizzle just above the freezing point. As we entered Central Park, a decrepit car about a hundred yards ahead of us went into a skid, did a wild sideways slalom off the road, and smashed into a colossal tree; the car split open and at least a dozen people flew out, rocketing off in all directions. I braked in a hurry, for some of the victims were practically in my path. Heads were cracked, necks were broken, people were moaning in Spanish. I stopped the car and said to Oliver, "We better get out and see if there's anything we can do." Oliver looked stunned. He has this thing about death: it guts him just to run over a squirrel. Coping with a carload of damaged Puerto Ricans was enough to send our sterling pre-med into a state of shock. As he began to mumble something, Judy From Nebraska peered around his shoulder and said with real frenzy, "No! Keep going, Tim!"

"People are hurt," I said.

"There'll be cops here any minute. They see eight kids in a car, they'll search us before they bother with *them*. And I'm *holding*, Tim, I'm *holding!* We'll all get busted!"

She was on the edge of panic. What the crap, we couldn't afford to waste half our vacation being arraigned because one dumb cunt felt she had to carry her stash around with her, so I nudged the pedal and steered my way carefully through the dead and dying. Would the fuzzies really have paused to hunt for dope while the ground was strewn with bodies? I couldn't believe that, but maybe it's because I'm conditioned to think that the police are on my side; Judy might just have been right. Paranoia is contagious these days. Anyway, I drove on, and it wasn't until we emerged onto Central Park West that Oliver opined it had been wrong to leave the scene of the accident. Morality after the fact, said Eli from the rear, is worse than no morality at all. And Ned cried bravo. What a routine, those two.

Bess and Judy lived up around 100th Street, in a huge, decaying apartment house that must have been a palace in 1920. Their apartment was an endless flat, room after room after room, high ceilings, gingerbread moldings, cracked lumpy plaster that had been patched and patched down through the centuries. Fifteenth floor or so: a magnificent view of New Jersey's squalor. Bess put on a stack of records—Segovia, Stones, Sergeant Pepper, Beethoven, you name it—and fetched a jug of Ripple. Judy produced the dope that had panicked her in the park: a lump of hash as big as my nose. "You keep it on you for a good luck charm?" I asked, but it turned out she'd had it laid on her at The Plastic Cave. The pipe passed. Oliver, as usual, let it go by; I think he thinks drugs of any sort will pollute his precious bodily fluids. Ned's Irish washerwoman also abstained—that much with-it she wasn't prepared to be.

"Come on," I heard Ned telling her, "it'll help you lose weight." She looked terrified. Expecting Jesus to stride through the window any moment and rip the immortal soul out of her throbbing sinful body. The rest of us got pleasantly stoned and drifted off to various bedrooms.

In the middle of the night I felt a certain pressure of the bladder and went searching for a john in that maze of hallways and doorways. I opened a few wrong doors. Heaps of humanity everywhere. Out of one room, sounds of passion, the regular, rhythmic bouncing of bedsprings. No need to peek: that had to be Oliver the Bull, giving his Judy her sixth or seventh ride of the night. She'd walk bowlegged for a week by the time he got through with her. Out of another room, snores and whistles: begorrah, kinky Ned's sweet sow at her slumbers. Ned was sleeping in the hall. Enough was enough, I guess. At last I found a john, only it was occupied by Eli and Mickey, taking a shower together. I didn't mean to intrude, but what the crap. Mickey struck a delicate Grecian pose, right hand over the black bush, left arm flung across the very minimal jugs. I would have believed she was fourteen or younger. "Excuse," I said, backing out. Eli, dripping, naked, came out after me. I said, "Don't make a hassle, I didn't intend to intrude on your privacy," but that wasn't what was on his mind at all. He asked me if we could swing a fifth passenger for the rest of the trip. "Her?" He nodded. Love at first sight; they had clicked, they had found real happiness in each other. Now he wanted to bring her along. "Christ," I said, coming close to waking everybody up, "have you told her about—"

"No. Just that we're going to Arizona."

"And what happens when we get there? Do you bring *her* to the skullhouse with us?"

He hadn't thought it through that far. Dazzled by her modest charms, he could see only as far as his next fuck, our brilliant Eli. Of course it was impossible. If this had been planned as an erotica trip, I'd have brought Margo and Oliver would have brought LuAnn. We were stagging it, though, excepting only such stuff as we foraged along the way, and Eli would have to abide by that. At his insistence we were a closed foursome, hermetically sealed. Now Eli wouldn't abide. "I can drop her off in a Phoenix motel while we're in the desert," he argued. "She doesn't have to know what we're going there for."

"No."

"And anyway, does it have to be such a fucking secret, Timothy?"

"Are you out of your tree? Aren't you the very one who practically made us take a blood oath never to reveal a single syllable of the Book of Skulls to—"

"You're shouting. They'll hear everything."

"Right on. Let them hear. You don't want that, do you? To have these chicks here find out about your Fu Manchu project. And yet you're ready to let her in on the whole thing. You aren't thinking, Eli."

"Maybe I'll forget about Arizona, then," he said.

I wanted to take him and shake him. Forget about Arizona? *He* organized it. *He* lured the necessary three other males into it. *He* went on for hours and hours to us about the importance of opening your soul to the inexplicable and the implausible and the fantastic. *He* goaded us to set aside mere pragmaticism and empiricism and perform an act of faith, et cetera, et cetera. Now a winsome daughter of Israel spreads her legs for him and he's willing in a flash to give the whole thing up, just to be able to spend Easter holding hands with her at the Cloisters and the Guggenheim and other metropolitan cultural shrines. Well, crap on that. He got us into this, and, entirely leaving out of the picture the question of how much faith we really had in his weirdo immortality cult, he wasn't going to shuck us that simply. The Book of Skulls says that candidates have to present themselves in fours. I told him that we wouldn't let him drop out. He was silent a long while. Much gulping of the Adam's apple: sign of Great Internal Conflict. True love versus eternal life. "You can look her up when we come back east," I reminded him. "Assuming that you're one of those who comes back." He was pronged on one of his own existential dilemmas. The bathroom door opened and Mickey peered chastely out, bath-toweled. "Go on," I said. "Your lady's waiting. I'll see you in the morning." Finding another john somewhere beyond the kitchen, I relieved myself and groped through the darkness back to Bess, who greeted me with little snorting sighs. Caught me by the ears, pulled me down between her bouncy, rubbery knockers. Large breasts, my father told me when I was fifteen, are rather vulgar; a gentleman chooses his women by other criteria. Yes, Dad, but they make groovy pillows. Bess and I celebrated the rites of spring one final time. I slept. At six in the morning Oliver, fully dressed, woke me. Ned and Eli were up and dressed already, too. All the girls were asleep. We break-fasted silently, rolls and coffee, and were on the road before seven, the four of us, up Riverside Drive to the George Washington Bridge, across into Jersey, westward on Interstate 80. Oliver did the driving. Old Iron Man.

eight

OLIVER

Don't go, LuAnn said, whatever it is, don't go, don't get involved, I don't like the sound of it. And I hadn't told her much at all, really. Just the externals of it: a religious group in Arizona, see, a sort of monastery, in fact, and Eli thinks it could be of great spiritual value for the four of us to pay it a visit. We might gain a whole lot from going, I told LuAnn. And her immediate response was one of fear.

The housewife syndrome: *if you don't know what it is, don't go near it.* Frightened, in-drawing. She's a sweet kid but she's too predictable. Perhaps if I had told her about the never-dying aspect she might have reacted differently. But of course I'd sworn not to breathe a word. And in any case, even immortality would scare LuAnn. Don't, she'd say, there's a catch in it, something awful will come out of it, it's strange and mysterious and frightening, it isn't God's will that such things should be. Each of us owes God a death. Beethoven died. Jesus died. President Eisenhower died. Do you think you should be excused from dying, Oliver, if *they* had to go? Please don't get mixed up in this.

Death. What does poor simpleheaded LuAnn know about death? She even has her grandparents still alive. Death is an abstraction for her, something that happened to Beethoven and Jesus. I know death better, LuAnn. I see his grinning skullface every night. And I have to fight him. I have to spit at him. Eli comes to me, he says, I know where you can get excused from dying, Oliver, it's just out yonder in Arizona. Visit the Brotherhood and play their little game, and they'll release you from the wheel of fire. Do not pass Go, do not descend into the grave, do not put on corruption. They can pluck his sting. How can I pass up the chance?

Death, LuAnn. Think about the death of LuAnn Chambers, say, next Thursday morning. Not in 1997, but next Thursday morning. You're walking down Elm Street on your way to visit your grandparents, and a car comes flying out of control at you the way the car of those poor Puerto Ricans went out of control last night, and—no, I take that back. I don't think even the Brotherhood can protect you against accidental death, violent death; whatever process they have, it doesn't work miracles, only retards physical decay. We start again, LuAnn. You're walking down Elm Street on your way to visit your grandparents and a blood vessel treacherously bursts in your temple. Cerebral hemorrhage. Why not? It can happen to nineteen-year-olds once in a while, I suppose. The blood bubbles through your skull and your legs fold up and you hit the sidewalk, wriggling and kicking, and you know something bad is happening to you but you can't even scream, and in ten seconds you're dead. You have been subtracted from the universe, LuAnn. No, the universe has been subtracted from *you*. Forget what's going to happen to your body now, the worms in your gut, the pretty blue eyes turning to muck, and just think about all you've lost. You've lost it all, sunrise and sunset, the smell of broiling steak, the feel of a cashmere sweater, the touch of my lips that you like so much against your little hard nipples. You've lost the Grand Canyon and Shakespeare and London and Paris and champagne and your big church wedding and Paul McCartney and Peter Fonda and the Mississippi River and the moon and the stars. You'll never have babies and you'll never taste real caviar, because you're dead on the sidewalk and the juices are already going sour in you. Why should that be, LuAnn? Why should we be put into such a wonderful world and then have everything taken away from us? God's will? No, LuAnn, God is love, and God wouldn't have done such a cruel thing to us, so therefore there is no God, there's only death, Death, whom we must reject. Not everyone dies at nineteen? That's true, LuAnn. I loaded the dice a little there. What if you hung on until 1997, yes, you had your church wedding and your babies, you saw Paris and Tokyo, too, you tasted champagne and caviar, and you went to the moon for a Christmas trip with your husband the rich doctor? And then Death came to you and said, Okay, LuAnn, it was a good trip, wasn't it, baby, only it's over now. Zap and you have cancer of the cervix, rotting ovaries, one of those female things, and it metastasizes overnight and you come apart, turning into a puddle of stinking fluids in the county hospital. Does the fact that you lived a full life for forty or fifty years make you any more willing to check out? Doesn't that just make the joke sicker, to find out how groovy life can be and then to be cut off? You've never thought about these things, LuAnn, but I have. And I tell you: the longer you live, the longer you want to live. Unless, of course, you're in pain or deformed or alone in the world and it's all become a terrible burden. But if you love life, you'll never have enough of it. Even you, you sweet placid nothinghead, you won't want to go. And I don't want to go. I've thought about the death of Oliver Marshall, believe you me, and I reject the concept entirely. Why did I go into pre-med program? Not so I could make a fortune prescribing pills for suburban ladies, but so I could do research in geriatrics, in senility phenomena, in life extension. So I could stick my finger in Death's eye. That was my big dream, still is; but Eli tells me of the Keepers of the Skulls, and I listen to him. I listen. At sixty miles an hour we roll westward. The death of Oliver Marshall could happen eight seconds from now—whiz, crash, smash!—and it could happen ninety years from now and perhaps it will never happen. *Perhaps it will never happen.*

Consider Kansas, LuAnn. You only know Georgia, but for a moment consider Kansas. Miles of corn, and the dusty wind whipping off the plains. Growing up in a town with 953 inhabitants. Give us this day our daily death, O Lord. The wind, the dust, the highway, the thin sharp faces. You want to see a movie? You drive half a day to Emporia. You want to buy a book? I guess you go to Topeka for that. Chinese food? Pizza? Enchiladas? Don't be funny. Your school has eight grades and nineteen students. One teacher. He doesn't know much, he grew up around here, too; too sickly to farm, he got a job teaching. The dust, LuAnn. The waving corn. The long summer afternoons. Sex. Sex isn't a mystery there, LuAnn, it's a necessity. Thirteen years old, you go behind the barn, you go to the far side of the creek. It's the only game there is. We all played it. Christa pulls down her jeans; how strange she looks, she's got nothing between her legs but yellow curls. Now you show me yours, she says. Here, get on top of me. Is it a thrill, LuAnn? It's no thrill. You're desperate, so you do it, and all the girls are pregnant by the time they're sixteen, and the wheel keeps turning. It's death, LuAnn, death in life. I couldn't take it. I had to escape. Not to Wichita, not to Kansas City, but east, to the real

world, the world on the TV. Do you know how hard I
worked to get out of Kansas? Saving to buy books. Sixty
miles twice a day to get to high school and back. The
whole Abe Lincoln bit, yes, because I was living the one
and irreplaceable life of Oliver Marshall, and I couldn't
afford to waste it raising corn. Fine, a scholarship to an Ivy
League school. Fine, straight-A average in the pre-med
program. I'm a climber, LuAnn, the devil's burning my tail
and I have to keep going higher. But for what? For what?
For thirty or forty or fifty pretty decent years, and then
the exit? No. No. I reject that. Death may have been good
enough for Beethoven and Jesus and President Eisenhower,
but, meaning no offense, I'm different, I can't just lie
down and go. Why is it all so short? Why does it come so
soon? Why can't we drink the universe? Death's been
hovering over me all my life. My father, he died at thirty-
six, stomach cancer, he coughed blood one day and said,
Hon, I think I've been losing a lot of weight lately, and ten
days later he looked like a skeleton, and ten days after that
he *was* a skeleton. They let him have thirty-six years. What
kind of life is that? I was eleven when he died. I had a dog,
the dog died, muzzle turning gray, ears going limp, tail
hanging, good-bye. I had grandparents once, just like you,
four of them, they died, one two three four, the leathery
faces, the gravestones in the dust. Why? Why? Why? I want
to see so much, LuAnn! Africa and Asia and the South
Pole, and Mars, and the planets out by Alpha Centauri! I
want to watch the sunrise the day the twenty-first century
starts, and the twenty-second century, too. Am I greedy?
Yes, I'm greedy. I have it now. I have it all. I'm scheduled
to lose it all, just like everyone else, and I refuse to
surrender. So I drive west with the morning sun at my
back and Timothy snoring next to me and Ned writing
poetry back there and Eli brooding about the girl Timothy
wouldn't let him keep, and I think all this to you, LuAnn,
these things I couldn't explain. Oliver Marshall's Meditation on Death. Soon we'll be in Arizona. Then will come
the disappointment and the disillusionment, and we'll have
some beers and tell ourselves the whole thing was

obviously a crock, and we'll drive east to resume the process of dying. But maybe not, LuAnn, maybe not. The chance exists. The barest merest chance that Eli's book is legitimate.

The chance exists.

nine

ned

We have driven four or five or six hundred miles so far today, and hardly a word has been spoken since early morning. Patterns of tension rivet us and hold us apart. Eli angry at Timothy; myself angry at Timothy; Timothy annoyed with Eli and me; Oliver bothered by all of us. Eli is angry at Timothy for not permitting him to bring with us that little dark-haired girl he picked up last night. My sympathies are with Eli; I know how hard it is for him to find women who are simpatico, and what anguish he must have felt at having to part with her. Yet Timothy was right: to take her along was unthinkable. I have my own grudge with Timothy for his interference in *my* sex life at the singles bar; he could just as easily have let me go with that boy to his pad and picked me up there in the morning. But no, Timothy was afraid I'd get beaten to death in the night—you know how it is, Ned, they always beat queers to death sooner or later—and so he wouldn't let me out of his sight. What is it to him if I'm beaten to death while pursuing my dirty pleasures? It would shatter the mandala, is what. The four-cornered framework, the holy diamond. Three could not present themselves to the Keepers of the Skulls; I am the necessary fourth. So Timothy, who makes it very clear that he believes scarcely a shred of the skullhouse mythos, nevertheless is sternly determined to shepherd the group intact to the shrine. I like that determination of his: it has the proper contradictory resonances, the appropriate ring of clashing absurdities. This is a half-assed trip, says Timothy, but I'm going to go through with it and by crap you guys are going to go through with it too!

There are other tensions this morning. Timothy is sullen and withdrawn, I suppose because he dislikes the paternal/schoolmastery role he had to play last night and resents our having forced it on him. (He surely thinks we deliberately set him up for it.) Also, I suspect Timothy is subliminally peeved at me for having bestowed my favors on sad bestial Mary: gay is gay, in Tim's book, and he believes, probably correctly, that I'm simply jeering at straights when I dabble in ugly-girl heterosex.

And Oliver is even more quiet than usual. I guess we seem frivolous to him and he detests us for it. Poor purposeful Oliver! A self-made man, as he reminds us now and then by implicit rather than explicit disapproval of our attitudes—a consciously Lincolnesque figure who has pulled himself up out of the corny wastelands of Kansas to attain the lofty status of a pre-med student at the nation's most tradition-encrusted college, bar one or two, and who through some fluke of fate has found himself sharing an apartment and a destiny with: (1) a poetic pansy, (2) a member of the idle rich, (3) a neurotic Jewish scholastic. While Oliver dedicates himself to preserving lives through the rites of Asklepios, I am content to scribble contemporary incomprehensibilities, Eli is content to translate and elucidate ancient and forgotten incomprehensibilities, and Timothy is content to clip coupons and play polo. You alone, Oliver, have social relevance, you who have vowed to be a healer of mankind. Ha! What if Eli's temple really does exist and we are granted what we seek? Where's your healing art then, Oliver? Why be a doctor if mumbo jumbo can let you live forever? Ah, then! Farewell! Oliver's occupation's gone!

We are in western Pennsylvania, now, or else eastern Ohio, I forget which. Tonight's destination is Chicago. The miles click by; one turnpike looks like another. We are flanked by barren wintry hills. A pale sun. A bleached sky. Occasionally a filling station, a restaurant, the hint of a drab, soulless town behind the woods. Oliver drove for two silent hours and tossed the keys to Timothy; Timothy drove half an hour, grew bored, asked me to take over. I am the Richard Nixon of the automobile—tense, overeager, bumptious, forever miscalculating and apologizing, ultimately incompetent. Despite his handicaps of the soul, Nixon became president; despite my lapses of coordination and attention, I have a driver's license. Eli has a theory that all American males can be divided into two moieties, those capable of driving and those who cannot drive, the former being suitable only for breeding and manual labor, the latter embodying the true genius of the race. He regards me as a traitor to the clerisy because I know which foot to put on the brake and which on the accelerator, but I think after experiencing an hour of my driving he's begun to revise his harsh placement of me. I am no driver, I merely masquerade. Timothy's Lincoln Continental is like a bus to me; I oversteer, I wobble. Give me a VW and I'll show my stuff. Oliver, never a good passenger, eventually lost his nerve and told me he'd take over the wheel again. There he sits now, our golden charioteer, flogging us toward sundown.

A book I was reading not long ago drew a structural metaphor of society from an ethnographical film about some African bushmen out hunting a giraffe. They had wounded one of the big beasts with their poisoned arrows, but now they had to follow their prey across the bleak Kalahari, chasing him until he dropped, which would take a week or more. There were four of them, bound in tight alliance. The Headman, the leader of the hunting unit. The Shaman, the craftsman and magician, who invoked supernatural aid when needed and otherwise served as the conduit between the divine charisma and the realities of the desert. The Hunter or Beautiful One, famous for his grace, speed, and physical strength, who bore the hardest burdens of the hunt. Lastly, the Clown, small and freaky, who mocked the mysteries of the Shaman, the beauty and strength of the Hunter, the self-importance of the Headman. These four constituted a single organism, each essential to the whole of the chase. From this the writer developed the polarities of the group, invoking a couple of Yeatsian counterrotating gyres: Shaman and Clown are the left gyre, the Ideational; and Hunter and Headman are the right gyre, the Operational. Each gyre realizes possibilities inaccessible to the other; each is useless without the other, but together they form a stable group in which all the skills are balanced. Onward from there to develop the ultimate metaphor, rising from the tribal to the national: the Headman becomes the State, the Hunter becomes the Military, the Shaman becomes the Church, the Clown becomes Art. We carry the macrocosm in this car. Timothy, our Headman; Eli, our Shaman; Oliver, our Beautiful One, our Hunter. And I, the Clown. And I, the Clown.

ten

olíveR

Eli saved the nasty part for last, after we were hooked on the idea of going. Leafing through the pages of his translation, frowning, nodding, pretending to have trouble finding the passage he wanted, though you bet he knew all the time where it was. And then reading to us:

"The Ninth Mystery is this: that the price of a life must always be a life. Know, O Nobly-Born, that eternities must be balanced by extinctions, and therefore we ask of thee that the ordained balance be gladly sustained. Two of thee we undertake to admit to our fold. Two must go into darkness. As by living we daily die, so then by dying we shall forever live. Is there one among thee who will relinquish eternity for his brothers of the four-sided figure, so that they may come to comprehend the meaning of self-denial? And is there one among thee whom his comrades are prepared to sacrifice, so that they may come to comprehend the meaning of exclusion? Let the victims choose themselves. Let them define the quality of their lives by the quality of their departures."

Cloudy stuff. We poked and prodded at it for hours, Ned exercising all his Jesuitical muscle on it, and even so we could only pull one meaning from it, an ugly one, the obvious one. There had to be a volunteer for suicide. And two of the remaining three had to murder the third. Those are the terms of the deal. Are they for real? Maybe it's all metaphorical. Meant to be interpreted in a symbolic way. Instead of actual deaths, say, one of the four simply has to volunteer to give up taking part in the ritual and goes away still mortal. Then two of the others have to gang up on the third and force him to leave the shrine. Could that be it? Eli believes literal deaths are involved. Of course, Eli is very literal-minded about this mysticism; he takes the irrational things of life extremely seriously and doesn't seem to care much about the rational things at all. Ned, who doesn't take *anything* seriously, agrees with Eli. I don't think Ned has much faith in the Book of Skulls, but his position is that if any of it is true, then the Ninth Mystery must be interpreted as demanding two deaths. Timothy also doesn't take anything seriously, though his way of laughing at the world is altogether different from Ned's: Ned's a conscious cynic, Timothy just doesn't give a damn. It's a deliberately demonic pose for Ned and a matter of having too much family money for Timothy. So Timothy doesn't fret much about the Ninth Mystery; to him it's bullshit, like all the rest of the Book of Skulls.

What about Oliver?

Oliver doesn't know. I have faith in the Book of Skulls, yes, because I have faith in it, and so I suppose I accept the literal interpretation of the Ninth Mystery, too. But I've gone into this in order to live, not to die, and so I haven't really thought much about the chances of my drawing the short straw. Assuming the Ninth Mystery is what we think it is, who, then, will the victims be? Ned has already let it be known that he doesn't care much whether he lives or dies; one night in February when he was stoned he delivered a two-hour speech on the esthetics of suicide. Red in the face, sweating and puffing, waving his arms, Lenin on a soapbox; we tuned in now and then and got his drift. Okay, we apply the usual Ned discount and conclude that his death talk is nine-tenths a romantic gesture; that will still leave him the outstanding candidate for voluntary exit. And the murder victim? Eli, of course. It couldn't be me; I'd fight too hard, I'd take at least one of the bastards with me, and they all know it. And Timothy, he's built like a mountain, you couldn't kill him with hammers. Whereas Timothy and I could polish off Eli in two minutes or less.

Christ, how I hate this kind of speculation!

I don't want to kill anybody. I don't want anyone to die. I only want to go on living, myself, as long as I possibly can.

But if those are the terms? If the price of a life is a life?

Christ. Christ. Christ.

eleven

eli

We came into Chicago at twilight, after a long day of driving. Sixty, seventy miles an hour, hour after hour after hour broken only by infrequent rest stops. The last four hours we didn't even stop, Oliver hurtling like a madman down the turnpike. Cramped legs. Stiff ass. Glazed eyes. My brain fuggy, blurred by excessive traveling. Highway hypnosis. As the sun sank, all color seemed to leave the world; an all-pervading blue engulfed everything—blue sky, blue fields, blue pavement, the whole spectrum draining toward the ultraviolet. It was like being on the ocean, unable to distinguish what lies above the horizon from what lies below. I had very little sleep last night. Two hours at the very most, probably less. When we weren't actually talking or making love, we lay side by side in a groggy doze. Mickey! Ah, Mickey! The scent of you is on my fingertips. I inhale. Three tumbles between midnight and dawn. How shy you were at first, in the narrow bedroom, flaking pale green paint, psychedelic posters, John Lennon and saggy-cheeked Yoko looking down on us as we stripped, and you huddled your shoulders together, you tried to hide your breasts from me, you slipped into bed quickly, seeking the safety of the sheets. Why? Do you think your body's so deficient? All right, you're thin, your elbows are sharp, your breasts are small. You're not Aphrodite. Do you need to be? Am I Apollo? At least you didn't shrink from my touch. I wonder if you came. I can never tell if they come. Where are the great wailing, shrieking, whooping spasms I read about? Other girls, I suppose. Mine are too polite for such volcanic orgasmic eruptions. I should become a monk. Leave screwing for the screwers and channel my energies into the pursuit of the profound. I'm probably not much good at fuckery away. Let Origen be my guide: in a moment of exaltation I'll perform an autoorchidectomy and deposit my balls on the holy altar as an offering. Thereafter no longer to feel the distractions of passion. Alas, no, I enjoy it too much. Grant me chastity, God, but, please, not just yet. I have Mickey's phone number. When I come back from Arizona I'll give her a ring. (*When I come back.* If I come back! And when and if, what will I be?) Mickey's the right sort of girl for me, indeed. I must set modest sexual goals. Not for me the blonde sex bomb, not for me the cheerleader, not for me the sophisticated society-girl contralto. For me the sweet shy mice. Oliver's LuAnn would bore me flaccid in fifteen minutes, though I imagine I could tolerate her once for the sake of her breasts. And Timothy's Margo? Let's not think about her, shall we? Mickey for me. Mickey: bright, pale, retiring, available. Eight hundred miles east of me at the moment. I wonder what she's telling her friends about me. Let her magnify me. Let her romanticize me. I can use it.

So we are in Chicago. Why Chicago? Does it not lie somewhat off the direct route between New York and Phoenix? I think it does. If I were navigating, I'd have plotted a course that sagged from one corner of the continent to the other, through Pittsburgh and Cincinnati, but maybe the fastest highways don't take the most direct line,

and in any event here we are up in Chicago, apparently on
Timothy's whim. He has a sentimental fondness for the
city. He grew up here; at least, that part of his childhood
that he didn't spend on his father's Pennsylvania estate he
spent in his mother's penthouse on Lake Shore Drive. Are
there any Episcopalians who *don't* get divorced every
sixteen years? Are there any who don't have two full sets
of mothers and fathers, as a bare minimum? I see the
wedding announcements in the Sunday newspapers. "Miss
Rowan Demarest Hemple, daughter of Mrs. Charles Holt
Wilmerding of Grosse Pointe, Michigan, and Mr. Dayton
Belknap Hemple of Bedford Hills, New York, and Montego
Bay, Jamaica, were married here this afternoon in All Saints
Episcopal Chapel to Dr. Forrester Chiswell Birdsall the
4th, son of Mrs. Elliott Moulton Peck of Bar Harbor,
Maine, and Mr. Forrester Chiswell Birdsall the 3rd of East
Islip, Long Island." *Et cetera ad infinitum.* What a con-
clave such a wedding must be, with the multiple couples
gathering round to jubilate, everybody cousin to everyone
else, all of them married two or three times apiece. The
names, the triple names, sanctified by time, girls named
Rowan and Choate and Palmer, boys named Amory and
McGeorge and Harcourt. I grew up with Barbaras and
Loises and Claires, Mikes and Dicks and Sheldons.
McGeorge becomes "Mac," but what do you call young
Harcourt when you're playing ring-a-levio? What about a
girl named Palmer or Choate? A different world, these
Wasps, a different world. Divorce! The mother (Mrs.
X.Y.Z.) lives in Chicago, the father (Mr. A.B.C. the 3rd)
lives just outside Philadelphia. My parents, who are going
to observe their thirtieth anniversary come August,
screamed at each other all through my boyhood: divorce,
divorce, divorce, I've had enough, I'm going to walk out
and never come back! The normal middle-class incom-
patibility. But divorce? Call a lawyer? My father would
have himself uncircumcized first. My mother would walk
naked into Gimbels first. In every Jewish family there's an
aunt who got divorced once, a long time ago, we don't talk
about it now. (You always find out by overhearing two of

your elderly relatives in their cups, reminiscing.) But never anyone with children. You never have these clusters of parents, requiring such intricate introductions: I'd like you to meet my mother and her husband, I'd like you to meet my father and his wife.

Timothy didn't visit his mother while we were in Chicago. We stayed not very far south of her, in a lake-front motel opposite Grant Park (Timothy paid for the room, with a credit card, no less) but he didn't even phone her. The warm, strong bonds of *goyishe* family life, yes, indeed. (Call up, have a fight, so why not?) Instead he took us on a nighttime tour of the city, behaving in part as though he were its sole proprietor and in part as if he were the guide on a Gray Line bus tour. Here we have the twin towers of Marina City, here we have the John Hancock Building, this is the Art Institute, this is the fabulous shopping district of Michigan Avenue. Actually, I was impressed, I who had never been west of Parsippany, New Jersey, but who had a clear and vivid impression of the probable nature of the great American heartland. I had expected Chicago to be grimy and cramped, the summit of midwestern dreariness, with nineteenth-century red-brick buildings seven stories high and a population made up entirely of Polish, Hungarian, and Irish workmen in over-alls. Whereas this was a city of broad avenues and glowing towers. The architecture was stunning; there was nothing in New York to equal it. Of course, we stayed close to the lake. Go five blocks inland, you'll see all the dreariness you want, Ned promised. The narrow strip of Chicago we saw was a wonderland. Timothy took us to dinner at a French restaurant, his favorite, opposite a curious monument of antiquity known as the Water Tower. One more reminder of the truth of Fitzgerald's maxim about the very rich: they *are* different from you and me. I know from French restaurants the way you know from Tibetan or Martian ones. My parents never took me to Le Pavillon or Chambord for celebrations; I got the Brass Rail for my high school graduation, Schrafft's the day I won my scholarship, dinner for three something under twelve dollars, and considered myself lucky at that. On those infrequent occasions when I take a girl out to dinner, the cuisine necessarily is no hauter than pizza or kung po chi ding. The menu at Timothy's place, an extravaganza of engraved gold lettering on sheets of vellum somewhat larger than the *Times,* was a mystery to me. Yet here was Timothy, my classmate, my roommate, making his way easily through its arcana, suggesting to us that we try the quenelles aux huîtres, the crêpes farcies et roulées, the escalopes de veau à l'estragon, the tournedos sautés chasseur, the homard à l'américaine. Oliver, naturally, was as much adrift as I, but to my surprise, Ned, with a lower-middle-class background not much different from my own, proved knowledgeable, and learnedly discussed with Timothy the relative merits of the gratin de ris de veau, the rognons de veau à la bordelaise, the caneton aux cerises, the suprêmes de volaille aux champignons. (The summer he was sixteen, he explained afterward, he had served as catamite to a distinguished Southampton gourmet.) It was ultimately impossible for me to cope with the menu, and Ned selected a dinner for me, Timothy doing the same for Oliver. I remember oysters, turtle soup, white wine followed by red, a marvelous something of lamb, potatoes made mostly of air, broccoli in a thick yellow sauce. Snifters of cognac for everyone afterward. Legions of waiters hovered over us as solicitously as though we were four bankers out on a binge, not four shabbily dressed college boys. I caught a glimpse of the check and it stunned me: $112, exclusive of tip. With a grand flourish Timothy produced his credit card. I felt feverish, dizzy, overstuffed; I thought I might vomit at the table, there amid the crystal chandeliers, the red plush wallpaper, the elegant linens. The spasm passed without disgrace and once outside I felt better, though still queasy. I made a mental note to spend forty or fifty years of my immortality in a serious study of the culinary arts. Timothy spoke of forging onward to groovy coffeehouses farther to the north, but the rest of us were tired and we voted him down. Back to the hotel, a long walk, perhaps an hour through the cutting cold.

We had taken a suite, two bedrooms, Ned and I in one, Timothy and Oliver in the other. I dumped my clothes and collapsed quickly into bed. Not enough sleep, too much food: ghastly, ghastly. Exhausted though I was, I remained awake, more or less, dozing, stupefied. The rich dinner lay like stones in my gut. A good puking, I decided some hours later, would be best for me. Purge-bound, I staggered naked toward the bathroom separating the two bedrooms. And encountered a terrifying apparition in the dark corridor. A naked girl, taller than I, with long heavy breasts, startlingly flaring hips, a corona of short curling brown hair. A succubus of the night! A phantom spawned by my overheated imagination! "Hi, handsome," she said, and winked, and passed me in a miasma of perfume and lust-smells, leaving me to stare in astonishment at her opulent retreating buttocks until the bathroom door closed behind them. I shivered with fright and horniness. Not even on acid had I experienced such tangible hallucinations; could Escoffier achieve what LSD could not? How beautiful, how meaty, how elegant she was. I heard water running in the john. Peered into the far bedroom, my eyes fully adjusted to the darkness now. Frilly feminine clothes scattered everywhere. Timothy snoring in one bed; in the other, Oliver, and on Oliver's pillow, a second head, female. No hallucinations, then. Where had they found these girls? The room next door? No. I understood. Call girls supplied by room service. The trusty credit card strikes again. Timothy comprehends the American way as I, poor cramped studious ghetto lad, never could hope to do. Want a woman? You have but to lift the phone and ask. My throat was dry; my mast was raised; I felt thunder in my chest. Timothy sleeps; very well, since she's been hired for the night, I'll borrow her awhile. When she comes out of the john I'll swagger up to her, one hand on her tits, one to the rump, feel the silky satiny smoothness of her, give her the Bogart rumble deep down in the throat, invite her to my bed. Indeed. And the bathroom door opened. She glided forth, breasts swaying, ding-dong-ding-dong. Another wink. And past me, gone. I groped air. Her long, lean back, swelling into two astounding globular cheeks; the scent of cheap musky fragrance; the fluid, hip-wiggling stride; the bedroom door closing in my face. She is hired, but not for me. She is Timothy's. I went into the john, knelt before the throne, spent eons upchucking. Then to my lonely bed for cold bad-trip dreams. In the morning, no girls visible. We were on the road before nine, Oliver at the wheel, St. Louis our next port of call. I sank into apocalyptic gloom. I would have shattered empires that morning, if my thumb had been on the right button. I would have unleashed Strangelove. I would have set free the Fenris wolf. I would have zapped the universe, had the chance been mine.

twelve

OLIVER

I drove for five hours without a break. It was beautiful. They wanted to stop, to piss, to stretch their legs, to get hamburgers, to do this, to do that, but I didn't pay any attention, I just went driving on. My foot glued to the accelerator, my fingers resting lightly on the steering wheel, my back absolutely straight, my head almost motionless, my eyes trained on a point twenty or thirty feet in front of the windshield. The rhythm of motion possessed me. It was almost a sexual thing: the long glossy car leaping forward, raping the highway, me in command. I took real pleasure from it. I actually got hard for a while.

Last night, with those whores Timothy found, my heart wasn't really in it. Oh, I went three rounds, but only because it was expected of me, and in my thrifty hayseed way I didn't want to waste Timothy's money. Three pops I had, the way the girl said it: "You want to work off another pop now, sweet?" But this, with the car, the long sustained unending thrust of the cylinders, this is practically a kind of intercourse, this is ecstasy. I think I understand now what the motorcycle freaks feel. On and on and on. The throbbing underneath you. We took Route 66, down through Joliet, through Bloomington, on towards Springfield. Not much traffic, lines of trucks in some places but otherwise hardly anything, and the telephone poles going flick-flick-flick past me all the time. A mile a minute, three hundred miles in five hours, even for me an excellent average for driving in the East. Bare, flat fields, some of them still covered with snow. Complaints from the peanut gallery, Eli calling me a goddamn driving machine, Ned nagging me to stop. I pretended I didn't hear them. Eventually they left me alone. Timothy slept, mostly. I was king of the road. By noon it was apparent we'd be in St. Louis in another couple of hours. The plan had been to spend the night there, but that no longer made sense, and when Timothy woke up he got out his maps and tourist guides and started figuring the next lap of the trip. He and Eli had a fight over the way Timothy had planned things. I didn't pay much attention. I think Eli's point was that we should have headed for Kansas City, not St. Louis, coming out of Chicago. I could have told them that a long time ago, but I didn't care what route they took; anyway I wasn't keen on passing through Kansas again. Timothy hadn't realized Chicago and St. Louis were so close together when he first sketched our route.

I tuned out on their squabbling and spent some time thinking about something Eli had said last night while we were running around sightseeing in Chicago. They hadn't been moving fast enough for me, and I tried to nag them into hustling some, and Eli said, "You're really devouring this city, aren't you? Like a tourist doing Paris."

"I haven't ever seen Chicago before," I told him. "I want to get in as much of it as I can."

"Okay, that's cool," he said. But I wanted to know why he was so surprised that I was curious about strange cities. He looked uncomfortable and seemed eager to change the subject. I prodded him. Finally he said, with the little laugh he uses to tell you that he's going to say something with insulting implications but you mustn't think he's serious, "I just wondered why someone who seems so normal. so well-adjusted, is all that interested in sightseeing so intensely." He amplified, unwillingly: to Eli, the hunger for experience, the quest for knowledge, the eagerness to see what's over the next hill are all traits that pertain primarily to those who are underprivileged in some way—members of minority groups, people who have physical blemishes or handicaps, those troubled by social hangups, and so forth. A big good-looking muscular clod like me isn't supposed to have the neuroses that engender intellectual curiosity; he's supposed to be relaxed and easygoing, like Timothy. My little display of intensity was out of character, according to Eli's reading of what my character ought to be. Because he's so far into the ethnic thing, I was ready to have him tell me that the desire to learn is fundamentally a trait found in his people, with a few honorable exceptions. But he didn't quite come out with that, though he was probably thinking it. I wondered then, and still do, why he thinks I'm so well adjusted. Must you be five feet seven, with one shoulder a little higher than the other, in order to have the obsessions and compulsions that Eli equates with intelligence? Eli underestimates me. He's got me stereotyped: big dumb handsome *goy*. I'd like to let him look inside my Gentile skull for five minutes.

We were approaching St. Louis, now. Racing along an empty interstate highway through open farmland; then into something dank and dismal calling itself East St. Louis; and finally the gleaming Gateway Arch, looming up on the far side of the river. We came to a bridge. The idea of crossing the Mississippi absolutely left Eli stoned; he stuck his head and shoulders out of the car, staring out, as though he were crossing the Jordan. When we were on the St. Louis side, I stopped the car in front of a shiny circular mote. The three of them rushed out and scampered around like lunatics. I didn't leave the driver's seat. Wheels were going round in my head. Five unbroken hours of driving. Ecstasy! At last I got up. My right leg was numb. I had to limp for the first few minutes. But it was worth it for those five beautiful hours, those private hours, alone with the car and the highway. I was sorry we had to stop at all.

thirteen

#

A cold blue Ozark evening. Exhaustion, anoxia, nausea: the dividends of auto-fatigue. Enough is enough; here we halt. Four red-eyed robots stagger out of the car. Did we really drive more than a thousand miles today? Yes, a thousand and some, clear across Illinois and Missouri into Oklahoma, long stretches at seventy or eighty miles per, and if Oliver had had his way we'd have driven five hundred more before knocking off. But we couldn't have gone on. Oliver himself admits the quality of his performance began to decline after his six-hundredth mile of the day. He nearly totaled us outside of Joplin, glassy-faced and groggy, wrists failing to deal with the curve his eyes registered. Timothy drove perhaps a hundred miles today, a hundred fifty; I must have done the rest, several stints amounting to three or four hours' worth, sheer terror all the way. But now we must stop. The psychic toll is too great. Doubt, despair, depression, dejection have seeped into our sturdy band. Dejected, disheartened, discouraged, disillusioned, dismayed, we slither into our chosen motel, wondering in our various ways how we could have persuaded ourselves to undertake this expedition. Aha! The Moment-of-Truth Motor Lodge, Nowhere, Oklahoma! The Edge of Reality Motel! Skepticism Inn! Twenty units, fake Colonial, plastic red-brick facing and white wooden columns flanking the entrance. We are the only guests, it seems. Gum-chewing female night clerk, about seventeen years old, her hair teased up into a fantastic 1962 beehive and held in place with embalming fluid. She looks at us languidly, no flicker of interest. Heavy eye makeup, turquoise with black edging. A doxy, a drab, too dumb-whorish even to be a successful whore. "Coffee shop closes at ten," she tells us. Bizarre twanging drawl. Timothy is thinking about inviting her to his room for some fucking, that's obvious to us all; I think he wants to add her to some collection he's making of all-American types. Actually—let me say it in my capacity as objective observer, subspecies polymorphous perverse—she wouldn't really be bad-looking, given a good scrubbing to get rid of all that makeup and hair spray. Fine high breasts jutting against her green uniform; outstanding cheekbones and nose. But the dull eyes, the slack pouting lips, can't be washed away. Oliver gives Timothy a fiery scowl, warning him not to start anything with her. For once Timothy yields: the prevailing mood of depression has him down, too. She assigns us to adjoining double rooms, thirteen dollars apiece, and Timothy offers her his omnipotent slice of plastic. "Room's around to the left," she says, doing her thing with the credit-card machine, and, having done it, disconnects completely from our presence, returning her attention to a Japanese television set with a five-inch screen perched on her counter. We go out to the left, past the drained swimming pool, and let ourselves into our rooms. We must hurry or we'll miss dinner. Drop the luggage, splash water in the faces, out to the coffee shop. One waitress, slouch-backed, gum-chewing; could be the sister of the desk clerk. She too has had a long day; there is an acrid cunty smell about her that hits us hard as she bends over us to plunk silverware on the Formica tabletop. "What'll it be, boys?" No escalopes de veau tonight, no caneton aux cerises. Dead hamburgers, oily coffee. We eat in silence and silently shuffle back to our lodgings. Off with the sweaty clothes. Into the shower, Eli first, then me. The door connecting our room to theirs can be opened. It is opened. Dull boomings from beyond: Oliver, naked, is kneeling before the television set, twiddling dials. I survey him, his taut rear, broad back, the dangling genitals visible below his muscle-bunched thighs. I repress my warped lustful thoughts. These three humanitarians have coped quite well with the problem of living with a bisexual roommate; they pretend that my "sickness," my "condition," does not exist, and carry on from there. The prime liberal rule: don't patronize the handicapped. Pretend that the blind man can see, that the black man is white, that the gay man feels no stirrings at the sight of Oliver's smooth firm ass. Not that I have ever overtly offered at him. But he knows. He knows. Oliver's no fool.

Why are we so depressed tonight? Why this loss of faith?

It must have come from Eli. He was bleak all day, lost in realms of existential despondency. I think it was a purely personal gloom, born of Eli's difficulties in relating to the immediate environment and to the cosmos at large, but it subtly, surreptitiously generalized itself and infected us all. It takes the form of grinding doubts:

1. Why have we bothered to make this trip?
2. What do we really expect to gain?
3. Can we really hope to find what we're looking for?
4. If we find it, do we want it?

So it must begin again, the task of self-hyping, of self-conversion. Eli has his papers out and studies them intently: the manuscript of his translation of the Book of

Skulls, the Xeroxes of the newspaper clippings that led him to connect the place in Arizona with the antique and implausible cult whose scripture the book may have been, and his mass of peripheral documents and references. He looks up after some time and says, " 'All at present known in medicine is almost nothing in comparison of what remains to be discovered . . . we could free ourselves from an infinity of maladies of body as well as of mind, and perhaps also even from the debility of age, if we had sufficiently ample knowledge of their causes, and of all the remedies provided for us by nature.' That's Descartes, *Discourse on Method.* And Descartes again, age forty-two, writing to Huygens's father: 'I never took so much care to conserve myself as I do now, and, though I had thought formerly that death could not rob me of more than thirty or forty years, henceforth it cannot surprise me without depriving me of the hope of more than a century: since it seems to me evident that if we guard ourselves from certain errors which we customarily commit in our way of life, we will be able without other inventions to achieve an old age much longer and happier than now.' "

Not the first time I've heard this. Eli presented all his data to us long before. The decision to go to Arizona ripened exceedingly slowly and was forced along to maturity by acres of pseudophilosophical palaver. Then I said, now I say, "Descartes died at fifty-four, didn't he?"

"An accident. A surprise. Besides, he hadn't perfected his theories of longevity yet."

Timothy: "A pity he didn't work faster."

"A pity, yes, for all of us," Eli said. "But we have the Keepers of the Skulls to look forward to. *They've* perfected their techniques."

"So you say."

"So I believe," said Eli, striving to make himself believe. And the familiar routines came forth once more. Eli, eroded by weariness, teetering on the brink of disbelief, trotting out his arguments to get his head together once more. His hands upraised, fingers outspread, the pedagogical gesture. "We agree," he said, "that coolness is out, pragmatism is through, sophisticated skepticism is obsolete. We've tried that whole pack of attitudes and they don't work. They cut us off from too much that's important. They don't answer enough of the real questions; they just leave us looking wise and cynical, but still ignorant. Agreed?"

"Agreed." Oliver, eyes rigid.

"Agreed." Timothy, yawning.

"Agreed." Even me. A grin.

Eli, again: "There's no mystery left in modern life. The scientific generation killed it all. The rationalist purge, driving out the unlikely and the inexplicable. Look how hollow religion has become in the last hundred years. God's dead, they say. Sure he is: murdered, assassinated. Look, I'm a Jew, I took Hebrew lessons like a good little Yid, I read the Torah, I had a Bar Mitzvah, they gave me fountain pens—did anybody once mention God to me in any context worth listening to? God was somebody who talked to Moses. God was a pillar of fire four thousand years ago. Where's God now? Don't ask a Jew. We haven't seen Him in a while. We worship rules, dietary laws, customs, the words of the Bible, the paper the Bible's printed on, the bound book itself, but we don't worship supernatural beings such as God. The old man in the whiskers, counting sins—no, no, that's for the *shvartzer,* that's for the *goy.* Only what about you three *goyim?* You've got empty religions, too. You, Timothy, high church, what do you have, clouds of incense, brocaded robes, the choir boys singing Vaughan Williams and Elgar. You, Oliver, Methodist, Baptist, Presbyterian, I can't even keep them straight, they're nothing, nothing at all, no spiritual content, no mystery, no ecstasy. Like being a Reform Jew. And you, Ned, the papist, the priest who didn't make it, what do you have? The Virgin? The saints? The Christ Child? You can't believe that crap. It's been burned out of your brain. It's for peasants, it's for the lumpenproletariat. The ikons and the holy water. The bread and the wine. You'd like to believe it—Jesus, I'd like to believe it myself, Catholicism's the only complete reli-

gion in this civilization, the only one that even tries to do
the mystery thing, the resonances with the supernatural,
the awareness of higher powers. Only they've ruined it,
they ruined *us,* you can't accept a thing. It's all Bing
Crosby and Ingrid Bergman now, or the Berrigans writing
manifestos, or Polacks warning against godless communism
and X-rated movies. So religion's gone. It's over. And
where does that leave us? Alone under an awful sky,
waiting for the end. Waiting for the end."

"Plenty of people still go to church," Timothy
pointed out. "Even to synagogue, I suppose."

"Out of habit. Out of fear. Out of social necessity.
Do they open their souls to God? When did you last open
your soul to God, Timothy? Oliver? Ned? When did I?
When did we even think of doing anything like that? It
sounds absurd. God's been so polluted by the evangelists
and the archaeologists and the theologists and the fake-
devout that it's no wonder He's dead. Suicide. But where
does that leave us? Are we all going to be scientists and
explain everything in terms of neutrons and protons and
DNA? Where's mystery? Where's depth? *We have to do it
all ourselves,"* Eli said. "There's a lack of mystery in
modern life. All right, then, it becomes the intelligent
man's task to create an atmosphere in which surrender to
the implausible is possible. A closed mind is a dead mind."
He was warming up, now. Fervor taking hold of him. The
Billy Graham of the Stoned Age. "For the last eight, ten
years, we've all been trying to stumble toward some kind
of workable synthesis, some structural correlative that'll
hold the world together for us in the middle of all the
chaos. The pot, the acid, the communes, the rock, the
whole transcendentalist thing, the astrology, the macro-
biotics, the Zen—we're searching, right, we're always
searching? And sometimes finding. Not often. We look in a
lot of dumb places, because basically we're mostly dumb,
even the best of us, and also because we can't know the
answers until we've worked out more of the questions. So
we chase after flying saucers. We put on Scuba suits and
look for Atlantis, We're into mythology, fantasy, paranoia,

Middle Earth, freakiness, a thousand kinds of irrationality. Whatever *they've* rejected, we buy, often for no better reason than that they turned it down. The flight from reason. I don't entirely defend it. I just say it's necessary, it's a stage we all have to pass through, the fire, the annealing. Reason wasn't sufficient. Western man escaped from superstitious ignorance into materialistic emptiness: now we've got to continue on, sometimes down blind alleys and false trails, until we learn how to accept the universe again in all its mysterious inexplicable tremendousness, until we find the right thing, the synthesis, the getting together that lets us live the way we ought to be living. And then we can live forever. Or so close to forever as doesn't make any difference."

Timothy said, "And you want us to believe that the Book of Skulls shows the way, huh?"

"It's a possibility. It gives us a finite chance to enter the infinite. Isn't that good enough? Isn't that worth trying? Where did sneering get us? Where did doubt get us? Where did skepticism get us? Can't we *try*? Can't we *look?*" Eli had found his faith again. He was shouting, sweating, standing up stark naked and waving his arms around. His whole body was on fire. He was actually beautiful, just for that moment. Eli, beautiful!

I said, "I'm into this all the way, and at the same time I don't buy it for half an inch. Do you follow me? I dig the dialectic of the myth. Its implausibility batters against my skepticism and drives me onward. Tensions and contradictions are my fuel."

Timothy, devil's advocate, shook his head—a heavy taurine gesture, his big beefy frame moving like a slow pendulum. "Come on, man. What do you *really* believe? The Skulls, yes or no, salvation or crap, fact or fantasy. Which?"

"Both," I said.

"Both? You can't have it both."

"Yes I can!" I cried. "Both! Both! Yes and no! Can you follow me to where I live, Timothy? In the place where the tension's greatest, where the yes is drawn tight

against the no. Where you simultaneously reject the
existence of the inexplicable and accept the existence of
the inexplicable. Life eternal! That's crap, isn't it, a load of
wishful thinking, the old hogwash dream? And yet it's real,
too. We *can* live a thousand years, if we want to. But it's
impossible. I affirm. I deny. I applaud. I jeer."

"You don't make sense," Timothy grumbled.

"You make too much sense. I shit on your sense!
Eli's right: we need mystery, we need unreason, we need
the unknown, we need the impossible. A whole generation's been teaching itself to believe the unbelievable,
Timothy. And there you stand with your crew cut on,
saying it doesn't make sense."

Timothy shrugged. "Right. What do you want
from me? I'm just a dumb jock."

"That's your pose," Eli said. "Your persona, your
mask. Big dumb jock. It insulates you. It spares you from
having to make any commitment whatsoever, emotional,
political, ideological, metaphysical. You say you don't
understand, and you shrug, and you step back and laugh.
Why do you want to be a zombie, Timothy? Why do you
want to disconnect yourself?"

"He can't help it, Eli," I said. "He was bred to be a
gentleman. He's disconnected by definition."

"Oh, fuck you," Timothy said, in his most gentle-
manly way. "What do you know, either of you? And what
am I doing here? Dragged halfway across the Western
Hemisphere by a Jew and a queer to check out a
thousand-year-old fairy tale!"

I made a little curtsy. "Hey, well done, Timothy!
The mark of the true gentleman: he never gives offense
unintentionally."

"You asked it," said Eli, "so you answer it. What
are you doing here?"

"And don't blame me for dragging you here," I
said. "This is Eli's trip. I'm as skeptical as you are, maybe
even more so."

Timothy snorted. I think he felt outnumbered. He
said, very quietly, "I just came along for the ride."

"For the ride! For the ride!" Eli.

"You asked me to come. What the crap, you needed four guys, you said, and I had nothing better to do for Easter. My buddies. My pals. I said I'd go. My car, my money. I can play along with a gag. Margo's into astrology, you know, it's Libra this and Pisces that, and Mars transits the solar tenth house, and Saturn's on the cusp, and she won't fuck without first checking the stars, which can sometimes be quite inconvenient. And do I make fun of her? Do I laugh at her the way her father does?"

"Only inside," Eli said.

"That's my business. I accept what I can accept, and I have no use for the rest. But I'm good-hearted about it. I tolerate her witch doctors. I tolerate yours, too, Eli. That's another mark of the gentleman, Ned: he's amiable, he doesn't proselytize, he never pushes his thing at the expense of someone else's thing."

"He doesn't have to," I said.

"He doesn't have to, no. All right: I'm here, yes? I'm paying for this room, yes? I'm cooperating 400 per cent. Must I be a True Believer, too? Must I get your religion?"

"What will you do," Eli said, "when we're actually in the skullhouse and the Keepers are offering us the Trial? Will you still be a skeptic then? Will your habit of not believing be such a hassle for you that you won't be able to surrender?"

"I'll evaluate that," Timothy answered slowly, "when I have something to base my evaluation on." Suddenly he turned to Oliver. "You've been pretty quiet, All-American."

"What do you want me to say?" Oliver asked. His long lean body stretched out in front of the television set. Every muscle outlined against his skin: a walking anatomy textbook. His lengthy pink apparatus, drooping out of a golden forest, inspiring me with improper thoughts. *Retro me, Sathanas.* This way lies Gomorrah, if not Sodom.

"Don't you have anything to contribute to the discussion?"

"I really wasn't paying close attention."

"We were talking about this trip. The Book of Skulls and the degree of faith we have in it," said Timothy.

"I see."

"Would you care to make a profession of belief, Dr. Marshall?"

Oliver seemed to be midway in a journey to another galaxy. He said, "I give Eli the benefit of the doubt."

"You believe in the Skulls, then?" Timothy asked.

"I believe."

"Although we know the whole thing's absurd?"

"Yes," said Oliver. "Even though it's absurd."

"That was Tertullian's position, too," Eli put in. *Credo quia absurdum est.* I believe because it's absurd. A different context of belief, of course, but the psychology's right."

"Yes, yes, my position exactly!" I said. "I believe because it's absurd. Good old Tertullian. He says precisely what I feel. My position exactly."

"Not mine." Oliver.

"No?" Eli asked.

Oliver said, "No. I believe *despite* the absurdity."

"Why?" Eli said.

"Why, Oliver?" I said, a long moment later. "You know it's absurd, and yet you believe. Why?"

"Because I have to," he said. "Because it's my only hope."

He stared straight at me. His eyes held a peculiarly devastated expression, as though he had looked into the face of Death with them and had come away still alive, but with every option blasted, every possibility shriveled. He had heard the drums and fifes of the dead-march, at the edge of the universe. Those frosty eyes withered me. Those strangled words impaled me. *I believe,* he said. *Despite the absurdity. Because I have to. Because it's my only hope.* A communique from some other planet. I could feel the chilly presence of Death there in the room with us, brushing silently past our rosy boyish cheeks.

fourteen

timothy

We're a heavy mixture, we four. How did we ever get together? What tangling of lifelines dumped us all into the same dormitory suite, anyway?

In the beginning it was just me and Oliver, two freshmen who'd been computer-assigned to a double room overlooking the quadrangle. I was straight out of Andover and very full of my own importance. I don't mean that I was impressed by the family money. I took that for granted, always had: everybody I grew up with was rich, so I had no real sense of how rich we were, and anyway *I* had done nothing to earn the money (nor my father, nor my father's father, nor my father's father's father, et cetera et cetera), so why should it puff me up? What swelled my head was a sense of ancestry, of knowing that I had the blood of Revolutionary War heroes in me, of senators and congressmen, of diplomats, of great nineteenth-century financiers. I was a walking slab of history. Also I enjoyed knowing that I was tall and strong and healthy—sound body, sound mind, all the natural advantages. Out beyond the campus was a world full of blacks and Jews and spastics and neurotics and homosexuals and other misfits, but I had come up three cherries on the great slot machine of life and I was proud of my luck. Also I had an allowance of one hundred dollars a week, which was convenient, and I may not actually have been aware that most eighteen-year-olds had to get along on somewhat less.

Then there was Oliver. I figured the computer had given me a lucky dip again, because I might have been assigned somebody weird, somebody kinky, somebody with a squashed, envious, embittered soul, and Oliver seemed altogether normal. Good-looking corn-fed pre-med from the wilds of Kansas. He was my own height—an inch or so taller, in fact—and that was cool; I'm ill at ease with short men. Oliver had an uncomplicated exterior. Almost anything made him smile. An easygoing type. Both parents dead: he was here on a full scholarship. I realized right away that he had no money at all and was afraid for a minute that would cause resentment between us, but no, he was altogether levelheaded about it. Money didn't appear to interest him as long as he had enough to pay for food and shelter and clothing, and he had that—a small inheritance, the proceeds of selling the family farm. He was amused, not threatened, by the thick roll I always carried. He told me the first day that he was planning on going out for the basketball team, and I thought he had an athletic scholarship, but I was wrong about that: he liked basketball, he took it very seriously, but he was here to *learn*. That was the real difference between us, not the Kansas thing or the money thing, but his sense of dedication. I was going to college because all the men of my family go to college between prep school and adulthood; Oliver was here to transform himself into a ferocious intellectual machine. He had—still has—tremendous, incredible, overwhelming inner drive. Now and then, those first few weeks, I caught him with his mask down; the sunny farm-boy grin vanished and his face went rigid, the jaw muscles clamping, the eyes radiating a cold gleam. His intensity could be scary. He had to be perfect in everything. He had a straight-A average, close to the absolute top of our class, and he made the freshman basketball team and broke the college scoring record in the opening game, and he was up half of every night studying, hardly sleeping at all. Still, he managed to seem human. He drank a lot of beer, he balled any number of girls (we used to trade with each other), and he could play a decent guitar. The only place where he revealed the other Oliver, the machine-Oliver, was when it came to drugs. Second week on campus I scored some groovy Moroccan hash and he absolutely wouldn't. Told me that he'd spent 17½ years calibrating his head properly and he wasn't about to let it get messed up now. Nor has he blown so much as a single joint, as far as I'm aware, in the four years since. He tolerates our smoking dope but he won't have any.

The spring of our sophomore year we acquired Ned. Oliver and I had signed up to room together again that year. Ned was in two of Oliver's classes: physics, which Ned needed to fulfill his minimum science requirement, and comparative lit, which Oliver needed to fulfill his minimum humanities requirement. Oliver had a little trouble digging Joyce and Yeats, and Ned had a lot of trouble digging quantum theory and thermodynamics, so they worked out a reciprocal coaching arrangement. It was an attraction of opposites, the two of them. Ned was small, soft-spoken, skinny, with big gentle eyes and a delicate way of moving. Boston Irish, strong Catholic background, educated in parochial schools; he still wore a crucifix when we were sophs and sometimes even went to mass. He intended to be a poet and short-story writer. No, "intended" isn't the right word. As Ned explained it once, people with talent don't *intend* to be writers. Either you have it or you don't. Those who have it, write, and those who don't, intend. Ned was always writing. Still is. Carries a spiral-bound notebook, jots down everything he hears. Actually I think his short stories are crap and his poetry is nonsense, but I recognize that the fault probably lies in my taste, not in his talent, since I feel the same way about a lot of writers much more famous than Ned. At least he works at his art.

He became a kind of mascot for us. He was always much closer to Oliver than he was to me, but I didn't mind having him around; he was somebody different, somebody with a whole other outlook on life. His husky voice, his sad-dog eyes, his freaky clothes (he wore robes a lot, I suppose by way of pretending he had gone into the priesthood after all), his poetry, his peculiar brand of sarcasm, his complicated head (he always took two or three sides of every issue and managed to believe in everything and nothing simultaneously)—they all fascinated me. We must have seemed just as foreign to him as he to us. He spent so much time around our place that we invited him to room with us for our junior year. I don't remember whose idea that was, Oliver's or mine. (Ned's?)

I didn't know he was queer, at the time. Or rather, that he was gay, to use the term he prefers. The problem with leading a sheltered Wasp life is that you see only a narrow slice of humanity, and you don't come to expect the unexpected. I knew such things as fags existed, of course. We had them at Andover. They walked with their elbows out and combed their hair a lot and talked with a special accent, the universal faggot accent that you hear from Maine to California. They read Proust and Gide all the time and some of them wore brassieres under their T-shirts. Ned wasn't outwardly swishy, though. And I wasn't the sort of meatball who automatically assumed that anyone who wrote (or read!) poetry had to be queer. He was arty, yes, he was hip, he was nonjock all the way, but you don't expect a man who weighs 115 pounds to have much interest in football. (He did go swimming almost every day. We swim bare-ass at the college pool, of course, so for Ned it was like a free beaver flick, but I didn't think of that then.) One thing, he didn't go around with girls that I noticed. Still, that in itself isn't a condemnation. The week before finals, two years ago, Oliver and I and a few other guys had what I guess you'd call an orgy in our room, and Ned was there, and he didn't seem turned off by the idea. I saw him balling a chick, a pimply waitress in from town. It was a long time afterward that I realized: one, that Ned might find an orgy useful to him as material to write about, and two, that he doesn't really *despise* cunt, he just doesn't care for it as much as he does for boys.

Ned brought us Eli. No, they weren't lovers, just buddies. That was practically the first thing Eli said to me: "In case you're wondering, I'm hetero. Ned doesn't go for my type and I don't go for his." I'll never forget it. It was the first hint I had had that Ned was that way, and I don't think Oliver had realized it either, though you never really know what's going on in Oliver's mind. Eli had spotted Ned right away, of course, A city boy, a Manhattan intellectual, he could put everybody into the proper category with one glance. He didn't like his roommate and wanted out, and we had a huge suite, so he said something to Ned and Ned asked if he could transfer in with us, the November of our junior year. My first Jew. I didn't know *that*, either—oh, Winchester, you naive prick, you! Eli Steinfeld from West Eighty-third Street, and you can't guess he's a Hebe! Honestly, I thought it was just a German name: Jews are called Cohen or Katz or Goldberg. I wasn't really captivated by Eli's personality, you might say, but once I found out he was Jewish I felt I had to let him room with us. For the sake of broadening myself through diversity, yes, and also because I had been raised to dislike Jews and I had to rebel against that. My grandfather on my father's side had had some bad experiences with clever Jews around 1923; some Wall Street Abies suckered him into investing heavily in a radio company they were organizing, and they were crooks and he lost about five million, so it became a family tradition to mistrust Jews. They were vulgar, pushy, sly, et cetera et cetera, always trying to do an honest Protestant millionaire out of his hard-inherited wealth, et cetera et cetera. In fact, my Uncle Clark once admitted to me that Grandfather would have doubled his money if he'd sold out within eight months, which is what his Jewish partners secretly did, but no, he hung on waiting for still fatter profits, and got clobbered. Anyway I don't uphold *all* the family traditions. Eli moved in. Short, somewhat swarthy, a lot of body hair, quick nervous bright little eyes, big nose. A brilliant mind. An expert on medieval languages; already recognized as an important scholar in his field and still an undergraduate. On the other side of the ledger, he was pretty pathetic—tongue-tied, neurotic, hypertense, worried about his masculinity. Forever prowling after girls, usually getting nowhere. Doggish girls, too. Not the spectacularly ugly broads that Ned prefers, God knows why; Eli went after a different sort of female loser—shy, scrawny, inconspicuous girls, thick glasses, flat chests, you know the bit. Naturally, they're as neurotic as he is, terrified of sex, and they wouldn't come across for him, which only made his problems worse. He seemed absolutely afraid to approach a normal, attractive, sensual chick. One day last fall as an act of Christian charity I turned Margo on to him and he screwed things up something unimaginable.

Quite a foursome. I doubt that I'll ever forget the first (and probably only) time all of our parents got together, in the spring of our junior year, at the big Carnival weekend. Up till then I don't think any of the parents had visualized their son's roommates in any clear way. I had Oliver home to meet my father a couple of Christmases, but not Ned or Eli, and I hadn't seen their folks either. So here we all were. No family for Oliver, of course. And Ned's father was dead. His mother was a gaunt hollow-eyed bony woman nearly six feet tall, in black clothes, speaking with a brogue. I couldn't connect her with Ned at all. Eli's mother was plump, short, a waddler, very much overdressed; his father was almost invisible, a tiny sad-faced man who sighed a lot. They both looked much older than Eli. They must have had him when they were thirty-five or forty. Then there was my father, who looks the way I imagine I'll look twenty-five years from now—smooth pink cheeks, thick hair shading from blond to gray, a moneyed look about the eyes. A big man, a handsome man, the board-of-directors type. With him was Saybrook, his wife, who I guess is thirty-eight and could pass for ten years younger, tall, well-scrubbed, long straight yellow hair, big-boned athletic body, very much the fox-and-hounds sort of woman. Imagine this group sitting under a parasol at a table in the quandrangle, trying to make conversation. Mrs. Steinfeld trying to mother Oliver, the poor dear orphan. Mr. Steinfeld eyeing my father's $450 Italian silk suit in horror. Ned's mother completely out of it, understanding neither her son, her son's friends, their parents, nor any other aspect of the twentieth century. Saybrook coming on all hearty and horsey, talking blithely about charity teas and her step-daughter's imminent debut. ("Is she an actress?" Mrs. Steinfeld asked, baffled. "I mean her coming-out party," said Saybrook, just as baffled.) My father studying his fingernails a lot, staring hard at the Steinfelds and at Eli, not wanting to believe any of this. Mr. Steinfeld, to make conversation, talking about the stock market to my father. Mr. Steinfeld doesn't have investments but he reads the *Times* very carefully. My father knows nothing about the market; so long as the dividends come on time, he's happy; besides, it's part of his religion never to talk about money. He flashes a signal to Saybrook, who deftly changes the subject, starts telling us about how she's chairman of a committee to raise funds for Palestinian Arab refugees, you know, she says, the ones who were driven out by the Jews when Israel got started. Mrs. Steinfeld gasps. Such a thing to say in front of a Hadassah member! My father then points across the quadrangle to a particularly long-haired classmate who had just turned around and says, "I could have sworn that fellow was a girl, until he looked this way." Oliver, who has let his hair grow to his shoulders, I suppose to show what he thinks of Kansas, gives my father his coldest, coldest smile. Undaunted, or unnoticing, my father continues, "Perhaps I'm wrong about this, but I can't help suspecting that many of those young men with flowing locks are, you know, a trifle homosexual." Ned laughs out loud at this. Ned's mother turns red and coughs—not because she knows her boy is gay (she doesn't—the idea would be incredible to her) but because that fine-looking Mr. Winchester has said a nasty word at the table. The Steinfelds, who are quick on the uptake, look at Ned, then at Eli, then at each other—a very complex bit of reaction. Is their boy safe with such a roommate? My father can't comprehend what his casual remark has started and doesn't know who to apologize to for what. He frowns and Saybrook whispers something to him—tsk, Saybrook, whispering in public, what would Emily Post say?—and he responds with a magnificent blush extending far into the infrared. "Perhaps we can order some wine," he says, loudly, to cover his confusion, and imperiously summons a student-waiter. "Do you have Chassagne-Montrachet '69?" he asks. "Sir?" the waiter replies blankly. An ice bucket is fetched, containing a bottle of three-buck Liebfraumilch, the best they can offer, and my father pays for it with a brand-new fifty. Ned's mother stares at the bill in disbelief; the Steinfelds scowl at my father, thinking he's trying to put them down. A beautiful, beautiful episode, this whole lunch. Afterward Saybrook draws me aside and says, "Your father feels very embarrassed. If he had known Eli was, well, attracted to other boys, he would never have made that remark."

"Not Eli," I said. "Eli's straight. Ned."

Saybrook is flustered. She thinks I may be putting her on. She wants to say that she and my father hope I'm not fucking around with either of them, whichever one may be queer, but she's much too well bred to tell me that. Instead she slides into neutral chitchat for the pre-scribed three minutes, gracefully breaks free, goes back to explain to my father the latest twist. I see the Steinfelds conferring in anguish with Eli, no doubt giving him hell for rooming with a snotty Gentile and warning him sternly to keep away from that little *faygeleh,* too, if it isn't *(oy! veh!)* already too late. Ned and his mother are generation-gapping also, not far away. I pick up stray phrases: "The sisters are praying for you . . . transfer to Holy Cross . . . novena . . . rosary . . . your angel father . . . novitiate . . . Jesuit . . . Jesuit . . . Jesuit. . . ." To one side, alone, is Oliver. Watching. Smiling his Venusian smile. Just a visitor on Earth, he is, is Oliver, the man from the flying saucer.

I'd rate Oliver as the deepest mind of the group. He doesn't know as much as Eli, he doesn't give the same appearance of brilliance, but he has a more powerful intelligence, I'm sure. He's also the strangest of us, because on the surface he appears so wholesome and normal, and he really isn't. Eli has the quickest wits among us, and he's also the most tormented, the most troubled. Ned poses as our weakling, our fairy, but don't underestimate him: he knows what he wants all the time, and he sees that he gets it. And me? What's there to say about me? Good old Joe College. The right family connections, the right fraternity, the right clubs. In June I graduate and begin to live happily ever after. An Air Force commission, yes, but no combat duty—it's all arranged, our genes are deemed too good to waste—and then I find an appropriate Episcopalian debutante, certified virgin and belonging to one of the Hundred Families, and settle down to be a gentleman. Jesus! Thank God Eli's Book of Skulls is nothing but superstitious crap. If I had to live forever I'd bore myself to death in twenty years.

fifteen

oliver

When I was sixteen I gave a great deal of thought to killing myself. Honestly. It wasn't a pretense, a romantic adolescent drama, an expression of what Eli would call a willed persona. It was a genuine philosophical position, if I can use so impressive-sounding a term, which I arrived at logically and rigorously.

What led me to the contemplation of suicide was, above all, my father's dying at thirty-six. That seemed like such an unbearable tragedy to me. Not that my father was in any way a special human being, except to me. He was just a Kansas farmer, after all. Up at five in the morning, in bed by nine at night. No education to speak of. All he read was the county newspaper, and sometimes the Bible, though most of that was over his head. But he worked hard all his short life. He was a good man, a dedicated man. It was his father's land first, and my father worked it from the age of ten, with a few years out for the army; he brought in his crops, he retired his debt, he made a living, more or less, he even was able to buy forty acres more and think of expanding beyond that. Meanwhile he married, he gave pleasure to a woman, he sired children. He was a simple man—he would never have understood anything that's happened in this country in the ten years since he died—but he was a decent man, in his way, and he had earned the right to a happy old age. Sitting on the porch, puffing his pipe, going hunting in the fall, letting his sons do the really back-breaking work, watching his grand-children grow up. He didn't get a happy old age. He didn't even get a middle age. Cancer sprouted in his guts and he died fast, he died in agony but fast.

That started me thinking. If you can be cut off like that, if you must live under a sentence of death all your days and never know when it will be carried out, why live at all? Why give Death the satisfaction of coming to claim you when you're least ready for it? Get out, get out early. Avoid the irony of being chopped down as punishment for having made something of your life.

My father's goal in life, as I understood it, was to keep to the way of the Lord and pay off the mortgage on his land. He succeeded with the first and came pretty close with the second. My goal was more ambitious: to get an education, to rise above the dirt of the fields, to become a doctor, a scientist. Doesn't that sound grand? *The Nobel Prize in Medicine to Dr. Oliver Marshall, who climbed out of the tobacco-chewing ignorance of the Corn Belt to become an inspiration for us all.* But did my goal differ in anything but degree from my father's? What it boiled down to, for both of us, was a life of hard work, honest toil.

I couldn't face it. Saving money, taking tests, ap-plying for the scholarship, learning Latin and German, anatomy, physics, chemistry, biology, breaking my skull with labors tougher than anything my father had known—

and then to die? To die at forty-five, or fifty-five, or sixty-five, or maybe, like my father, at thirty-six? Just when you're ready to start to live, it's time to go. Why bother to make the effort? Why submit to the irony? Look at President Kennedy: all that outlay of energy and skill to get himself into the White House, and then the bullet in his skull. Life is a waste. The more you succeed in making out of yourself, the more bitter a thing it is to have to die. Me, with my ambitions, my drives, I was only setting myself up for a bigger downfall than most. Inasmuch as I would have to die eventually, I resolved to cheat Death by doing away with myself before I began forcing myself toward the inevitable sick joke that was waiting for me.

So I told myself, age sixteen. I made lists of possible ways to bug out. Cut my wrists? Turn on the gas? Plastic bag over my head? Rack up my car? Look for thin ice in January? I had fifty different plans. I arranged them in order of desirability. I rearranged them. I balanced quick painful deaths against slow easy ones. For half a year, maybe, I studied suicide the way Eli studies irregular verbs. Two of my grandparents died in those six months. My dog died. My older brother was killed in the war. My mother had her first bad heart attack, and the doctor privately told me she wouldn't last another year, which was correct. All this should have reinforced my decision: get out, Oliver, get out, get out now, before life's tragedies come even closer to you! You've got to die, just like the others, so why stall for time? Die now. Die now. Save yourself a load of trouble. Curiously, though, my interest in suicide rapidly waned, even though my philosophy didn't really change. I stopped making lists of ways to kill myself. I started planning ahead, instead of assuming that I'd be gone within the next few months. I decided I would fight Death rather than surrender to him. I *would* go to college, I *would* become a scientist, I *would* learn all I could, and perhaps I'd push the border of Death's country back a little. Now I know that I'll never kill myself. I'm just not going to do it, ever. I'll go on fighting to the end, and if Death comes to laugh in my face, why, I'll laugh in his. And, after all, suppose the Book of Skulls is authentic! Suppose an escape from him really exists! The joke would have been on me, then, if I'd cut my wrists five years ago.

I must have driven four hundred miles already today, and it isn't even noon yet. The roads here are great—wide, straight, empty. Amarillo is just ahead. And then Albuquerque. And then Phoenix. And then, at last, we start to find out a lot of things.

sixteen

eli

How strange the world looks here. Texas; New Mexico. A lunar landscape. Why did anyone ever want to settle in this kind of country? The broad brown plateaus, no grass, only twisted scrubby greasy gray-green plants. The bare purple mountains, jagged, sharp, rimming the harsh blue horizon like eroded teeth. I thought the mountains out west were bigger than these. Timothy, who's been everywhere, says that the really big mountains are in Colorado, Utah, California; these are just hills, five or six thousand feet high. I was shaken by that. The biggest mountain east of the Mississippi is Mount Mitchell, North Carolina, something like sixty-seven hundred feet. I lost a bet about that when I was ten and never forgot it. The biggest mountain I had ever seen before this trip was Mount Washington, sixty-three hundred feet or so, New Hampshire, where my parents took me the one year we didn't go to the Catskills.

(I was betting on Mount Washington. I was wrong.) And here all around me are mountains the size of those, and they're just hills. They probably don't even have names. Mount Washington hung in the sky like a giant tree, about to fall and crush me. Of course, here the view is broader, the landscape is wide open; even a mountain is dwarfed by the immense perspective.

The air is crisp and cold. The sky is improbably blue and clear. This is apocalyptic country: I keep expecting to hear the crack of trumpet calls resounding out of the "hills." Wondrous sound the trumpet flingeth, through earth's sepulchres it ringeth, all before the throne it bringeth. Yes. And death will be stupefied. We go thirty, forty miles between towns, seeing only jackrabbits, deer, squirrels. The towns themselves seem new: filling stations, a row of motels, small square aluminum houses that look as though they can be attached to an automobile and driven off to some other place. (Probably they can be.) On the other hand, we have passed two pueblos, six or seven hundred years old, and there will be more. The idea that there are actually Indians, live Indians, walking around all over the place, blows my Manhattanized mind. There were Indians galore in the technicolor movies I saw every Saturday afternoon for years on Seventy-third Street and Broadway, but I was never taken in, I knew with my cool small-boy wisdom that they were just Puerto Ricans or maybe Mexicans togged out in fancy feathers. Real Indians were nineteenth-century stuff, they had died out long ago, none of them left except on the nickel with the buffalo on the other side, and when did you last see one of those? (When did you last see a buffalo?) Indians were archaic, Indians were extinct, Indians, to me, were in a class with the mastodon, the tyrannosaurus, the Sumerians, the Carthaginians. But no, here I am in the Wild West for the first time in my life, and the flat-faced, leather-colored man who sold us our lunchtime beer in the grocery store was an Indian, and the roly-poly kid who filled our gas tank was an Indian, and those mud huts on the far side of the Rio Grande there are inhabited by Indians, even though I can see a forest of television aerials rising above the adobe rooftops. See the Indians, Dick! See the giant cactus plants! Look, Jane, look, the Indian drives a Volkswagen! Watch Ned cut the Indian off! Listen to the Indian honk his horn!

I think our commitment to this adventure has deepened since we reached the desert's edge. Certainly mine has. That terrible day of doubt, while we were driving across Missouri, now seems as far in the past as the dinosaurs. I know now (how do I know? how can I say?) that what I have read in the Book of Skulls is real, and what we have come to find in the wastes of Arizona is real, and that if we persevere we will be granted that which we seek. Oliver knows it, too. A weird freaky intensity has surfaced in him these last few days. Oh, it was always there, that tendency toward monomania, but he did a better job of concealing it. Now, sitting behind the wheel ten or twelve hours a day, needing virtually to be forced to stop driving, he makes it altogether clear that nothing is more urgent for him than to reach our destination and submit himself to the disciplines of the Keepers of the Skulls. Even our two unbelievers are catching the faith. Ned oscillates between absolute acceptance and absolute rejection, as ever, and often holds both positions simultaneously; he mocks us, he needles us, and yet he studies maps and mileage charts as though he, too, is seized by impatience. Ned is the only man I know capable of attending a mass at sunrise and a black mass at midnight, all the while feeling no sense of incongruity, devoting himself with equal fervor to each rite. Timothy still remains aloof, a genial scoffer, protesting that he's merely humoring his far-out roommates by undertaking this pilgrimage—but how much of that is just a front, a show of proper aristocratic coolness? More than a little, I suspect. Timothy has less reason than the rest of us to hunger after metaphysical life-extensions, because his own life as presently constituted offers him such an infinity of possibilities—his financial resources being what they are. But money isn't everything, and you can do only so much in the standard threescore and ten, even if you've inherited Fort Knox. He's tempted by the vision of the skullhouse, I believe. He's tempted.

By the time we reach our goal, tomorrow, the day after tomorrow, I think we'll have drawn together into that cohesive four-sided unit that the Book of Skulls calls a Receptacle: that is, a group of candidates. Let's hope so. It was last year, wasn't it, that so much fuss was made over those midwestern students who carried out a suicide pact? Yes. A Receptacle can be considered to be the philosophical antithesis of a suicide pact. Both represent manifestations of alienation from present-day society. I reject your loathsome world entirely, says the member of a suicide pact; therefore I choose to die. I reject your loathsome world entirely, says the member of a Receptacle; therefore I choose never to die, in the hope that I will live to see better days.

seventeen

Albuquerque. A dreary city, miles of suburbs, an endless string of gaudy motels along Route 66, a pathetic schlocky touristy Old Town down at the far end of things. If I have to have tourist-west, let me have Santa Fe, at least, with its adobe shops, its pretty hilltop streets, its few genuine remnants of the Spanish colonial past. But we aren't going that way. Here we part from U.S. 66, finally, and roll

southward on 85 and 25 almost to the Mexican border,
down to Las Cruces, where we pick up Route 70 that
shoots us toward Phoenix. How long have we been driving
now? Two days, three, four? I've lost all track of time. I sit
here hour after hour watching Oliver drive, and occasionally I do some of the driving myself, or Timothy does, and
the wheels impinge on my soul, the carburetor fires in my
gut, the interface between passenger and vehicle dissolves.
We are all parts of this snorting monster rolling westward.
America lies sprawling, gassed, behind us. Chicago is only a
memory now. St. Louis is only a bad dream. Joplin,
Springfield, Tulsa, Amarillo—unreal, lacking in substance.
A continent of pinched faces and small souls back there.
Fifty million cases of severe menstrual cramps erupt to the
east, and we couldn't care less. A plague of premature
ejaculation spreads through the great urban metropolises.
All heterosexual males over the age of seventeen in Ohio,
Pennsylvania, Michigan, and Tennessee have been smitten
by an outbreak of hemorrhaging hemorrhoids, and Oliver
drives on, giving no damns.

   I like this part of the country. It's open, unclut-
tered, vaguely Wagnerian, with a good campy westernness
about it: you see the men in their string ties and ten-gallon
hats, you see the Indians sleeping in the doorways, you see
the sagebrush swarming up the hillsides, and you know it's
right, it's all the way it's supposed to be. I was here the
summer I was eighteen, mostly in Sante Fe, bunking with
an agreeable weather-beaten suntanned fortyish dealer in
Indian artifacts. A member of the Homintern, he. A card-
carrying official of the International Pervo-Devo Conspiracy. They say it takes one to tell one, but in his case it
took no great amount of telling: he did the lisp thing, the
accent thing, he was plainly a squaw. He taught me, among
much else, how to drive a car. All during August I made his
collecting rounds for him, visiting his suppliers; he buys
old pots for five bucks, sells them to antiquity-minded
tourists for fifty. Low overhead, quick turnover. I under-
took solitary terrifying voyages, hardly knowing my clutch
from my elbow, driving down to Bernalillo, up to Farming-

ton, over to the Rio Puerco country, even making a vast
expedition out to Hopi, going to all sorts of places where,
in violation of local archaeological ordinances, the farmers
raid unexcavated ruined pueblos and winkle out salable
merchandise. Also I met a number of Indians, many of
them (surprise!) gay. I remember fondly a certain groovy
Navaho. And a swaggering buck from Taos who, once he
was sure of my credentials, took me down into a kiva and
initiated me into some of the tribal mysteries, giving me
access to ethnographical data for which many scholars no
doubt would sell their foreskins. A profound experience. A
mind-blower. I mean to tell the world that it's not just
your asshole that gets broadened, when you're gay.

Trouble with Oliver this afternoon. I was driving,
rocketing down 25 somewhere between Belen and Socor-
ro, feeling ballsy and light, for once the master of the car
and not just something caught in the machinery. Half a
mile ahead I spotted a figure, walking on our side of the
road, evidently a hitchhiker. On impulse, I slowed. A
hitcher, right: more than that, a hippie, the genuine 1967
article, long scruffy hair, sheepskin vest over bare chest,
stars-and-stripes patch on the seat of his tie-dyed jeans,
knapsack, no shoes. I suppose heading toward one of the
desert communes, trudging alone from nowhere to nowhere. Well, in a sense we were heading toward a commune, too, and I felt we could accommodate him. I braked
the car almost to a halt. He looked up, maybe flashing
quickly on paranoia, saw *Easy Rider* once too often and
was expecting a blast of good Amurrican gunfire, but the
fear went out of his face when he saw we were kids. He
grinned, gap-toothed, and I could almost hear the
mumbled little courtesies, like I mean, wow, sure is cool of
you to pick me up, man, like I mean, you know, it's a long
walk, the straights around here won't help you nohow,
man, when Oliver said, simply, "No."

"No?"

"Keep on driving."

"We've got room in the car," I said.

"I don't want to take the time."

"Christ, Oliver, the guy's harmless! And he gets maybe one car an hour out here. If you were in his position—"

"How do you know he's harmless?" Oliver asked. By now the hippie was less that a hundred feet to the rear of where I'd stopped. "Maybe he's part of Charles Manson's family," Oliver went on quietly. "Maybe his thing is knifing guys who sentimentalize hippies."

"Oh, wow! How sick can you get, Oliver?"

"Start the car," he said, in his ominous flat prairie voice, his tornado's-a-comin' voice, his out-of-this-town-by-nightfall-nigger voice. "I don't like him. I can smell him from here. I don't want him in the car."

"I'm driving now," I answered. "I'll make the decisions about—"

"Start the car," Timothy said.

"You, too?"

"Oliver doesn't want him, Ned. You aren't going to impose him on Oliver against his wishes, are you?"

"Jesus, Timothy—"

"Besides, it's my car, and I don't want him either. Put the foot on the gas, Ned."

Out of the back came Eli's voice, soft, perplexed. "Wait a second, guys, I think we have a moral issue to consider here. If Ned wants—"

"Will you drive?" Oliver said, in as close to a shout as I've ever heard from him. I glanced at him in my rear-view mirror. His face was red and sweat-beaded, and a vein stood out terrifyingly on his forehead. A manic face, a psychotic face. He might do anything. I couldn't risk a blowup over one hitchhiking hippie. Shaking my head sadly, I put my foot to the accelerator, and, just as the hippie was reaching to open the door on Oliver's side in back, we blasted off with a roar, leaving him standing alone and astonished in a cloud of exhaust fumes. To his credit, he didn't shake his fist at us, he didn't even spit at us, he just let his shoulders slump and went on walking. Maybe he was expecting a rip-off all the time. When I could no longer see the hippie, I looked at Oliver again. His

face was more calm now; the vein had receded, the color had ebbed. But there was still a weird chilling fixity about it. Rigid eyes, a muscle flickering in his pretty-boy cheek. We were twenty miles down the highway before the electricity had stopped crackling in the car.

Finally I said, "Why'd you do that, Oliver?"

"Do what?"

"Force me to screw that hippie."

"I want to get where I'm going," Oliver said. "Have you seen me pick up any hitchhikers so far? Hitchhikers mean trouble. They mean delay. You would have taken him down some side road to his commune, an hour, two hours off the schedule."

"I wouldn't have. Besides, you complained about his smell. You worried about getting knifed. What was that all about, Oliver? Haven't you picked up enough paranoid shit yourself on account of *your* long hair?"

"Perhaps I wasn't thinking clearly," said Oliver, who had never thought any other way but clearly in his life. "Perhaps I'm in such a rush to get a move on that I say things I don't mean," said Oliver, who never spoke except from a prepared script. "I don't know. I just had this gut feeling that we shouldn't pick him up," said Oliver, who last gave way to a gut feeling when he was being toilet-trained. "I'm sorry I leaned on you, Ned," said Oliver.

Ten minutes of silence later he said, "I think we ought to agree on one thing, though. From here to the end of the trip, no hitchhikers. Okay? No hitchhikers."

eighteen
eli

They were right to choose this cruel and shriveled terrain as the site of the skullhouse. Ancient cults need a setting of mystery and romantic remoteness if they are to maintain themselves against the clashing, twanging resonances of the skeptical, materialistic twentieth century. A desert is ideal. Here the air is painfully blue, the soil is a thin burnt crust over a rocky shield, the plants and trees are twisted, thorny, bizarre. Time stands still in a place like this. The modern world can neither intrude nor defile. The old gods can thrive. The old chants rise skyward, undamped by the roar of traffic and the clatter of machines. When I told this to Ned he disagreed; the desert is stagy and obvious, he said, even a little campy, and the proper place for such survivors of antiquity as the Keepers of the Skulls is the heart of a busy city, where the contrast between their texture and ours would be greatest. Say, a brownstone on East 63rd Street, where the priests could go complacently about their rites cheek by jowl with art galleries and poodle parlors. Another possibility, he suggested, would be a one-story brick-and-plate-glass factory building in a suburban industrial park devoted to the manufacture of air-conditioners and office equipment. Contrast is everything, Ned said. Incongruity is essential. The secret of art lies in attaining a sense of proper juxtapositions, and what is religion if not a category of art? But I think Ned was putting me on, as usual. In any case I can't buy his theories of contrast and juxtaposition. This desert, this dry wasteland, is the perfect place for the headquarters of those who will not die.

Crossing from New Mexico into southern Arizona we left the last traces of winter behind. Up by Albuquerque the air had been cool, even cold, but the elevation is greater there. The land dipped as we drove toward the Mexican border and made our Phoenixward turn. The temperature rose sharply, from the fifties into the seventies, or even higher. The mountains were lower and seemed to be made of particles of reddish-brown soil compressed into molds and sprayed with glue; I imagined I could rub a deep hole in such rock with a fingertip. Soft, vulnerable, sloping hills, practically naked. Martian-looking. Different vegetation here, too. Instead of dark sweeps of sagebrush and gnarled little pines, we now traveled through forests of widely spaced giant cacti surging ithyphallically out of the brown, scaly earth. Ned botanized for us. Those are saguaros, he said, those big-armed cacti taller than telephone poles, and these, the shrubby spiky-branched blue-green leafless trees that might have been native to some other planet, these are palo verde, and those, the knobby upthrust clusters of jointed woody branches, they call that ocotillo. Ned knows the Southwest well. Feels quite at home here, having spent some time in New Mexico a couple of summers ago. Feels quite at home everywhere, Ned. Likes to speak of the international fraternity of the gay; wherever he goes, he's sure of finding lodging and companionship among His Own Kind. I envy him sometimes. It might be worth all the peripheral traumas of being gay in a straight society to know that there are places where you're always welcome, for no other reason than that you're a child of the tribe. My own tribe isn't quite as hospitable.

We crossed the state border and zoomed westward toward Phoenix, the land becoming more mountainous again for a while, the terrain less forbidding. Indian country here—Pimas. We caught a glimpse of Coolidge Dam: memories of third-grade geography lessons. When we were still a hundred miles east of Phoenix, we began to see billboards inviting, no, commanding, us to stay at a downtown motel: "Have a Happy Holiday in the Valley of the

Sun." The sun already impinged on us, here in late afternoon, hanging suspended over the windshield and hurling
bolts of red-gold fire into our eyes. Oliver, driving like a
robot, produced glittering silvered wraparound sunglasses
and kept right on going. We shot through a town called
Miami. No beaches, no matrons in mink. The air was
purple and pink from the fumes belching out of smoke-
stacks; the odor of the atmosphere was sheer Auschwitz.
What were they cremating here? Just before the central
part of the town we saw the huge gray battleship-shaped
mound of a copper mine's discards, the great heap of
tailings flung up across many years. A gaudy giant motel
was right across the highway from it, I suppose for the
benefit of those who dig close-up views of environmental
rape. What they cremate here is Mother Nature. Sickened,
we hurried on, into uninhabited territory. Saguaro, palo
verde, ocotillo. We swooped through a long mountain
tunnel. Forlorn townless countryside. Lengthening
shadows. Heat, heat, heat. And then, abruptly, the ten-
tacles of urban life reaching out from still-distant Phoenix:
suburbs, shopping centers, gas stations, trading posts selling Indian souvenirs, motels, neon lights, fast-food stands
offering tacos, custard, hot dogs, fried chicken, roast beef
sandwiches. Oliver was persuaded to stop and we had tacos
under eerie yellow streetlamps. And onward. The gray
slabs of immense windowless department stores flanking
the road. This was money country, the home of the
affluent. I was a stranger in a strange land, poor disorien-
tated alienated Yidling from the Upper West Side whizzing
through the cactus and the palm trees. So very far from
home. These flat towns, these glistening one-story bank
buildings of green glass with psychedelic plastic signs.
Pastel houses, pink and green stucco. Land that has never
known snow. American flags aflutter. Love it or leave it,
Mac! Main Street, Mesa, Arizona. The University of Arizona Experimental Farm right up against the highway.
Far-off mountains glooming in the blue dusk. Now we are
on Apache Boulevard in the town of Tempe. Wheels
screeching; road turns. And suddenly we are in the desert.

No streets, no billboards, nothing: no-man's-land. Dark lumpy shapes on our left: hills, mountains. Headlights visible, far away. A few minutes more and the desolation ends; we have crossed from Tempe into Phoenix and now are on Van Buren Street. Shops, houses, motels. "Keep going till we're downtown," Timothy says. His family, it seems, has a major financial stake in one of the inner-city motels; we'll stay there. Ten minutes more, through a district of secondhand bookshops and five-dollar-a-night motor lodges, and we are downtown. Skyscrapers here, ten or twelve stories: bank buildings, a newspaper office, large hotels. The heat is fantastic, close to ninety degrees. This is late March; what is the weather like in August? Here is our motel. Statue of a camel out front. Big palm tree. Cramped, ungenerous lobby. Timothy registers. We'll have a suite. Second floor, in back. A swimming pool. "Who's for a swim?" Ned asks. "And then a Mexican dinner," says Oliver. Our spirits bubble. This is Phoenix, after all. We're actually here. We've almost reached our goal. Tomorrow we set out to the north in quest of the retreat of the Keepers of the Skulls.

It seems like years since all this began. That passing reference, offhand, casual, in the Sunday newspaper. A "monastery" in the desert, not far north of Phoenix, where twelve or fifteen "monks" practice some private brand of so-called Christianity. "They came up from Mexico about twenty years ago, and are believed to have gone to Mexico from Spain about the time of Cortes. Economically self-sufficient, they keep to themselves and do not encourage visitors, though they are cordial and civil to anyone who stumbles into their isolated, cactus-encircled retreat. The decor is strange, a combination of medieval Christian style and what seems to be Aztec motifs. A predominant symbol that gives the monastery a stark, even grotesque, appearance is the human skull. Skulls are everywhere, grinning, somber, in high relief or in three-dimensional representation. One long frieze of skull images seems patterned after designs to be seen at Chichén Itzá, Yucatán. The monks are lean, intense men, their skins tanned and toughened by exposure to desert sun and wind. They seem, oddly enough, both old and young at once. The one I spoke to, who declined to give his name, might have been thirty years old or three hundred, it was impossible to tell. . . ."

Only an accident that I happened to notice that as I glanced randomly through the newspaper's travel supplement. Only an accident that bits of strange imagery—that frieze of skulls, those old-young faces—lodged in my mind. Only an accident that I should, a few days later, come upon the manuscript of the Book of Skulls in the university library.

Our library has a *geniza,* a storehouse of culls and curios, of scraps of manuscript, of apocrypha and oddities that nobody had bothered to translate, decipher, classify, or even examine in any detail. I suppose every great university must have a similar repository, filled with a miscellanea of documents acquired through bequest or unearthed on expeditions, awaiting an eventual (twenty years? fifty?) scrutiny of scholars. Ours is more copiously stocked than most, perhaps because for three generations our empire-building librarians have been hungrily acquisitive, piling up the treasures of antiquity faster than any battalion of scholars could cope with the accessions. In such a system certain items invariably are laid aside, inundated by the torrent of new acquisitions, and eventually are hidden, forgotten, orphaned. So we have cluttered shelves of Sumerian and Babylonian cuneiform documents, most of them unearthed during our celebrated digs in southern Mesopotamia in 1902-05; we have whole barrels of untouched papyri of the later dynasties; we have pounds of material from Iraqi synagogues, not only Torah scrolls but also marriage contracts, court decisions, leases, poetry; we have inscribed sticks of tamarisk wood from the caves of Tun-huang, a neglected gift from Aurel Stein long ago; we have cases of parish records from the moldy muniment rooms of cold Yorkshire castles; we have scraps and strips of pre-Columbian Mexican codices; we have stacks of hymns and masses from fourteenth-century monasteries in the Pyrenees. For all anyone knows, our library may hold a Rosetta Stone to unlock the secrets of the Mohenjo-daro script, it may have the Emperor Claudius' textbook of Etruscan grammar, it may contain, uncatalogued, the memoirs of Moses or the diary of John the Baptist. Those discoveries, if they are to be made at all, will be made by other prowlers in the dim, dusty storage tunnels beneath the main library building. But I was the one who found the Book of Skulls.

Wasn't looking for it. Hadn't ever heard of it. Wangled permission to go into the storage vaults in quest of a collection of manuscripts of Catalan mystic verse, thirteenth-century, supposedly obtained from the Barcelonian dealer in antiquities, Jaime Maura Gudiol, in 1893. Professor Vasquez Ocaña, with whom I'm supposedly collaborating on a group of translations from the Catalan, had heard about the Maura hoard from *his* professor, thirty or forty years ago, and had some vague memories of having handled a few of the actual manuscripts. By checking faded accession cards in nineteenth-century sepia ink, I succeeded in learning where in the storage vaults the Maura collection was likely to be found, and went looking. Dark room; sealed boxes; an infinity of cardboard folders; no luck. Coughing, choking in the dust. My fingers blackened, my face grimy. We'll try one more box and call it quits. And then: a stiff red paper binder containing a handsome illuminated manuscript on sheets of fine vellum. Richly embellished title: **Liber Calvarium.** *The Book of Skulls.* A fascinating title, sinister, romantic. I turned a page. Elegant uncial lettering in a clear, bold hand of the tenth or eleventh century, the words not in Latin but in a heavily Latinate Catalan, which I automatically translated. *Hear this, O Nobly-Born: life eternal we offer thee.* The damnedest incipit I had ever encountered. Had I made a mistake? No. *Life eternal we offer thee.* The page held a paragraph of text, the rest of it not so easy to decipher as the incipit; along the bottom of the page and up the left side were eight beautifully painted human skulls, each set off from the next by a border of columns and a little

Romanesque vault. Only one skull still had its lower jaw. One was tipped on its side. But all were grinning, and there was mischief in their shadowy eyesockets: face after face saying, from beyond the grave, *It would do you some good to learn the things we have come to know.*

I sat down on a box of old parchments and leafed quickly through the manuscript. Twelve sheets or so, all embellished with grotesqueries of the grave—crossed thighbones, toppled tombstones, a disembodied pelvis or two, and skulls, skulls, skulls, skulls. Translating it on the spot was beyond me; much of the vocabulary was obscure, being neither Latin nor Catalan but some dreamy, flickering intermediate language. Yet the broad sense of what I had found quickly came clear. The text was addressed to some prince by the abbot of a monastery under his protection and was, essentially, an invitation to the prince to withdraw from the mundane world in order to partake of the "mysteries" of the monastic order. The disciplines of the monks, the abbot said, were aimed toward the defeat of Death, by which he meant not the triumph of the spirit in the next world but rather the triumph of the body in this one. *Life eternal we offer thee.* Contemplation, spiritual and physical exercises, proper diet, and so forth— these were the gateways to everlasting life.

An hour of sweaty toil gave me these passages:

"The First Mystery is this: that the skull lieth beneath the face, as death lieth alongside life. But, O Nobly-Born, there is no paradox in this, for death is the companion of life, life is the messenger of death. If one could but reach through the face to the underlying skull and befriend it, one might [unintelligible]. . . .

"The Sixth Mystery is this: that our gift shall always be despised, that we shall ever be fugitives among men, so that we flee from place to place, from the caves of the north to the caves of the south, from the [uncertain] of the fields to the [uncertain] of the city, and so has it been in the hundreds of years of my life and the hundreds of years of my forebears. . . .

"The Ninth Mystery is this: that the price of a life

must always be a life. Know, O Nobly-Born, that eternities must be balanced by extinctions, and therefore we ask of thee that the ordained balance be gladly sustained. Two of thee we undertake to admit to our fold. Two must go into darkness. As by living we daily die, so then by dying we shall forever live. Is there one among thee who will relinquish eternity for his brothers of the four-sided figure, so that they may come to comprehend the meaning of self-denial? And is there one among thee whom his comrades are prepared to sacrifice, so that they may come to comprehend the meaning of exclusion? Let the victims choose themselves. Let them define the quality of their lives by the quality of their departures. . . ."

There was more, eighteen Mysteries in all, plus a peroration in absolutely opaque verse. I was captured. It was the intrinsic fascination of the text that caught me, its somber beauty, its ominous embellishments, its gonglike rhythms, rather than any immediate connection with that Arizona monastery. Taking the manuscript from the library was impossible, of course, but I went upstairs, emerging from the vaults like Banquo's grimy ghost, and arranged for the use of a study cubicle deep in the recesses of the stacks. Then I went home and bathed, saying nothing to Ned about my discovery, though he saw I was preoccupied with something. And returned to the library armed with notepaper, pencils, my own dictionaries. The manuscript was already on my assigned desk. Until ten that evening, until closing time, I wrestled with it in my badly lit cloister. Yes, no doubt of it: these Spaniards were claiming a technique for attaining immortality. The manuscript gave no actual clues to their processes, but merely insisted that they were successful. There was much symbology of the-skull-beneath-the-face; for a life-oriented cult, they were greatly attracted to the imagery of the grave. Perhaps that was the necessary discontinuity, the sense of jarring juxtapositions, that Ned makes so much of in his esthetic theories. The text made it plain that some of these skull-worshipping monks, if not all, had survived for centuries. (Even for thousands of years? An ambiguous passage in the Sixteenth Mystery implied a lineage older than the pharaohs.) Their longevity evidently earned them the resentment of the mortals around them, the peasants and shepherds and barons; many times had they moved their headquarters, seeking always a place where they could practice their exercises in peace.

Three days of hard work gave me a reliable translation of perhaps 85 per cent of the text and a working understanding of the rest. I did it mostly by myself, though I consulted Professor Vasquez Ocaña about some of the more troublesome phrases, concealing from him, however, the nature of my project. (When he asked if I had found the Maura Gudiol cache I replied vaguely.) At this point I still thought of the whole thing as a charming fantasy. I had read *Lost Horizon* when I was a boy; I remembered Shangri-la, the secret monastery in the Himalayas, the monks practicing yoga and breathing pure air, that wonderful shocker of a line, *"That you are still alive, Father Perrault."* One didn't take such stuff seriously. I visualized myself publishing my translation in, say, *Speculum,* with appropriate commentary on the medieval belief in immortality, references to the Prester John mythos, to Sir John Mandeville, to the Alexander romances. The Brotherhood of the Skulls, the Keepers of the Skulls who are its high priests, the Trial which must be undergone by four simultaneous candidates, only two of whom are permitted to survive, the hint of ancient mysteries passed down across millennia—why, this might have been some tale told by Sheherazade, might it not? I went to the trouble of carefully checking Burton's version of the *Thousand Nights and a Night,* all sixteen volumes, thinking that the Moors might have brought this tale of skulls to Catalonia in the eighth or ninth century. No. Whatever I had found, it was no free-floating fragment of the Arabian Nights. Perhaps part of the Charlemagne cycle, then? Or some unattributed Romanesque yarn? I prowled through bulky indices of medieval mythological motifs. Nothing. I went further back. I became an expert on the whole literature of immortality and longevity, all in a single week. Tithonus, Methuselah, Gilgamesh, the Uttara-kurus and the Jambu tree, the fisherman Glaukus, the Taoist immortals, yes, the whole bibliography. And then, the burst of insight, the pounding of the forehead, the wild shout that brought student couriers running from all corners of the stacks. Arizona! Monks who came from Mexico and before that went to Mexico from Spain! The frieze of skulls! I hunted for that article in the Sunday supplement again. Read it in a kind of delirium. Yes. "Skulls are everywhere, grinning, somber, in high relief or in three-dimensional representation. . . . The monks are lean, intense men. . . . The one I spoke to . . . might have been thirty years old or three hundred, it was impossible to tell." *That you are still alive, Father Perrault.* My astounded soul recoiled. Could I believe such things? I, skeptic, scoffer, materialist, pragmatist? Immortality? An age-old cult? Could such a thing be? The Keepers of the Skulls thriving among the cactus? The whole thing no myth of the medievals, no legend, but an actual continuing establishment that has penetrated even our automated world, one which I could visit whenever I chose to make the trip? Offering myself as candidate. Undergoing the Trial. Eli Steinfeld living to see the dawn of the thirty-sixth century. It was beyond all plausibility. I rejected the juxtaposition of manuscript and newspaper article as a wild coincidence; then, meditating, I succeeded in rejecting my rejection; and then I moved beyond that toward accept-ance. It was necessary for me to make a formal act of faith, the first I had ever achieved, in order to begin to accept it. I compelled myself to agree that there could be powers outside the comprehension of contemporary science. I forced myself to shed a lifelong habit of dismiss-ing the unknown until it has been made known by rigor-ous proofs. I allied myself willingly and gladly with the flying saucerites, with the Atlanteans, with the scientolo-gists, with the flat-earthers, with the Forteans, with the macrobioticists, with the astrologers, with that whole legion of the credulous in whose company I had rarely felt comfortable before. At last I believed. I believed fully, though allowing for the possibility of error. I believed. Then I told Ned, and, after a while, Oliver and Timothy. Dangling the bait before them. Life eternal we offer thee. And here we are in Phoenix. Palm trees, cactus, the camel outside the motel: here we are. Tomorrow to commence the final phase of our quest for the House of Skulls.

nineteen

oliver

Maybe I did make too much fuss over picking up that hitchhiker. I don't know. The whole episode puzzles me. Usually my motives for anything are clear, right out on the surface, but not this time. I was really shouting and rampaging at Ned. Why? Eli chewed me out for it afterward, saying that I had no business interfering with Ned's freely taken decision to offer help to another human being. Ned was driving; he was in charge. Even Timothy, who backed me up when it happened, told me later that he thought I'd overreacted to the situation. The only one who didn't say anything in the evening was Ned; but I knew Ned was burning about it.

Why did I do it, I wonder? I couldn't have been in that much of a hurry to get to the skullhouse. Even if the hitchhiker had taken us fifteen minutes out of our way, so what? Throw a fit over fifteen minutes, with all of eternity

g me. It
wasn't that garbage about Charles Manson, either. It was
something deeper, that I know.

I had this flash of intuition just as Ned was slowing
down to offer the hippie a ride. *The hippie is a fag,* I
thought. In just those words. *The hippie is a fag.* Ned has
spotted him, I told myself; using the ESP that his kind
seems to have, Ned has spotted him right on the highway,
and Ned's going to pick him up and bring him to the motel
tonight. I have to be honest with myself. That was what I
thought. Accompanied by an image of Ned and the hitchhiker in bed together, kissing, gasping, rolling around,
fingering each other, doing whatever it is that homos like
to do. I didn't have any reason for suspecting stuff like
that. The hippie was just a hippie, like five million others:
barefoot, long messy hair, furry vest, tie-dyed jeans. Why
did I think he was a fag? And even if he was a fag, so
what? Didn't Timothy and I pick up girls in New York and
Chicago? Why shouldn't Ned get some action of the kind
he prefers? What do I have against homosexuals? One of
my own roommates is one, isn't he? One of my closest
friends? I knew what Ned was when he moved in with us. I
didn't care, so long as he didn't make passes at me. I liked
Ned for himself, I didn't give a shit about his sexual
preferences. So why this sudden bigotry on the highway?
Think about it some, Oliver. Think.

Maybe you were jealous. Eh? What about that
possibility, Oliver? Maybe you didn't want Ned carrying
on with somebody else? Would you care to examine that
notion a little while?

All right. I know he's interested in me. He always
has been. That puppydog look in his eyes when he looks at
me, that dreamy wistfulness—I know what that means. Not
that Ned's ever approached me. He's afraid to, afraid to
explode a pretty useful friendship by stepping across the
line. But even so, the desire's there. Was I a dog in the
manger, then, not giving Ned what he wants from me but
not letting him get it from that hippie, either? What a
tangled mess this is. But I have to sort everything out. My

anger when Ned slowed the car. The shouting. The hysteria. Obviously something was being triggered in me. I've got to think some more about this. I've got to get it together. This frightens me. I'm likely to find out something about myself that I don't want to know.

twenty
ned

And now we've become detectives. Scouting all over Phoenix, trying to trace the skullhouse. I find it amusing: to come this far and not to be able to make the final connection. But all Eli has to go by is his newspaper clipping, which places the monastery "not far north of Phoenix." That's a big place, though, "not far north of Phoenix." It covers everything between here and the Grand Canyon, say, from one side of the state to the other. We need help. After breakfast this morning Timothy took Eli's clipping to the desk clerk, Eli feeling too shy or too eastern-looking to want to do the asking himself. The desk clerk didn't know anything about any monastery anywhere, though, and suggested we inquire at the newspaper office, just across the street. But the newspaper, being an afternoon journal, didn't open shop till nine, and we, still living on eastern standard time, had awakened very early this morning. It was even now only a quarter past eight. So we wandered around town to kill the forty-five minutes, peering at barber shops, at newsstands, at the

windows of stores selling Indian pottery and cowboy ac-
cessories. The sun was already bright and the thermometer
on a bank building announced that the temperature was
seventy-nine degrees. It promised to be a stifling day. The
sky was that fierce desert blue; the mountains just beyond
the edge of town were pale brown. The city was silent,
scarcely a car in the streets. Unrush hour in downtown
Phoenix.

We hardly said a thing to one another. Oliver
seemed still to be sulking over the ruckus he had started
about that hitchhiker: he apparently felt embarrassed, and
with good reason. Timothy acted bored and superior. He
had expected Phoenix to be much livelier, the dynamic
center of the dynamic Arizona economy, and the quiet
here offended him. (Later we discovered that things are
dynamic enough a mile or two north of downtown, where
the real growth is taking place.) Eli was tense and withdrawn, no doubt wondering whether he had led us across
the continent for nothing. And I? Edgy. Dry lips, dry
throat. A tightness of the scrotum that comes over me
only when I'm very, very, very nervous. Flexing and un-
flexing my gluteal muscles. What if the skullhouse doesn't
exist? Worse, what if it does? An end, then, to my
elaborate oscillating dance; I would have to take sides at
last, commit myself to the reality of the thing, give myself
up wholly to the rites of the Keepers, or else, jeering,
depart. What would I do? Always the threat of the Ninth
Mystery lurked in the wings, shadowy, menacing,
tempting. *Eternities must be balanced by extinctions.* Two
live forever, two die at once. That proposition holds
tender, quavering music for me; it shimmers afar; it sings
seductively out of the naked hills. I fear it and yet I cannot
resist the gamble it offers.

At nine we presented ourselves at the newspaper
office. Again Timothy did the talking; his easy, self-
assured, upper-class manners carry him smoothly through
any kind of situation. The advantages of breeding. He
identified us as college students doing research for a thesis
on contemporary monasticism, which swept us past a

receptionist and a reporter to one of the feature editors, who looked at our clipping and said that he knew nothing about any such monastery in the desert (dejection!) but that there was a man on his staff who specialized in keeping track of all the communes, cult headquarters, and similar settlements on the fringes of the town (hope!). Where was this man now? Oh, he's on vacation, said the editor (despair!). When will he be back in town? Didn't leave town, matter of fact (hope reborn!). Spending his holiday at home. He might be willing to talk. At our request, the editor phoned and got us invited out to the house of this specialist in crackpottery. "He lives up past Bethany Home Road, just off Central, the sixty-four hundred block. You know where that is? You just go up Central, past Camelback, past Bethany Home—"

A ten-minute drive. We left sleepy downtown behind, plunging northward through the busy uptown section, all glass skyscrapers and sprawling shopping centers, and passed through that into a district of impressive-looking modern homes half concealed by thick gardens of tropical vegetation. Beyond that a short way, into a more modest residential zone, and we came to the house of the man who had the answers. His name was Gilson. Forty, deep tan, open blue eyes, high shiny forehead. A pleasant sort. Keeping track of the lunatic fringe was plainly a hobby, not an obsession, with him; this wasn't the sort of man who had obsessions. Yes, he knew about the Brotherhood of the Skulls, though he didn't call it that. "The Mexican Fathers" was the term he used. Hadn't been there himself, no, though he had talked to someone who had, visitor from Massachusetts, maybe even the same one who wrote the newspaper article. Timothy asked if Gilson could tell us where the monastery was. Gilson invited us inside: small house, clean, typical southwestern decor— Navaho rugs on the wall, half a dozen Hopi pots in cream and orange occupying the bookshelves. He produced a map of Phoenix and environs. "Here you are, now," he said, tapping the map. "To get out of town you go over here, Black Canyon Highway, that's a freeway, you pick it up

here and ride north. Follow the signs to Prescott, though
of course you don't want to go anywhere near that far.
Now, here, you see, not much past city limits, a mile, two
miles, you get off the freeway—you got a map? Here, let
me mark it. And you follow this road here—then you turn
onto this one, see, going northeast—I guess you drive six,
seven miles—" He sketched a series of zigzags on our
roadmap and finally a big X. "No," he said "that isn't
where the monastery is. That's where you leave your car
and walk. The road becomes just a trail, there, no car
could possibly get through, not even a jeep, but young
fellers like you, you won't have any problems, it's just
three, four miles straight east." "What if we miss it?"
Timothy asked. "The monastery, not the road." "You
won't," Gilson told us. "But if you come to the Fort
McDowell Indian Reservation, you'll know you've gone a
little too far. And when you see Roosevelt Lake, you'll
know you've gone a whole lot too far."

He asked us, as we left, to stop by at his house on
our way back through town and tell him what we had
discovered up there. "Like to keep my files up to date," he
said. "Been meaning to have a look at the place myself,
only, you know how it is, lot of things to do and so little
time for doing them."

Sure, we told him. We'll give you the whole story.

Into the car. Oliver driving, Eli navigating, the map
spread out wide in his lap. Westward to Black Canyon
Highway. A broad superhighway, frying in the midmorning
heat. No traffic other than a few huge trucks. We headed
north. All our questions would shortly be answered;
doubtless some new ones would be asked. Our faith, or
perhaps merely our naivete, would be repaid. I felt a chill
in the midst of the torrid zone. I heard a brawling, surging
overture rising from the pit, ominous, Wagnerian, tubas
and trombones making a dark, throbbing music. The curtain was going up, though I was not sure if we were
entering the last act or the first. No longer did I doubt that
the skullhouse would be there. Gilson had been too
matter-of-fact about it; it was no myth, just another mani-

festation of the urge to spirituality that this desert seemed to awaken in mankind. We would find the monastery, and it would be the right one, the lineal descendant of the one described in the Book of Skulls. Another delicious shiver: what if we came face to face with the very author of that ancient manuscript, millennial, timeless? Anything is possible, if ye have faith.

Faith. How much of my life has been shaped by that five-letter Anglo-Saxon word? Portrait of the artist as a young snot. The parochial school, its leaky roof, wind whistling through the windows so sorely in need of puttying, the pale sisters steely in their severe eyeglasses scowling at us in the hall. The catechism. The well-scrubbed little boys, white shirts, red ties. Father Burke instructing us. Plump, young, pink-faced, always beads of sweat on his upper lip, a bulge of soft flesh hanging over his clerical collar. He must have been, oh, twenty-five, twenty-six years old, a young priest, itchy in his celibacy, dong not yet withered, wondering in the dark hours whether it all was worth it. To Ned, age seven, he was the embodiment of Holy Writ, fierce, immense. Always a yardstick in his hand, and he used it, too: he'd read his Joyce, he played the role, wielding the pandybat. Asking me now to stand. I rise, trembling, wanting to shit in my pants and run. My nose running. (My nose dripped constantly until I was twelve; my image of my child-self is marred by a dark smudge, a sticky dirt-mustache. Puberty shut off the tap.) My wrist goes now to my snout: a quick wipe. "Don't be disgusting!" from Father Burke, watery blue eyes flashing. God is love, God is love; what then is Father Burke? The yardstick whooshing through the air. The lightnings of his terrible swift sword. He gestures irritably at me. "The Apostles' Creed, now, out with it!"

I say, stammering, "I believe in God the Father Almighty, creator of heaven and earth, and in Jesus Christ—and in Jesus Christ—"

Faltering. From behind me, a hoarse whisper, Sandy Dolan: "His only son, our Lord." My knees shake. My soul quakes. Last Sunday, after mass, Sandy Dolan

and I went peering into windows and saw his sister changing her clothes, fifteen years old, little pink-tipped breasts,
dark hair below. Dark hair. We'll grow hair too, Sandy
whispered. Did God see us spying on her? The Lord's Day,
and such a sin! Now the yardstick flicks warningly.

"—his only son, our Lord, who was conceived by
the Holy Spirit, born from the Virgin Mary—" Yes. Now
I'm into the heart of it, the melodramatic part that I love
so much. I speak more confidently, loudly, my voice a
clear fluting soprano. "—suffered under Pontius Pilate,
was crucified, dead, and buried, descended to Hell, on the
third day rose again from the dead, ascended to the
heavens—ascended to the heavens—"

I am lost again. Sandy, help me! But Father Burke
is too close. Sandy does not dare speak.

"—ascended to the heavens—"

"He's up there already, boy," the priest snaps.
"Get on with it! Ascended to the heavens—"

My tongue cleaves to the roof of my mouth. They
all stare at me. Can't I sit down? Can't Sandy continue?
Seven years old, Lord, must I know the whole creed?

The yardstick—the yardstick—

Incredibly, the father himself prompts me. "Sits at
the right hand—"

Blessed clue. I seize on it. "Sits on the right
hand—"

"*At* the right hand!" And my left hand gets the
pandybat. A hot burning stinging tingling blow like the
loud crack of a broken stick makes my trembling hand
crumple together like a leaf in the fire: and at the sound
and the pain scalding tears are driven into my eyes. May I
sit down, now? No, I must go on. They expect so much of
me. Old Sister Mary Joseph, face a mass of wrinkles,
reading one of my poems aloud in the auditorium, my ode
on Easter Sunday, telling me afterward I have great gifts.
Go on, now. The creed, the creed, the creed! It isn't fair.
You hit me, now I ought to be allowed to sit. "Continue,"
says the inexorable father. "Sits at the right hand—"

I nod. "Sits at the right hand of God the Father

Almighty, thence will come to judge the living and the dead." The worst is over. Heart pounding, I rush through the rest. "I believe in the Holy Spirit, the Holy Catholic Church, the communion of saints, the remission of sins, the resurrection of the flesh, and eternal life." A mumbled torrent of words. "Amen." Should one finish with amen? I am so confused I don't know. Father Burke smiles sourly; I tumble into my seat, drained. There's faith for you. Faith. The Christ Child in the manger and the yardstick descending toward your knuckles. Cold hallways; scowling faces; the dry, powdery smell of the holy. One day Cardinal Cushing paid us a visit. The whole school was in terror; it couldn't have been more frightening if the Savior Himself had stepped out of a textbook closet. The angry glances, the furious whispered warnings: stay in line, sing in tune, keep your mouth shut, show your respect. God is love, God is love. And the beads, the crucifixes, the pastel portraits of the Virgin, the Friday fish, the nightmare of first communion, the terror of stepping into the confessional—all the apparatus of faith, the debris of centuries— well, of course, I had to junk all that. Escaping from the Jesuits, from my mother, from the apostles and martyrs, St. Patrick, St. Brendan, St. Dionysius, St. Ignatius, St. Anthony, St. Theresa, St. Thais the penitent harlot, St. Kevin, St. Ned. I became a stinking accursed apostate, not the first of my family to fall away from truth. When I go to damnation I'll meet uncles and cousins galore, turning on their spits. And now Eli Steinfeld demands new faith of me. As we all know, says Eli, God is irrelevant, an embarrassment; to admit in our modern age that you have faith in His existence is something like admitting you have pimples on your ass. We sophisticates, we who have seen everything and know it for the shuck it is, can't bring ourselves to surrender to Him, much as we'd like to let the obsolete old bastard make all the hard decisions for us. But wait, crieth Eli! Give up your cynicism, give up your shallow mistrust of the invisible! Einstein, Bohr, and Thomas Edison have destroyed our capacity to embrace the Hereafter, but would you not gladly embrace the

Here-and-Now? Believe, says Eli. Believe in the impossible. Believe because it *is* impossible. Believe that the received history of the world is a myth and that myth is what survives of the true history. Believe in the Skulls, believe in their Keepers. Believe. Believe. Believe. Make an act of faith, and life eternal shall be your reward. Thus speaketh Eli. We go north, east, north, east again, zigzagging into the thorny wilderness, and we must have faith.

twenty-one

timothy

I try to be cheerful, I try not to complain, but sometimes I get pushed too far. This trek through the desert at high noon, for example. You have to be a masochist to impose something like this on yourself, even for the sake of living ten thousand years. That part of it is crap, of course: unreal, idiotic. What *is* real is the heat. My guess is that it's 95, 100, even 105 degrees out here. Not even April yet, and we're in a furnace. The famous dry heat of Arizona that they keep telling you about; sure, it's hot, but it's dry heat, you don't feel it. Crap. *I* feel it. My jacket is off and my shirt is open and I'm roasting. If I didn't have this crappy fair skin of mine I'd take the shirt off altogether, but then I'd fry. Oliver already has his shirt off, and he's blonder than I am; maybe his skin doesn't burn, peasant skin, Kansas skin. Every step is a struggle. And how much farther do we have to go, anyway? Five miles? Ten?

The car is a long way behind us. It's half past twelve now, and we've been walking since noon, quarter of, something like that. The pathway is about eighteen inches wide, and in places it's narrower than that. In places, actually, there isn't any pathway at all, and we have to hop and scramble over tangles of underbrush. We plod single file like four freaked-out Navahos stalking Custer's army. Even the lizards laugh at us. Jesus, I don't know how anything manages to stay alive here, the lizards, the plants, baked to pieces like this. The ground isn't really soil and it isn't really sand; it's something dry and crumbly that makes a soft crunching sound as we step on it. The silence here magnifies the sound. The silence is scary. We haven't been talking. Eli plods ahead as though he's rushing toward the Holy Grail. Ned huffs and puffs: he isn't strong and this hike is using him up. Oliver, bringing up the rear, is, as usual, completely sealed into himself. He could be an astronaut marching across the moon. Occasionally Ned cuts in to tell us something about the plant life. I never realized he was such a botany freak. There are very few of the tremendous vertical cacti here, the saguaros, though I see a few, fifty or sixty feet tall, some way back from the path. What we have instead, thousands of them, is a weird thing about six feet high, with a gnarled gray woody trunk and a lot of long dangling clusters of spines and green bumpy things. The chainfruit cholla, Ned calls it, and warns us to keep far away from it. The spines are sharp. So we avoid it; but there's another cholla here, the teddybear cholla, that's not so easy to avoid. The teddybear is a bummer. Little stubby plants a foot or two high, covered with thousands of fuzzy straw-colored spines: you look at a teddybear the wrong way, and the spines jump up and bite you. I swear they do. My boots are covered with prickles. The teddybear breaks easily and chunks come loose and roll away; they lie scattered everywhere, a lot of them right in the path. Ned says that each chunk will take root eventually and become a whole new plant. We have to watch our steps all the time for fear of coming down on one. You can't just kick a teddybear chunk aside if it's in your way, either. I tried that and the cactus stuck to my boot, and I reached down to pull it off, only to get it stuck to my fingertips next. A hundred needles jabbing me at once. Like fire. I yelled. Most uncool screams. Ned had to pry it away, using two twigs as handles. My fingers still burn. Dark, tiny points are buried in the flesh. I wonder if they'll get infected. There's plenty of other cactus here, too—barrel cactus, prickly pear, six or seven more that not even Ned can put names to. And leafy trees with thorns, mesquite, acacia. All the plants here are hostile. Don't touch me, they say, don't touch me or you'll be sorry. I wish I was anywhere else. But we walk on, on, on. I'd trade Arizona for the Sahara, even up, throwing in half of New Mexico to sweeten the deal. How much longer? How much hotter? Crap. Crap. Crap. Crap.

"Hey, look here!" Eli, pointing. To the left of the path, half hidden in a yellow tangle of cholla: a big round boulder, as big as a man's torso, dark rough stone different in texture and composition from the local chocolate-colored sandstone. This is black volcanic rock, basalt, granite, diabase, one of those. Eli crouches by it and, picking up a piece of wood, begins to push the cactus away from it. "See?" he says. "The eyes? The nose?" He's right. Great deep eyesockets are visible. A tremendous triangular gouge of a nose-hole. And down at ground level, a row of immense teeth, an upper jaw, the teeth biting into the sandy soil.

A skull.

It looks a thousand years old. We can see traces of more delicate carving, indicating cheekbones, brow ridges, and other features; but most of this has been obliterated by time. A skull, though. Unmistakably a skull. It's a road marker, telling us that that which we seek is not much farther down the road—or perhaps warning us that we ought to turn back now. Eli stands a long time, studying the skull. Ned. Oliver. They're fascinated by it. A cloud passes over us, shadowing the boulder, changing our view of its contours, and it seems to me now that the empty eyes have turned and are staring at us. The heat's getting me. Eli says, "It's probably pre-Columbian. They brought it with them from Mexico, I'd imagine." We peer ahead, into the heat haze. Three great saguaros, like columns, block our view. We must pass between them. And beyond? The skullhouse itself? No doubt. Suddenly I wonder what I'm doing here, how I ever let myself into this craziness. What had seemed like a joke, a lark, now seems all too real.

Never to die. Oh, crap! How can such things be? We'll waste days here, finding out. An adventure in lunacy. Skulls in the road. Cactus. Heat. Thirst. Two must die if two are to live. All the mystical garbage Eli's been spouting now is summed up for me in that globe of rough black stone, so solid, so undeniable. I've committed myself to something that's altogether beyond my understanding, and there may well be danger in it for me. But there's no turning back now.

twenty-two

eli

And if there had been no skullhouse here? And if we had come to the end of the path, only to find a wall of impenetrable thorns and spines? I confess I was expecting that. This whole expedition just one more failure, one more fiasco of Eli the *schmeggege*. The skull by the road turning out to be a false clue, the manuscript a dreamy fable, the newspaper article a hoax, the X on our map a mere pointless prank. Nothing before us but cactus and mesquite, a scraggly wasteland, an armpit of a desert where not even pigs would deign to shit, and then what would I have done? I would have turned with great dignity to my three weary companions and said, "Gentlemen, I have been deceived, and you have been misled. We have chased the wild goose." With an apologetic half-smile playing about the corners of my lips. And then they seize me calmly, without malice, having known all along that it was bound to come to this in the end, and they strip me, they thrust the wooden stake into my heart, they nail me to a towering saguaro, they press me to death beneath flat rocks, they rub chollas into my eyes, they burn me alive, they bury me chest-deep in an anthill, they castrate me with their fingernails, all the while solemnly chanting, *Schmeggege, schlemihl, schlemazel, schmendrick, schlep!* Patiently I accept my well-earned punishment. I am no stranger to humiliation. I am never surprised by disaster.

Humiliation? Disaster? As in the Margo fiasco? My most recent major debacle. It still stings. Last October, early in the semester, a rainy, foggy night. We had some first-rate pot, alleged Panama Red that had come to Ned through the alleged homosexual underground, and we passed the pipe, Timothy, Ned, and I, with Oliver, of course, abstaining, piously sipping some cheap red wine. One of the Rasoumovsky quartets played in the background, rising eloquently above the drumbeats of the rain: as we soared high, Beethoven gave us a mystic noise, a second cellist unaccountably seeming to join the group, even an oboe at odd moments, a transcendental bassoon below the strings. The beserk five-dimensional musicology of the stoned. Ned hadn't hyped us: the dope was superb. And somehow I found myself drifting, getting into a talking trip, a confessional trip, unloading everything, saying suddenly to Timothy that what I regretted most of all was that I have never in my life made it even once with what I'd consider a really beautiful girl.

Timothy, sympathetic, concerned, asked me who I'd consider a really beautiful girl. I was silent, contemplating my options. Ned, being helpful, suggested Raquel

Welch, Catherine Deneuve, Lainie Kazan. At last, coming on with marvelous ingenuousness, I blurted, "I consider Margo a really beautiful girl." Timothy's Margo. Timothy's *goyishe* goddess, the golden *shikse*. Having said it, I felt a swiftly sketched series of quick interchanges of dialog resonating through my cannabis-ridden mind, a lengthy passage of words, and then time, as it will do when it is under the influence of pot, inverted itself so that I heard my entire scenario being performed, each line arriving strictly on cue. Timothy was asking me, quite earnestly, if Margo turned me on. I assured him, just as earnestly, that she did. He wanted to know, then, if I'd feel less inadequate, more fulfilled, if I were to make it with her. Hesitantly now, wondering what his game was, I answered in vague circumlocutions, only to hear him say, astoundingly, that he would arrange everything for tomorrow night. Arrange what, I asked? Margo, he said. He would set me up with Margo, as an act of Christian charity.

"And would she—"

"Sure she would. She thinks you're cute."

"We all think you're cute, Eli." That was Ned.

"But I couldn't—she wouldn't—how—what—"

"I bestow her upon you," said Timothy magnificently. The grand seigneur, making a lordly gesture. "I can't let my friends walk around in a state of frustration and unrequited longing. Tomorrow at eight, her place. I'll tell her to expect you."

"It seems like a cheat," I said, growing morose. "Too easy. Unreal."

"Don't be an ass. Accept it as vicarious experience. Like going to the movies, only more intimate."

"And more tactile," said Ned.

"I think you're putting me on," I told Timothy.

"Scout's honor! She's yours!"

He began describing Margo's preferences in bed, her special erogenous zones, the little signals they used. I caught the spirit of the thing, flew high and higher, got myself into a laughter trip, began capping Timothy's graphic descriptions with scabrous fantasies of my own. Of course, when I crashed an hour or two later I was certain Timothy *had* been putting me on, and that tumbled me into a dark abyss. For I had always been convinced that the Margos of this world are not for me. The Timothys would fuck their way through whole brigades of Margos, but I would have never a one. In truth I worshiped her from afar. The prototypical *shikse,* the flower of Aryan womanhood, slim and long-legged, two inches taller than I am (it seems so much more, when the girl is taller than you!), silky golden hair, sly blue eyes, upturned button nose, wide agile lips. A strong girl, a lively girl, a star basketball player (Oliver himself respected her abilities on the court), an outstanding scholar, a wry and supple wit: why, she was frightening, numbingly perfect, one of those flawless female creatures that our aristocracy spawns in such multitudes, born to rule serenely over country estates or to prance with poodles down Second Avenue. Margo for me? My sweaty hairy body to cover hers? My stubbly cheek to rub against her satiny skin? Yes, and frogs would couple with comets. To Margo I must seem something coarse and grubby, the pathetic representative of an inferior species. Any commerce between us would be unnatural, an alloying of silver and brass, a mixing of alabaster and charcoal. I dismissed the whole project from my mind. But at lunch Timothy reminded me of my date. It's impossible, I said, giving him six swift excuses—study, a paper due, a difficult translation, and so forth. He swept my feeble temporizings aside. Report to her apartment at eight, he said. I felt a wave of terror. "I can't," I insisted. "You're prostituting her, Timothy. What am I supposed to do, walk in, unzip my fly, jump on top? There's no way it would work out. You can't make a fantasy come true just by waving your magic wand." Timothy shrugged.

I assumed that the matter was ended. Oliver had basketball practice that night. Ned went to the movies. About half past seven Timothy excused himself. Library work, he said, see you at ten. I was alone in the apartment we shared. Unsuspecting. Busied myself with my paper. At eight a key turning in the door; Margo entered; a ravishing

smile, molten gold. For me, panic, consternation. "Timothy here?" she asked, casually locking the door behind her.
Thunder in my chest. "Library," I blurted. "Back at ten."
No place to hide for me. Margo pouted. "I was sure I'd
find him here. Well, it's his tough luck. Are you very busy,
Eli?" A sparkling blue-eyed wink. She draped herself
serenely on the couch.

"I've been doing this paper," I said. "On the irregular forms of the verb *to—*"

"How fascinating! Would you like to smoke?"

I understood. They had set it up. A conspiracy to
make me happy, whether I liked it or not. I felt patron-
ized, used, mocked. Should I order her to leave? No,
schmendrick, don't be dumb. She's yours for two hours.
To hell with the moral frills. The end justifies the means.
Here's your chance and you won't get another. I swaggered
toward the couch. Eli, swaggering, yes! She had two fat
joints, professionally rolled. Coolly she lit one, pulled
deep, handed it to me; my wrist shook, I nearly jabbed the
burning end of the joint into her arm in my tremor as I
took it from her. Raw stuff; I coughed; she patted my
back. *Schlemihl. Schlep.* She inhaled and flashed her eyebrows in an "oh, wow!" at me. The pot did nothing for me
at all, though; I was too tense, and the adrenalin in me
burned away the effect before it could take hold. I was
conscious of the reek of my perspiration. Rapidly the stick
was down to a roach. Margo, already looking stoned,
proffered the other one. I shook my head. "Later," I said.

She rose and prowled around the room. "It's awfully hot in here, don't you think?" What a cliché number! A clever girl like Margo could have been capable of
better. She stretched. Yawned. She was wearing tight
white hip-huggers and a skimpy top, flat tawny midriff
bare. No bra, no panties, obviously: the little hummocks
of her nipples were visible, and the slacks, clinging skin-
tight to her round, small buttocks, revealed no telltale
underwear creases. Ah, Eli, you observant devil, you suave
and skillful manipulator of womanflesh! "So hot in here,"
she said, stony-dreamy. Off with the top. Favoring me

with an innocent smile, as if to say: we're all old friends, we don't need to fret about silly taboos, why should tits be more sacred than elbows? Her breasts were medium-big, full, high, marvelously firm, undoubtedly the most successful breasts I had ever seen. I sought ways of looking at them without seeming to. At the movies it's easier; you don't have an I-thou relationship with what's happening on screen. She began an astrology rap, trying to put me at ease, I suppose. Much stuff about the conjunction of planets in the so-and-so house. I could only jabber in response. Smoothly she glided into palm reading: that was her new bag, the mysteries of the crevices. "The gypsies mostly rip the public off," she said seriously, "but that doesn't mean there isn't some substance to the basic idea. You see, your whole future life is programed into the DNA molecules, and they govern the patterns of the palm of your hand. Here, let me have a look." Taking my hand, drawing me down next to her on the couch. How idiotic I felt, practically a male virgin in my attitude if not in actual experiential qualifications, needing to be coaxed into the obvious. Margo bent low over my palm, tickling me. "This, you see, that's the life line—oh, it's long, it's *very* long!" I sneaked covert glances at her headlights while she did her palmistry number. "And this," she said, "that's the mount of Venus. You see this line angling in here? It tells me that you're a man of powerful passions but that you restrain them, you repress a lot. Isn't that so?" All right. I'll play your game, Margo. My arm suddenly around her shoulders, my hand groping for her breasts. "Oh, yes, Eli, yes, yes!" Hamming it up. A clinch; a smeary kiss. Her lips were parted and I did the expected. But I felt no passions, powerful or otherwise. All this seemed formal, a minuet, something programed from outside; I couldn't relate to it, to the whole idea of making it with Margo. Unreal. unreal, unreal. Even when she slithered free of me and dropped the hip-huggers, revealing sharp hipbones, taut boyish buttocks, tight off-yellow curls, I felt no desire. She smiled at me, beckoned, invited me. For her this was no more apocalyptic than a handshake, a peck on the cheek. For me the galaxies upheaved. How easy it should have been for me. Drop the pants, get on her, inside her, move the hips, oh ah oh ah, hey wow groovy! But I suffered from sex-in-the-head; I was too preoccupied with the notion of Margo as unattainable symbol of perfection to realize that Margo was very much attainable and not even all that perfect—pale scar of appendectomy; faint stretch marks on her hips, the terminal moraines of a much chunkier preadolescent girl; thighs a shade too thin.

So I blew it. Yes, I stripped, and yes, we scampered to the bed, and yes, I couldn't get it up, and yes, Margo helped me, and at last libido triumphed over mortification and I became properly stiff and throbbing, and then, wild bull of the pampas, I flung myself at her, clawing, grappling, frightening her with my ferocity, practically raping her, only to have the wick soften at the critical instant of insertion, and then—oh, yes, blunder upon blunder, gaucherie upon gaucherie, Margo alternately terrified and amused and solicitous, until at last came consummation, followed almost instantly by eruption, followed by chasms of self-contempt and craters of revulsion. I couldn't bear to look at her. I rolled free, hid in the pillows, reviled myself, reviled Timothy, reviled D. H. Lawrence. "Can I help you?" Margo asked, stroking my sweaty back. "Please go," I said. "Please. And don't say anything to anyone." But of course she did. They all knew. My clumsiness, my absurd incompetence, my seven varieties of ambiguity culminating eventually in seven species of impotence. Eli the *schmeggege*, blowing his big chance with the grooviest wench he'll ever touch. Another in his long series of lovingly crafted fiascos. And we might have had another here, slogging through cactusville to ultimate disappointment, and the three of them might well have said, at the end of our trek, "Well, what else should we have expected from Eli?" But the skullhouse was there.

The pathway wound up a gentle grade, taking us through ever more dense thickets of cholla and mesquite, until, abruptly, we came to a broad sandy clearing. From left to right stretched a series of black basalt skulls, similar to the one we had seen farther back but much smaller, about the size of basketballs, set in the sand at intervals of perhaps twenty inches. On the far side of the row of skulls, some fifty yards beyond, we saw the House of Skulls crouching like a sphinx in the desert: a fairly large one-story building, flattopped, with coarse yellow-brown stucco walls. Seven columns of white stone decorated its windowless facade. The effect was one of stark simplicity, broken only by the frieze running along the pediment: skulls in low relief, presenting their left profiles. Sunken cheeks, hollow nostrils, huge round eyes. The mouths gaped wide in grisly grins. The large sharp teeth, carefully delineated, seemed poised for a fierce snap. And the tongues—ah, a truly sinister touch, skulls with tongues!—the tongues were twisted into elegant, horrid sideways S-curves, the tips protruding just past the teeth, flickering like the forked tongues of serpents. There were dozens of these reduplicated skulls, obsessively identical, frozen in weird suspension, one after another after another marching out of sight around the corners of the building; they had the nightmarish quality I detect in most pre-Columbian Mexican art. They would have been more appropriate, I felt, along the rim of some altar on which living hearts were cut with obsidian knives from quivering breasts.

The building appeared to be U-shaped, with two long subordinate wings sprouting behind the main section. I saw no doors. Perhaps fifteen yards in front of the facade, though, the entrance to a stone-lined vault could be seen at the center of the clearing: it yawned, dark and mysterious, like the gateway to the underworld. Immediately I realized that this must be a passage leading into the House of Skulls. I walked toward it and peered in. Darkness within. Do we dare enter? Should we not wait for someone to emerge and summon us? But no one emerged; and the heat was brutal. I felt the skin over my nose and cheeks already stiffening and swelling, going red and glossy from sunburn, winter's paleness exposed to this desert sun for half a day. We stared at each other. The Ninth Mystery was hot in my mind and probably in theirs. We may go in, but we shall not all come forth. Who to live, who to die? I found myself unwillingly contemplating candidates for destruction, weighing my friends in the balance, quickly surrendering Timothy and Oliver to death and then pulling back, reconsidering that too ready judgment, substituting Ned for Oliver, Oliver for Timothy, Timothy for Ned, myself for Timothy, Ned for myself, Oliver for Ned, around and around, inconclusively, indecisively. My faith in the truth of the Book of Skulls had never been stronger. My sense of standing at the brink of infinity had never been greater or more terrifying. "Let's go," I said hoarsely, my voice splitting, and took a few uneasy steps forward. A stone staircase led steeply down into the vault. Five, six, seven feet underground, and I found myself in a dark tunnel, wide but low-roofed, at best five feet high. The air was cool. By dim strands of light I caught glimpses of embellishment on the walls: skulls, skulls, skulls. Not a shred of Christian imagery visible anywhere so far at this so-called monastery, but the symbolism of death was ubiquitous. From above Ned called: "What do you see?" I described the tunnel and told them to follow me. Down they came, shuffling, uncertain: Ned, Timothy, Oliver. Crouching, I went forward. The air grew much cooler. We could no longer see anything, other than the dim purplish glow at the entranceway. I tried to keep count of my paces. Ten, twelve, fifteen. Surely we should be under the building now. Abruptly there was a polished stone barrier in front of me, a single slab, completely filling the tunnel. I realized only at the last moment that it was there, catching an icy glint in the faint light, and halted before I crashed into it. A dead end? Yes, of course, and in another moment we would hear the clang behind us as a twenty-ton stone slab was lowered into place over the mouth of the tunnel, and then we would be trapped, left here to starve or asphyxiate, while peals of monstrous laughter rang in our ears. But nothing so melodramatic occurred. Tentatively I pressed my palm against the cold stone slab that blocked our way, and—the effect was pure Disneyland, wonderful hokum—the slab yielded, swinging smoothly away from me. It was perfectly counterbalanced; the lightest touch was enough to open it. Exactly right, I felt, that we should enter into the House of Skulls in this operatic manner. I expected melancholy trombones and basset horns and a chorus of basses intoning the Requiem in reverse: *Pietatis fons, me salva, gratis salvas salvandos qui, majestatis tremendae rex.* An opening above. Knees bent, we crept toward it. Stairs, again. Up. Emerging, one by one, into a huge square room whose walls were of some gritty pale sandstone. There was no roof, only a dozen or so black, thick beams spaced at intervals of three or four feet, admitting the sunlight and the choking heat. The floor of the chamber was of purple-green slate, somewhat oily and glossy of texture. In the middle of the room was a tub-sized fountain of green jade, with a human figure about three feet high rising from it; the figure's head was a skull, and a steady trickle of water dribbled from its jaws, splashing into the basin below. In the four corners of the room stood tall stone statuettes, Mayan or Aztec in style, depicting men with curved, angular noses, thin cruel lips, and immense ear-ornaments. There was a doorway at the side of the room opposite the exit from the subterranean vault, and a man stood framed in it, so motionless that I thought at first he was a statue, too. When all four of us were in the room, he said, in a deep, resonant voice, "Good afternoon. I am Frater Antony."

He was a short, stocky man, no more than five feet five, who wore only a pair of faded blue denims cut to midthigh. His skin was deeply tanned, almost to a mahogany color, and appeared to have the texture of very fine leather. His broad, high-domed skull was utterly bald, lacking even a fringe of hair behind the ears. His neck was short and thick, his shoulders wide and powerful, his chest deep, his arms and legs heavily muscled; he gave an impression of overwhelming strength and vitality. His general appearance and his vibrations of competence and power reminded me in an extraordinary way of Picasso: a small, solid, timeless man, capable of enduring anything. I had no idea how old he might be. Not young, certainly, but far from decrepit. Fifty? Sixty? A well-preserved seventy? His agelessness was the most disconcerting thing about him. He seemed untouched by time, wholly uncorroded: this, I thought, is what an immortal ought to look like.

He smiled warmly, revealing large flawless teeth, and said, "I alone am here to greet you. We get so few visitors, and we expect none. The other fraters are now in the fields and will not return until afternoon devotions." He spoke in perfect English of a peculiarly bloodless, unaccented kind: an IBM accent, so to speak. His voice was steady and musical, his phrasing was unhurried, self-assured. "Please consider yourselves welcome for as long as you wish to stay. We have facilities for guests, and we invite you to share our retreat. Shall you be with us longer than a single afternoon?"

Oliver stared at me. Timothy. Ned. I was to be spokesman, then. The taste of copper was in my throat. The absurdity, the sheer preposterousness, of what I had to say, rose up and sealed my lips. I felt my sunburned cheeks blazing with shame. *Turn and flee, turn and flee,* a voice cried between my ears. *Down the rabbit hole. Run. Run. Run while you can.* I forced out a single rusty syllable:

"*Yes.*"

"In that case you will require accommodations. Will you come with me, please?"

He began to leave the room. Oliver shot me a furious glance. "Tell him!" he whispered sharply.

Tell him. Tell him. Tell him. Go on, Eli, say it. What can happen to you? At worst you'll be laughed at. That's nothing new, is it? So tell him. It all converges on this moment, all the rhetoric, all the self-hyping hyperbole, all the intense philosophical debates, all the doubt and the counterdoubt, all the driving. You're here. You think it's the right place. So tell him what you're looking for here. Tell him. Tell him. Tell him.

Frater Antony, overhearing Oliver's whisper, halted and looked back at us. "Yes?" he said mildly.

I struggled dizzily for words and found the right ones at last. "Frater Antony, you ought to know—that we've all read the Book of Skulls—"

There.

The frater's mask of unshakable equanimity slipped for just a moment. I saw a brief flash of—surprise? puzzlement? confusion?—in his dark, enigmatic eyes. But he recovered quickly. "Indeed?" he said, voice as firm as before. "The Book of Skulls? What a strange name that is! What, I wonder, is the Book of Skulls?" The question was meant as a rhetorical one. He turned on me a brilliant, short-lived smile, like a lighthouse beam cutting momentarily through dense fog. But, after the fashion of jesting Pilate, he would not stay for an answer. Calmly he went out, indicating with a casual flip of his fingers that we were to follow him.

twenty-three

ned

We have something to stew about, now, but at least they're letting us do our stewing in style. A private room for each of us, austere but handsome, quite comfortable. The skull-house is much bigger than it seemed from outside: the two rear wings are extremely long, and there may be as many as fifty or sixty rooms in the entire complex, excluding the possibility of more subterranean vaults. No room that I've seen has a window. The central chambers, what I think of as "the public rooms," are open-roofed, but the side units in which the fraters live are completely enclosed. If there's an air-conditioning system, I'm unaware of it, having seen no vents or pipes, but when you pass from one of the roofless rooms to an enclosed one you are conscious of a sharp and definite drop in temperature, from desert-hot to motelroom-comfortable. The architecture is simple: bare rectangular rooms, the walls and ceilings made of rough, unplastered tawny sandstone, uninterrupted by moldings or visible beams or other decorative contrivances. All the floors are of dark slate; there are no carpets or rugs. There seems to be little in the way of furniture; my room offers only a low cot made of logs and thick rope and a short squat storage chest, I suppose for my belongings, fashioned quite superbly from a hard black wood. What does break up the prevailing starkness is a fantastic collection of bizarre pre-Columbian (I guess) masks and statuettes, mounted on walls, standing in corners, set into recessed niches—terrifying faces, all angles and harsh planes, gorgeous in their monstrosity. The imagery of the skull is ubiquitous. I have no idea what led that newspaper reporter to think that this place was occupied by "monks" practicing Christianity; the clipping Eli has speaks of the decor as "a combination of medieval Christian style and what seems to be Aztec motifs," but, though the Aztec influence is obvious enough, where is the Christian? I see no crosses, no stained glass windows, no images of the saints or the Holy Family, none of the proper paraphernalia. The whole texture of the place is pagan, primitive, prehistoric; this could be a temple to some ancient Mexican god, even to a Neanderthal deity, but Jesus simply isn't on the premises, or I'm not Boston Irish. Perhaps the clean cold austere refinement of the place gave the newspaperman the feel of a medieval monastery—the echoes, the hint of Gregorian chant in the silent hallways—but without the symbolism of Christianity there can't be Christianity, and such symbols as are on display here are alien ones. The total effect of the place is one of strange luxury combined with immense stylistic restraint: they have understated everything, but a sense of power and grandeur bursts from the walls, the floors, the endlessly receding corridors, the bare rooms, the sparse and lean furnishings.

Cleanliness is evidently important here. The plumbing arrangements are extraordinary, with bubbling fountains everywhere in the public rooms and the larger halls. My own room has a capacious sunken tub lined with rich green slate, which looks suitable for a maharajah or a Renaissance Pope. As he delivered me to my room, Frater Antony suggested that I might like to take a bath, and his polite statement had the force of an order. Not that I needed much urging, for the hike through the desert had coated me miserably with grime. I treated myself to a long voluptuous soaking, wriggling on the glossy slate, and when I came out I discovered that my filthy, sweaty clothing had disappeared, every scrap, shoes and all. To replace it I found on my cot a pair of worn-looking but clean blue shorts of the sort Frater Antony was wearing. Very well: the philosophy here seems to be that less is more. Good riddance to shirts and sweaters; I'll settle for shorts over my naked loins. We have come to an interesting place.

The question of the moment is, Does this place have any connection with Eli's medieval manuscript and with the supposed cult of immortality? I think it does, but I can't yet be sure of that. It was impossible not to admire the frater's sense of theatricality, his wondrously ambiguous handling of the moment when Eli sprang the Book of Skulls on him a few hours ago. His delicious, reverberating curtain line: *The Book of Skulls? What, I wonder, is the Book of Skulls?* And a fast exit, allowing him to take possession of all sides of the situation at once. Did he genuinely not know about the Book of Skulls? Why, then, did he seem so jarred, just for an instant, when Eli mentioned it? Can the fondness for skull imagery here be just a coincidence? Has the Book of Skulls been forgotten by its own adherents? Is the frater playing with us, trying to induce uncertainty in us? The esthetics of teasing: how

much great art is built on that principle! So we will be
teased for a while. I would like to go down the hall and
confer with Eli; his mind is quick, he interprets nuances
well. I want to know if he was thrown into perplexity by
Frater Antony's response to his statement. But I suppose
I'll have to wait till later to talk to Eli. Just now my door
appears to be locked.

twenty-four

timothy

Creepier and creepier. That mile-long hallway. Those skulls
all over the place, the Mexican-looking death-masks. Figures who've been flayed and still can grin, faces with
skewers jabbed through their tongues and cheeks, bodies
with flesh below and skulls on top. Lovely. And that weird
old man, speaking to us in a voice that could have come
out of a machine. I almost think he's some kind of robot.
He can't be real, with that smooth tight skin of his, that
bald head that looks as if it's never had any hair, those
peculiar glossy eyes—sheesh!

    At least the bath was good. Although they've taken
my clothes. My wallet, my credit cards, everything. I don't
like that angle much, though I suppose there isn't much
they can do with my things here. Maybe they just mean to
launder them. I don't mind wearing these shorts instead. A
little tight around the ass, maybe—I guess I'm bigger than

their usual run of guests—but in this heat it's all right to cut down on clothes.

What I do mind is being locked in my room. That bit reminds me of too many horror movies out of TV. Now a secret panel opens in the floor, yeah, and the sacred cobra comes slithering up, hissing and spitting. Or the poison gas enters by way of a hidden vent. Well, I don't mean that seriously. I don't think any harm's going to come to us. Still, it's offensive to be locked up, if you're a guest. Is this the hour for some very special prayer that they don't want us to interrupt? Could be. I'll wait an hour, and then I'll try to force the door. Looks pretty fucking solid, though, a big burly slab of wood.

No television set in this motel. Nothing much to read, except this booklet they've left on the floor next to my cot. And that's something I've read before. The Book of Skulls, no less. Typewritten, in three languages, Latin, Spanish, English. Cheerful decoration on the front cover: skull and crossbones. Hi ho for the Jolly Roger! But I'm really not amused. And inside the booklet, there's all the stuff Eli read us, that melodramatic crap about the eighteen Mysteries. The phrasing's different from his translation, but the meaning's the same. Much talk of eternal life, but much talk of death, too. Too much.

I'd like to get out of this place, if they ever unlock the door. A gag is a gag is a gag, and maybe it seemed a fun idea last month to go tear-assing out west on Eli's say-so, but now that I'm here I can't understand what could have led me to get into this. If they're for real, which I continue to doubt, I don't want any part of them, and if they're just a bunch of ritual-happy fanatics, which seems quite likely, I still don't want any part of them. I've had two hours here and I think that's about enough. All these skulls blow my mind. The locked-door number, too. The weird old man. Okay, boys, that'll do. Timothy's ready to go home.

twenty-five
eli

No matter how many times I replayed the little exchange with Frater Antony, I couldn't come to terms with it. Was he putting me on? Pretending ignorance? Pretending knowledge that he doesn't in fact have? Was that a sly smile of the initiate, or a dumb smile of bluffing?

It was possible, I told myself, that they might know the Book of Skulls under some other name. Or that in the course of their migration from Spain to Mexico to Arizona they had undergone some fundamental reshuffling of their theological symbology. I was convinced, despite the frater's oblique reply, that this place had to be the direct successor to the Catalonian monastery in which the manuscript I had discovered had been written.

I took a bath. The finest bath of my life, the ultimate in baths, the acme. I emerged from the splendiferous tub to discover that my clothes had disappeared and my door was locked. I put on the pair of faded, frayed, tight shorts they had left for me. *(They?)* And I waited. And I waited. And I waited. Nothing to read, nothing to look at except a fine stone mask of a goggle-eyed skull, mosaic work, an infinity of bits of jade and shell and obsidian and turquoise, a treasure, a masterpiece. I considered taking a second bath just to consume the time. Then my door opened—I heard no key, no click of a lock—and someone who at first glance seemed to be Frater Antony entered. Second glance told me he was someone else: a shade taller, a shade narrower through the shoulders, a shade lighter of skin, but otherwise the same sun-burnished sturdy stocky pseudo-Picassoid physique. In a curious quiet voice, furry-sounding, a Peter Lorre voice, he said, "I am Frater Bernard. Please accompany me."

The hallway seemed to grow longer as we traversed it. Onward we plodded, Frater Bernard leading the way, my eyes fixed for the most part on the oddly conspicuous ridge of his backbone. Bare feet against the smooth stone floor, a good feeling. Mysterious doors of sumptuous wood standing shut along both sides of the corridor: rooms, rooms, rooms, rooms. A million dollars' worth of grotesque Mexican artifacts mounted on the walls. All the gods of nightmare peered owlishly down at me. The lights had been turned on, and a soft yellow glow streamed from widely spaced skull-shaped sconces, another little melodramatic touch. As we neared the front section of the building, the crossbar of the U, I glanced past Frater Bernard's right shoulder and had a quick, startling glimpse of an unmistakably female figure some forty or fifty feet ahead of me. I saw her step out of the last room in this dormitory wing, unhurriedly cross my path—she seemed to be floating—and vanish into the main section: a short, slender woman wearing a kind of clinging minidress, barely thigh-length, of some soft, pleated white fabric. Her hair was dark and glossy, Latin hair, and hung well below her shoulders. Her skin was deeply tanned, offering a strong contrast to her white garment. Her breasts jutted forward spectacularly; I was in no doubt about her sex. I did not clearly see her face. It surprised me that there should be sorors as well as fraters in this House of Skulls, but perhaps she was a servant, for the place was impeccably clean. I knew there was no point in asking Frater Bernard about her; he wore silence as others might wear armor.

He ushered me into a large room of ceremonial nature, apparently not the same one in which Frater Antony had greeted us, for I saw no sign of a trapdoor leading to the tunnel. The fountain appeared to be of a different shape here, taller, more tulip-shaped, though the figure from which the water flowed looked much like the one in the other room's fountain. Through the openwork beams of the ceiling I saw the slanting light of very late afternoon. The air was hot but not so stifling as it had been before.

Ned, Oliver, and Timothy were already present, each clad only in shorts, all three looking tense and uncertain. Oliver had that peculiar glazed expression that comes over him at moments of great stress. Timothy was trying to look blasé, and was failing at it. Ned gave me a quick hard wink, perhaps congratulatory, perhaps in scorn.

There were about a dozen fraters also in the room.

They seemed all to have been stamped from one mold: if not in literal truth brothers, they must at least be cousins. Not one of them was taller than five feet seven, and some were five feet four or less. Bald. Deep-chested. Tanned. Durable-looking. Naked except for those shorts. One, who I thought I recognized to be Frater Antony—he was—wore a small green pendant on his breast; three of the others had similar pendants, but of a darker stone, perhaps onyx. The woman who had crossed my path was not in the room.

Frater Antony indicated that I should stand with my companions. I took up a position next to Ned. Silence. Tension. An impulse to burst out laughing, which I barely choked back. How absurd all this was! Who did these pompous little men think they were? Why this rigmarole of skulls, this ritual of confrontations? Solemnly Frater Antony studied us, as if judging us. There was no sound but that of our breathing and the merry dribble of the fountain. A little serious music in the background, please, maestro. *Mors stupebit et natura, cum resurget creatura, judicanti responsura.* Death and Nature stand amazed, when all Creation rises again, to answer the Judge. To answer the Judge. And are you our Judge, Frater Antony? *Quando Judex est venturus, cuncta stricte discussurus!* Will he never speak? Must we remain eternally suspended between birth and death, womb and grave? Ah! They're following the script! One of the lesser fraters, pendantless, goes to a niche in the wall and takes out a slender book, elaborately bound in glittering red morocco, which he hands to Frater Antony. Without needing to be told, I know what the book must be. *Liber scriptus proferetur, in quo totum continetur.* The written book will be brought forth, in which all is contained. *Unde mundus judicetur.* Whence the world is to be judged. What can I say? King of tremendous majesty, who saves freely those to be saved, save me, O fount of mercy! Frater Antony now was looking directly at me. "The Book of Skulls," he said, gently, quietly, resonantly, "has few readers these days. How did it come to pass that you encountered it?"

"An old manuscript," I said. "Hidden and forgotten in a university library. My studies—an accidental discovery—curiosity led me to translate—"

The frater nodded. "And then to come to us? How was this?"

"A newspaper account," I replied. "Something about the imagery, the symbolism—we chanced it, we were on holiday and we thought we'd come to see if—if—"

"Yes," said Frater Antony. No question implied. A serene smile. He faced me squarely, obviously waiting for me to say what came next. There were four of us. We had read the Book of Skulls, and there were four of us. A formal application seemingly was now in order. *Exaudi orationem meam, ad te omnis caro veniet.* I could not speak. I stood mute in the infinite blast of silence, hoping that Ned would utter the words that would not pass my lips, that Oliver would say them, even Timothy. Frater Antony waited. He was waiting for me, he would wait to the last trump if need be, to the clamor of the final music. Speak. Speak. Speak.

I said, hearing my own voice from outside my body as though I were listening to the playback of a tape, "We four—having read and comprehended the Book of Skulls—having read and comprehended—wish to submit—wish to undergo the Trial. We four—we four offer ourselves—as candidates—we four offer ourselves as—" I faltered. Was my translation correct? Would he understand my choice of language? "As a Receptacle," I said.

"As a Receptacle," said Frater Antony.

"A Receptacle. A Receptacle. A Receptacle," said the fraters in chorus.

How very operatic the scene had become! Yes, suddenly I was singing tenor in *Turandot,* crying out to be asked the fatal riddles. It seemed preposterously stagy, a fatuous and overblown bit of histrionics, taking place against all reason in a world in which signals bounced off orbiting satellites, long-haired boys foraged for pot, and the billyclubs of the *staatspolizei* shattered the heads of demonstrators in fifty American cities. How could we be standing here chanting of skulls and receptacles? But stranger strangenesses lay ahead. Portentously Frater Antony beckoned to the one who had brought him the book, and again the other frater went to the niche. From it now he took a massive, carefully polished stone mask; he gave it to Frater Antony, who clapped it over his face, as one of the other fraters with pendants came forward to fasten a thong in the rear. The mask covered Frater Antony from the upper lip to the top of his head. It gave him the aspect of a living skull; his cool bright eyes glistened at me through deep stony sockets. Of course.

He said, "You four are aware of the conditions imposed under the Ninth Mystery?"

"Yes," I said. Frater Antony waited: he got a yes apiece from Ned, Oliver, and, distantly, Timothy.

"You undertake this Trial in no frivolous spirit, then, cognizant of the perils as well as of the rewards. You offer yourselves fully and without inner reservations. You have come here to partake of a sacrament, not to play a game. You yield yourselves fully to the Brotherhood and especially to the Keepers. Are these things understood?"

Yes, yes, yes, and—eventually—yes.

"Come to me. Your hands to my mask." We touched it, delicately, as if fearing electricity from the cold gray stone. "Not in many years has a Receptacle entered our company," Frater Antony said. "We value your presence and extend to you our gratitude for your coming among us. But I must tell you now, if your motives in coming to us were trifling ones, that you may not leave this House until the completion of your candidacy. Our rule is one of secrecy. Once the Trial commences, your lives are ours, and we forbid any departure from these grounds. This is the Nineteenth Mystery, of which you cannot have read: if one of you leaves, the three who remain are forfeit to us. Is this fully understood? We can permit no second thoughts, and you will be each other's guardians, knowing that if there is one renegade among you, the rest perish without exception. This is the moment for withdrawal. If the terms are too stringent, take your hands from my mask, and we will let the four of you go in peace."

I wavered. This was something I hadn't expected: death the penalty for pulling out in mid-Trial! Were they serious? What if we found, after a couple of days, that they had nothing of value to give us? Were we bound, then, to remain here, month upon month upon month, until they told us at last that our Trial was ended and we were again free? Those terms seemed impossible; I nearly pulled my hand away. But I remembered that I had come here to make an act of faith, that I was surrendering a meaningless life in the hope of gaining a meaningful one. Yes. I am yours, Frater Antony, no matter what. I kept my hand to his mask. In any case, how could these little men harm us if we decided to walk out? This was merely more stage-ritual, like the mask, like the choral chanting. Thus I reconciled myself. Ned, too, seemed to have his doubts; warily I watched him and saw his fingers flicker momentarily, but they stayed. Oliver's hand never budged from the rim of the mask. Timothy seemed the most hesitant; he scowled, glared at us and at the frater, burst into a sweat, actually lifted his fingers for perhaps three seconds, and then, with a what-the-hell gesture, clamped them to the mask so vehemently that Frater Antony nearly stumbled from the impact. Done. We were pledged. Frater Antony removed his mask. "You will dine with us now," he said, "and in the morning it will begin."

twenty-six
OLIVER

So we're here and it's real and we're inside it and they'll take us on as candidates. Life eternal we offer thee. That much is established. It's real. But is it? If you go to church faithfully every Sunday and say your prayers and lead a blameless life and put two bucks in the tray, you'll go to heaven and live forever among the angels and apostles, so they say, but do you really go? Is there a heaven? Are there angels and apostles? What good is all that diligent churchgoing if none of the rest of the deal is real? And so there really is a House of Skulls, there really is a Brotherhood of the Skulls, there are Keepers—Frater Antony is a Keeper—and we are a Receptacle, there is to be a Trial, but is it real? Is any of it real? Life eternal we offer thee, but do they? Or is it all just a pipe dream, like the stories of how you'll go to live among the angels and apostles?

Eli thinks it's real. Ned seems to think it's real. Timothy is amused by the whole thing, or perhaps irritated by it; hard to tell. And I? And I? I feel like a sleepwalker. This is a waking dream.

I constantly wonder, not just here but wherever I go, whether things are real, whether I'm experiencing anything genuine. Am I truly connected, am I plugged in to things? What if I'm not? What if the sensations I feel are just the dimmest faintest echoes of what others feel? How can I tell? When I drink wine, do I taste all that there is to taste in it, what *they* taste? Or do I get only the ghost of the flavor? When I read a book, do I understand the words on the page, or do I only think I do? When I touch a girl's body, do I truly feel the texture of her flesh? Sometimes I think all my perceptions are too weak. Sometimes I believe that I'm the only one in the world who isn't feeling things in full, but I have no way of telling that, any more than a color-blind man is able to tell if the colors he sees are the true ones. Sometimes I think I'm living a motion picture. I'm just a shadow on a screen, drifting from episode to meaningless episode in a script somebody else has written, some moron has written, some chimpanzee, some berserk computer, and I have no depth, no texture, no tangibility, no reality. Nothing matters; nothing is real. It's all a big picture-show. And this is how it has to be for me, forever. A kind of desperation comes over me at times like that. I can't believe in anything, then. Words themselves lose their meanings and become empty sounds. Everything becomes abstract, not just cloudy words like *love* and *hope* and *death,* but even the concrete ones, words like *tree, street, sour, hot, soft, horse, window.* I can't trust anything to be what it's supposed to be, because its name is only a noise. All content gets washed out of nouns. *Life. Death. Everything. Nothing.* They're all the same, aren't they? So what's real and what's unreal, and does it make any difference? Isn't the whole universe just a bundle of atoms, which we arrange into meaningful patterns by means of our abilities to perceive? And can't the packets of perception that we assemble be disassembled just as easily, by our ceasing to believe in the whole process? I simply have to withdraw my acceptance of the abstract notion that what I see, what I think I see, really is there. So that I could walk through the wall of this room, once I succeeded in denying that wall. So that I could live forever, once I denied death. So that I could die yesterday, once I denied today. I get into a mood like this and I go spiraling down and down on the whirlpool of my own thoughts, until I'm lost, I'm lost, I'm lost forever.

But we're here. It's real. We're inside it. They'll take us on as candidates.

That's all established. That's all real. But "real" is just a noise. "Real" isn't real. I don't think I'm connected any more. I don't think I'm plugged in. The other three, they could go to a restaurant and they'd think they were biting into a rare juicy broiled steak; I'd know I'm biting into a bundle of atoms, an abstract percept that we've labeled "steak," and you can't get nourishment from abstract percepts. I deny the steakness of the steak. I deny the reality of the steak. I deny the reality of the House of Skulls. I deny the reality of Oliver Marshall. I deny the reality of reality.

I must have been out in the sun too long today.

I'm scared. I'm coming apart. I'm not plugged in. And I can't tell any of them about it. Because I deny them, too. I've denied everything. God help me, I've denied God! I've denied death and I've denied life. What do the Zen people ask? What's the sound of one hand clapping, eh? Where does the flame of the candle go when it's been snuffed?

Where does the flame go?

I think I'm going to go there too, soon.

twenty-seven

eli

So it begins. The rituals, the diet, the gymnastics, the spiritual exercises, and the rest. Doubtless we have seen only the tip of the iceberg. Much else remains to be revealed; and, for example, we still do not know when the terms of the Ninth Mystery must be carried out. Tomorrow, next Friday, Christmas, when? Already we eye one another in a sinister fashion, peering through the face to the skull beneath. You, Ned, will you kill yourself for us? You, Timothy, are you planning to kill me so you may live? We haven't speculated on that aspect of it aloud at all, not once; it seems too terrible and too absurd to bear discussing or even thinking about. Perhaps the requirements are symbolic ones, metaphorical ones. Perhaps not. I worry about that. I've sensed since the beginning of this project certain unvoiced assumptions about who is to go, if any of us must go: me to die at their hands, Ned to perish at his own. Of course I'll reject that. I came here to gain life eternal. I don't know if any of them really did. Ned, freaky Ned, he's capable of seeing suicide as his finest poem. Timothy doesn't seem really to care about life-extension, though I suppose he'll take it if it comes along without much effort. Oliver insists that he absolutely refuses to die, ever, and he gets quite impassioned on the subject; but Oliver's a lot less stable than he appears on the surface, and there's no accounting for his motives. With the right philosophical prompting he could get as enamored of dying as he claims to be of living. So I can't say who lives, who succumbs to the Ninth Mystery. Except that I'm watching my step, and I'll go on watching it for however long we stay here. (How long is that supposed to be? We never gave any thought to that, really. Easter holiday is over in six, seven more days, I imagine. Certainly the Trial won't be finished by then. I get the feeling it lasts months or even years. Will we leave next week, regardless? We swore not to, but of course there isn't much the fraters can do to us if we all slip away in the middle of the night. Except that I want to stay. Weeks, if necessary. Years, if necessary. They'll report us missing in the outer world. The registrars, the draft boards, our parents, they'll all wonder about us. As long as they don't trace us here, though. The fraters have brought our baggage from the car. The car itself remains parked by the edge of the desert path. Will the state troopers notice it, eventually? Will they send a man down the path looking for the owner of that glossy sedan? We dangle loose ends by the score. But here we stay for the duration of the Trial. Here *I* stay, at any rate.)

   And if the rite of the Skulls is genuine?

   I won't stay here, as the fraters seem to do, after I've won what I seek. Oh, I might hang around for five or ten years, out of a sense of propriety, a sense of gratitude. But then I take off. It's a big world; why spend eternity in a desert retreat? I have my vision of the life to come. In a way, it's like Oliver's: I mean to feed my hunger for experience. I'll live a sequence of lives, draining the utmost out of each. Say, I'll spend ten years on Wall Street, piling up a fortune. If my father's right, and I'm sure he is, any reasonably clever sort can beat the market, just by doing the opposite of what all the supposedly smart ones are doing. They're all sheep, cattle, a bunch of *goyishe kops*. Dumb, greedy, following this fad and that one. So I'll play the other side of the game and come away with two or three million, which I'll invest in the right blue chips, good dividends, nothing fancy, steady income-producers. After all, I mean to live off those dividends for the next five or ten thousand years. Now I'm financially independent. What next? Why, ten years in debauchery. Why not? With enough money and self-confidence, you can have any woman in the world, right? I'll have Margo and a dozen like her every week. I'm entitled. A little lust, sure: it's not intellectual, it's not Significant, but fucking has its place in a well-rounded existence. All right. Gold and lust. Then I look after my spiritual welfare. Fifteen years in a Trappist monastery. I say not a word to anyone; I meditate, I write poetry, I try to reach God, I break through to the itness of the universe. Make that twenty years. Purify the soul, purge it, lift it to heights. Then I come forth and devote myself to body-building. Eight years of full-time exercise. Eli the beach boy. No longer a ninety-seven-pound weakling. I surf, I ski, I win the East Village Indian Wrestling Championship. Next? Music. I've never gotten as far into music as I'd like. I'll enroll at Juilliard, four years, the full schtick, penetrating the innerness of the musical art, going deep into Beethoven's late quartets, the Bach forty-eight, Berg, Schoenberg, Xenakis, all the toughest stuff, and I'll use the techniques I learned in the monastery in order to enter the heart of the universe of sound. Perhaps I'll compose. Perhaps I'll do critical essays. Perform, even. Eli Steinfeld in a Bach series at Carnegie Hall. Fifteen years for music, right? That takes care of the first sixty-odd years of my immortality. What next? We're well into the twenty-first century by now. Let's see the world. Go traveling like the Buddha, wander from land to land on foot, let my hair grow, wear yellow robes, carry a begging-bowl, pick up my checks once a month at American Express in Rangoon, Katmandu, Djakarta, Singapore. Experiencing humanity at the gut level, eating every food, curried ants, fried balls, sleeping with women of all races and creeds, living in leaky huts, in igloos, in tents, in houseboats. Twenty years for that and I should have a good idea of humanity's cultural complexity. Then, I think, I'll return to my original specialty, linguistics, philology, and allow myself the career I'm presently abandoning. In thirty years I might produce the definitive treatise on irregular verbs in Indo-European languages, or crack the secret of Etruscan, or translate the complete corpus of Ugaritic verse. Whatever field strikes my fancy. Next I'll become a homosexual. With life eternal at your disposal, you have to try everything at least once, don't you, and Ned insists that the gay life is the good life. Personally I've always preferred girls, intuitively, instinctively—they're softer, smoother, nicer to touch—but somewhere along the line I ought to see what the other gender has to offer. *Sub specie aeternitatis,* why should it matter whether I plug this hole or that one? When I'm back in a heterosexual phase I'll go to Mars. It'll be about the year 2100 by then; we'll have colonized Mars, I'm sure. Twelve years on Mars. I'll do manual labor, pioneer stuff. Then twenty years for literature, ten for reading everything worthwhile that's ever been written, ten for producing a novel that will rank with the best of Faulkner, Dostoevsky, Joyce, Proust. Why shouldn't I be able to equal them? I won't be a snotty kid any more; I'll have had 150 years of engagement with life, the deepest and broadest self-education any human being every enjoyed, and I'll still be in full youthful vigor. So if I apply myself to the task, a page a day, a page a week, five years to plan the architectonics of the book before I write word one, I should be able to produce, well, an immortal masterpiece. Under a pseudonym, of course. That's going to be a special problem, shifting my identity every eighty or ninety years. Even in the shiny futuristic future, people are likely to be suspicious of someone who simply won't die. Longevity is one thing, immortality something else again. I'll have to transfer my investments to myself somehow, name my new identity as my old one's heir. I'll have to keep disappearing and resurfacing. Dye my hair, beards on and off, mustaches, wigs, contact lenses. Be careful not to come too close to the machinery of government: once my fingerprints get into the master computer, I'll have troubles. What will I use for birth certificates each time I reappear? I'll think of something. If you're smart enough to live forever, you're smart enough to be able to cope with the bureaucracy. What if I fall in love? Marry, have kids, watch my wife wither and grow old, watch my kids slide into old age too, while I remain every fresh and young? Probably I shouldn't marry at all, or else do it just for the experience, ten, fifteen years at most, then get a divorce even if I still love her, to avoid all the later complications. We'll see. Where was I? On into the 2100s, parceling out the decades with a free hand. Ten years as a lama in Tibet. Ten years as an Irish fisherman, if they still have any fish left by then. Twelve years as a distinguished member of the United States Senate. Then I should take up science, the great neglected area of my life. I'll be able to handle it, given the proper amount of patience and application—physics, math, whatever I need to learn. I'll allot forty years for science. I intend to get right up there with Einstein and Newton, a full career in which I function at the highest level of intellect. And then? I could return to the skullhouse, I guess, to see how Frater Antony and the rest of his crowd have been getting along. Five years in the desert. Out, out into the world again. What a world it il be! They'll have whole new careers available, things that haven't begun to be invented yet: I can spend twenty years as a demateriali- zation expert, fifteen in polyvalent levitation, a dozen as a symptom-peddler. And then? And then? On and on and on. The possibilities will be infinite. But I'd better keep close watch on Timothy and Oliver, and maybe even Ned too, because of the accursed thrice-fucked Ninth Mystery. That's something big to worry about. If a couple of my pals kill me next Tuesday, say, it's going to spoil some awfully elaborate long-term plans.

twenty-eight
ned

The fraters are in love with us. No other term applies. They try to be poker-faced, solemn, hieratic, aloof, but they cannot conceal the simple joy our presence brings them. We rejuvenate them. We have rescued them from an eternity of repetitious toil. Not for an eon and a half have they had novices here, have they had new young blood on the premises; just the same closed society of fraters, fifteen of them in all, going about their devotions, working in the fields, doing the chores. And now we are here to be led through the rituals of initiation, and it is something novel for them, and they love us for having come.

They all participate in our enlightenment. Frater Antony presides over our meditations, our spiritual exercises. Frater Bernard leads us in the physical exercises. Frater Claude, the kitchen-frater, supervises our diet. Frater Miklos instructs us circumvolutely in the history of the order, providing us in his ambiguous way with the proper background information. Frater Javier is the father-confessor who will guide us, some days hence, through the psychotherapy that seems to be a central part of the entire process. Frater Franz, the work-frater, shows us our responsibilities as hewers of wood and drawers of water. Each of the other fraters has his special role to play, but we have not yet had occasion to meet with them. Also there are women here, an unknown number of them, perhaps only three or four, perhaps a dozen. We see them peripherally, a glance now, a glance then. Always they move across our field of vision at a distance, going from room to room on mysterious private errands, never pausing, never looking at us. Like the fraters, the women all are garbed alike, in brief white frocks rather than ragged blue shorts. Those that I've seen have long dark hair and full breasts, nor have Timothy, Eli, and Oliver noticed any willowy blondes or redheads. They bear close resemblance to one another, which is why I'm uncertain of their number; I never can tell whether the women I see are different ones each time, or the same few. The second day here, Timothy asked Frater Antony about them, but he was told gently that it was forbidden to ask a direct procedural question of any member of the Brotherhood; all will be made manifest to us at the proper time, Frater Antony promised. With that we must be content.

Our day is fully programed. We rise with the sun; lacking windows, we depend on Frater Franz, who goes at dawn down the dormitory wing hammering on doors. A bath is the mandatory first deed. Then we go into the fields for an hour of labor. The fraters raise all their food themselves, in a garden about two hundred yards behind the building. An elaborate irrigation system pumps water from some deep spring; it must have cost a fortune to install, just as the House of Skulls must have cost a fortune and a half to build, but I suspect the Brotherhood is enormously wealthy. As Eli has pointed out, any self-perpetuating organization that can compound its assets at 5 or 6 percent for three or four centuries would end up owning whole continents. The fraters grow wheat, herbs, and an assortment of edible fruits, berries, roots, and nuts; I have no idea yet what most of the crops are that we weed and tend so lovingly, and I suspect that many of them are exotic plants. Rice, beans, corn, and "strong" vegetables such as onions are forbidden here. Wheat, I gather, is tolerated only grudgingly, deemed spiritually unworthy but somehow necessary: it undergoes a rigorous fivefold sifting and tenfold milling, accompanied by special meditations, before it is made into bread. The fraters eat no meat, nor shall we as long as we remain here. Meat, apparently, is a source of destructive vibes. Salt is banished. Pepper is outlawed. Black pepper, that is; chili pepper is within the pale, and the fraters dote on it, consuming it as the Mexicans do in any number of ways—fresh peppers, dried pods, chili powder, pickled peppers, etc., etc., etc. The stuff they grow here is fiery. Eli and I are spice freaks, and we use it liberally even though it sometimes brings tears to our eyes, but Timothy and Oliver, reared on blander diets, can't handle it at all. Another favorite food here is eggs. There's a hatchery out back full of busy hens, and eggs in some form appear on the menu three times a day. The fraters also produce certain mildly alcoholic herb-liqueurs, under the supervision of Frater Maurice, the distiller-frater.

When we have done our hour of service in the fields a gong summons us; we go to our rooms to bathe again, and then it is breakfast-time. Meals are served in one of the public rooms, at an elegant stone bench. The menus are calculated according to arcane principles not yet disclosed to us; it seems as if the color and texture of what we eat has as much to do with the planning of meals as the nutritional value. We eat eggs, soups, bread, vegetable mashes, and so forth, copiously seasoned with chili; for beverages we have water, a kind of wheat-beer, and, in the evening, the herb-liqueurs, but nothing else. Oliver, a steak-eater, complains a good deal about the lack of meat.

I missed it at first but by now have completely adapted to this odd regimen, as has Eli. Timothy grumbles to himself and swills the liqueurs. At lunch the third day he had too much beer and threw up on the marvelous slate floor; Frater Franz waited until he was finished, then handed him a cloth and wordlessly ordered him to clean up his own mess. The fraters plainly dislike Timothy, and perhaps fear him, for he's half a foot taller than any of them and must outweigh the heaviest by ninety pounds. The rest of us, as I say, they love, and in the abstract they love Timothy too.

After breakfast comes morning meditations with Frater Antony. He says little, merely provides a spiritual context for us with a minimum of words. We meet in the other long rear wing of the building, opposite the dormitory wing; this is entirely given over to the monastic functions. Instead of bedrooms, there are chapels, eighteen of them, I suppose corresponding to the Eighteen Mysteries; they are as sparsely furnished and as powerfully austere as the other rooms, and contain a series of overwhelming artistic masterpieces. Most of these are pre-Columbian, but some of the chalices and carvings have a medieval European look, and there are certain abstract objects (of ivory? bone? stone?) that are completely unfamiliar to me. This side of the building also has a large library, crammed with books, rarities, by the looks of the shelves; we are forbidden at present to enter that room, though its door is never locked. Frater Antony meets with us in the chapel closest to the public wing. It is empty except for the ubiquitous skull-mask on the wall. He kneels; we kneel; he removes from his breast his tiny jade pendant, which unsurprisingly is carved in the shape of a skull, and places it on the floor before us as a focus for our meditations. As frater-superior, Frater Antony has the only jade pendant, but Frater Miklos, Frater Javier, and Frater Franz are entitled to wear similar pendants of polished brown stone—obsidian, I imagine, or onyx. These four are the Keepers of the Skulls, an elite group within the fraternity. What Frater Antony urges us to contemplate is a paradox: the skull beneath the face, the presence of the death-symbol hidden under our living masks. Through an exercise of "interior vision," we are supposed to purge ourselves of the death-impulse by absorbing, fully comprehending, and ultimately destroying the power of the skull. I don't know how successful any of us has been at achieving this: another thing we are forbidden to do is compare notes on our progress. I doubt that Timothy is much good at meditation. Oliver evidently is; he stares at the jade skull with lunatic intensity, engulfing it, surrounding it, and I think his spirit goes forth and enters it. But is he moving in the correct direction? Eli, in the past, has complained to me of the difficulties he's had in reaching the highest levels of mystic experience on drugs; his mind is too agile, too jumpy, and he's spoiled several acid trips for himself by darting hither and thither instead of settling down and gliding into the All. Out here, too, I think he's having trouble getting it together; he looks tense and impatient during the meditation sessions and seems to be forcing it, trying to push himself into a region he can't really attain. As for me, I rather enjoy the daily hour with Frater Antony; the paradox of the skull is, of course, precisely my line of irrationality, and I think I'm grooving properly with it, though I recognize the possibility that I'm deceiving myself. I'd like to discuss the degree of my progress, if any, with Frater Antony, but all such self-conscious inquiries are prohibited for now. So I kneel and stare at the little green skull each day, and cast forth my soul, and conduct my perpetual internal struggle between corrosive cynicism and abject faith.

When we finish our hour with Frater Antony we go back to the fields. We pull weeds, spread fertilizer—it's all organic, naturally—and plant seedlings. Here Oliver is at his best. He's always tried to repudiate his farm-boy upbringing, but now suddenly he's flaunting it, the way Eli flaunts his Yiddish vocabulary despite not having been inside a synagogue since his bar mitzvah. The more-ethnic-than-thou syndrome, and Oliver's ethnos is rural-agricultural, so he goes at his hoeing and spading with formidable vim. The fraters try to slow him down: I think his energy appalls them, but also they worry about his chances of heatstroke; Frater Leon, the physician-frater, has spoken to Oliver several times, pointing out that the midmorning temperatures are in the low nineties and will soon be much higher than that. Still Oliver chugs furiously on. I find all this grubbing in the soil agreeably strange and strangely agreeable, myself. It appeals to the back-to-nature romanticism that I suppose lurks in the hearts of all excessively urbanized intellectuals. I've never done any manual labor more strenuous than masturbation before this, so the field chores are back-breaking as well as mindblowing for me, but I haul myself eagerly through the work. So far. Eli's relationship to the farm stuff is very similar to mine, though if anything more intense, more romantic; he talks about drawing physical renewal from Mother Earth. And Timothy, who of course had never had to do so much as tie his own shoelaces, takes a lordly gentleman farmer attitude: *noblesse oblige,* he says with every languid gesture, doing as the fraters tell him but making it quite plain that he deigns to dirty his hands only because he finds it amusing to play their little game. Well, we all dig, each in his own way.

By ten or half past ten in the morning it becomes unpleasantly hot, and we leave the fields, all except three farmer-fraters whose names I do not yet know. They spend ten or twelve hours outdoors each day: as a penance, perhaps? The rest of us, both fraters and the Receptacle, go to our rooms and bathe again. Then we four convene over in the far wing for our daily session with Frater Miklos, the history-frater.

Miklos is a compact, powerfully built little man, with forearms like thighs and thighs like logs. He gives the impression of being older than the other fraters, though I admit there's something paradoxical about applying a comparative like "older" to a group of ageless men. He speaks with a faint and indefinable accent, and his thought processes are distinctly nonlinear: he rambles, he wanders, he slides unexpectedly from theme to theme. I believe it's deliberate, that his mind is subtle and unfathomable rather than senile and undisciplined. Perhaps over the centuries he's grown bored with mere consecutive discourse; I know I would.

He has two subjects: the origin and development of the Brotherhood and the history of the concept of human longevity. On the first of these he is at his most elusive, as if determined never to give us a straightforward outline. We are very old, he keeps saying, very old, very old, and I have no way of knowing whether he means the fraters or the Brotherhood itself, though I think perhaps both; perhaps some of the fraters have been in it from the beginning, their lives spanning not merely decades or centuries but entire millennia. He hints at prehistoric origins, the caves of the Pyrenees, the Dordogne, Lascaux, Altamira, a secret confraternity of shamans that has endured out of mankind's dawn, but how much of this is true and how much is fable I cannot say, any more than I know if the Rosicrucians really do trace their genesis to Amenhotep IV. But as Frater Miklos speaks I have visions of smoky caverns, flickering torches, half-naked artists clad in the skins of woolly mammoths and daubing bright pigments on walls, medicine men conducting the ritual slaughter of aurochs and rhinoceros. And the shamans whispering, huddling, whispering, saying to one another, We shall not die, brothers, we will live on, we will watch Egypt rise out of the swamps of the Nile, we will see Sumer born, we will live to behold Socrates and Caesar and Jesus and Constantine, and yes! we will still be here when the fiery mushroom flares sun-bright over Hiroshima and when the men from the metal ship descend the ladder to walk the face of the moon. But did Miklos tell me this, or did I dream it in the haze of noonday desert heat? Everything is obscure; everything shifts and melts and runs as his mazy words circle round themselves, circle round themselves, twist, dance, tangle. Also he tells us, in riddles and periphrasis, of a lost continent, of a vanished civilization, from which the wisdom of the Brotherhood is derived. And we stare, wide-eyed, exchanging little covert glances of astonishment, not knowing whether to snicker in skeptical scorn or gasp in awe. *Atlantis!* How did Miklos do it, conjuring in our minds those images of a glittering land of gold and crystal, broad leafy avenues, towering white-walled buildings, shining chariots, dignified philosophers in flowing robes, the brassy instruments of forgotten science, the aura of beneficent karma, the twanging sound of strange music echoing through the halls of vast temples dedicated to unknown gods. Atlantis? How narrow a line we tread between fantasy and foolishness! I have never heard him utter the name, but he put Atlantis into my mind the first day, and now my conviction grows that I am correct, that he indeed claims for the Brotherhood an Atlantean heritage. What are these emblems of skulls on the temple facade? What are these jeweled skulls worn as rings and pendants in the great city? Who are these missionaries in auburn fabric, crossing to the mainland, making their way to the mountain settlements, dazzling the mammoth-hunters with their flashlights and pistols, holding high the sacred Skull and calling upon the cave-dwellers to drop down, give knee. And the shamans in the painted caves, crouched by their sputtering fires, whispering, conniving, at length rendering homage to the splendid strangers, bowing, kissing the Skull, burying their own idols, the fat-thighed Venuses and the carved slivers of bone. *Life eternal we offer thee,* say the newcomers, and they show a shimmering screen within which swim images of their city, towers, chariots, temples, jewels, and the shamans nod, they crack their knuckles and pass water on the holy fires, they dance, they clap hands, they submit, they submit, they stare into the shimmering screen, they kill the fatted mastodon, they offer their guests a feast of fellowship. And so it commences, that alliance between mountain-men and island-men, in that chilly dawn, so it starts, the flow of karma to the icebound mainland, the awakening, the transfer of knowledge. So that when the earthquake comes, when the veil is rent asunder and the pillars tremble and a black pall hangs over the world, when the avenues and the towers are swallowed by the angry sea, something lives on, something survives in the caves, the secrets, the rituals, the faith, the Skull, the Skull, the Skull! Is that how it was, Miklos? And is that how it has been, across ten, fifteen, twenty thousand years, out of a past that we choose to deny? Bliss was it in that dawn to be alive! And you are still here, Frater Miklos? You have come down to us out of Altamira, out of Lascaux, out of doomed Atlantis itself, you and Frater Antony and Frater Bernard and the rest, outlasting Egypt, outlasting the Caesars, giving knee to the Skull, enduring all things, hoarding wealth, tilling the soil, moving from land to land, from the blessed caves to the newborn neolithic villages, from the mountains to the rivers, across the earth, to Persia, to Rome, to Palestine, to Catalonia, learning the languages as they evolve, speaking to the people, posing as men of their gods, building your temples and monasteries, nodding to Isis, to Mithra, to Jehovah, to Jesus, this god and that, absorbing everything, withstanding everything, putting the Cross over the Skull when the Cross was in fashion, mastering the arts of survival, replenishing yourselves now and then by taking in a Receptacle, demanding always new blood though your own grew never thin. And then? Moving on to Mexico after Cortes broke her people for you. Here was a land that understood the power of death, here was a place where the Skull had always reigned, perhaps brought there as well as to your own land by the island-folk, eh, Atlantean missionaries in Cholula and Tenochtitlán also, showing the way of the deathmask? Fertile ground, for a few centuries. But you insist on constant renewal, and so you went onward, taking your loot with you, your masks, your skulls, your statues, your paleolithic treasures, north, into the new country, the empty country, the desert heart of the United States, into the bomb-land, into the pain-land, and with the compound interest of the ages you built your newest House of Skulls, eh, Miklos, and here you sit, and here sit we. Is that how it was? Or have I hallucinated it all, bum-tripping your vague and muddy words into a gaudy self-deceptive dream? How can I tell? How will I ever know? All I have is what you tell me, which blurs and trembles and flees my mind. And I see what is around me, this contamination of your primordial imagery by Aztec visions, by Christian visions, by Atlantean visions, and I can only wonder, Miklos, how is it you are still here when the mammoth has shuffled off the stage, and am I a fool or a prophet?

The other part of what Frater Miklos has to impart to us is less elliptical, more readily grasped and held in place. It constitutes a seminar on life-extension, in which he shuttles coolly across time and space in search of ideas that may well have entered the world long after he had. To begin with, why resist death at all, he asks us? Is it not a natural termination, a desirable release from toil, a consummation devoutly to be wished? The skull beneath the face reminds us that all creatures perish in their time, none is exempt: why then defy the universal will? Dust thou art, and unto dust shalt thou return, eh? All flesh shall perish together; we pass away out of the world as grasshoppers, and it is a poor thing for anyone to fear that which is inevitable. Ah, but can we be such philosophers? If it is our destiny to go, is it not also our desire to delay the moment of exit? His questions are rhetorical ones. Sitting cross-legged before that thick-thewed tower of years, we do not dare intrude on the rhythms of his thought. He looks at us without seeing us. What, he asks, what if one could indeed postpone death indefinitely, or at least thrust it far into the time to come? Of course, preserving one's health and strength is necessary to the bargain: there is no merit in becoming a struldbrug, is there, old and drooling, babbling and rheumy-eyed, a perambulatory mass of decay? Consider Tithonus, who petitioned the gods for exemption from death and was granted immortality but not eternal youth; gray, withered, he lies yet in a sealed room, forever growing older, locked within the constrictions of his corruptible and corrupt flesh. No, we must seek vigor as well as longevity.

There have been those, observes Frater Miklos, who scorn such quests and argue a passive acceptance of death. He reminds us of Gilgamesh, who strode from Tigris to Euphrates in search of the thorny plant of eternity and lost it to a hungry serpent. Gilgamesh, whither runnest thou? The life which thou seekest thou wilt not find, for when the gods created mankind, they allotted death to mankind, but life they retained in their keeping. Consider Lucretius, he says, Lucretius who observes that it is pointless to strive to extend one's life, for however many years we may gain through such activities, it is nothing to the eternities we must spend in death. By prolonging life, we cannot subtract or whittle away one jot from the duration of our death. . . . We may struggle to remain, but in time we must go, and no matter how many generations we have added to our span, there waits for us none the less the same eternal death. And Marcus Aurelius: Though thou shouldst be going to live three thousand years, and as many times ten thousand years, still remember that no man loses any other life than this which he now lives. . . . The longest and shortest are thus brought to the same . . . all things from eternity are of like forms and come round in a circle . . . it makes no difference whether a man shall see the same things during a hundred years or two hundred, or an infinite time. And from Aristotle, a snippet I take to heart: Hence all things on earth are at all times in a state of transition and are coming into being and passing away . . . never are they eternal when they contain contrary qualities.

Such bleakness. Such pessimism. Accept, submit, yield, die, die, die, die!

What saith the Judaeo-Christian tradition? Man that is born of a woman is of few days, and full of trouble. He cometh forth like a flower, and is cut down: he fleeth also as a shadow, and continueth not. Seeing his days are determined, the number of his months are with thee, thou hast appointed his bounds that he cannot pass. The funereal wisdom of Job, earned in the hardest way. What news from St. Paul? For me to live is Christ, and to die is gain. If it is to be life in the flesh, that means fruitful labor for me. Yet which I shall choose I cannot tell. I am hard pressed between the two. My desire is to depart and be with Christ, for that is far better. But, Frater Miklos demands, must we accept such teachings? (He implies that Paul, Job, Lucretius, Marcus Aurelius, Gilgamesh, all are johnny-come-latelies, wet behind the ears, hopelessly post-paleolithic; he gives us once again a glimpse of the dark caves as he winds back on his theme into the aurochs-infested past.) Now he emerges suddenly from that valley of despond and by a commodius vicus of recirculation we are back to a recitation of the annals of longevity, all the thundering names Eli dinned into our ears in the snowy months, as we sailed onward into this adventure, a way a lone a last a loved a long the riverrun, past Eve and Adam's from swerve of shore to bend of bay, and Miklos shows us the Isles of the Blest, the Land of the Hyper-boreans, the Keltic Land of Youth, the Persian Land of Yima, oh, even Shangri-la (see, the old fox cries, I am contemporary, I am aware!), and gives us Ponce de Leon's leaky fountain, gives us Glaukus the fisherman, nibbling the herbs beside the sea and turning green with immor-tality, gives us fables out of Herodotus, gives us the Uttara-kurus and the Jambu tree, dangles a hundred gleaming myths before our bedazzled ears, so that we want to cry out, Here! Come, Eternity! and kneel to the Skull, and then he twists again, leading us on a Möbius-dance, hauling us back into the caves, letting us feel the gusts of glacial winds, the frigid kiss of the Pleistocene, and taking us by the ears, turning us westward, letting us see that hot sun blazing over Atlantis, shoving us on our way, stumbling, shuffling, toward the sea, toward the sunset lands, toward the drowned wonders and past them, to Mexico and her demon-gods, her skull-gods, toward leering Huitzilopochtli and terrible snaky Coatlicue, toward the red altars of Tenochtitlán, toward the flayed god, toward all the para-doxes of life-in-death and death-in-life, and the feathered serpent laughs and shakes his rattling tail, click-click, and we are before the Skull, before the Skull, before the Skull, with a great gong tolling through our brains out of the labyrinths of the Pyrenees, we drink the blood of the bulls of Altamira, we waltz with the mammoths of Lascaux, we hear the tambourines of the shamans, we kneel, we touch stone with our foreheads, we pass water, we weep, we shiver in the reverberations of the Atlantean drums hammering three thousand miles of ocean in the fury of irretrievable loss, and the sun rises and the light warms us and the Skull smiles and the arms open and the flesh takes wing and the defeat of death is at hand, but then the hour has ended and Frater Miklos has departed, leaving us blinking and stumbling in sudden disarray, alone, alone, alone, alone. Until tomorrow.

We go from our history lesson to lunch. Eggs, mashed chilis, beer, thick dark bread. After lunch, an hour of private meditations, each to his own room, as we struggle to make sense of all that has been poured into our heads. Then the gong sounds, calling us again to the fields. Now the full heat of afternoon has descended, and even Oliver shows some restraint: we move slowly, cleaning the hen house, staking the seedlings, providing extra hands for the tireless farmer-fraters who have labored most of the day. Two hours of this; the entire Brotherhood is side by side, all but Frater Antony, who stays alone in the House of Skulls. (It was at such a time that we first arrived here.) At last we are released from servitude. Sweaty, sun-annealed, we shamble to our rooms, bathe yet once again, and rest, each by himself, until the time of dinner.

Another meal, then. The usual fare. After dinner, we serve on cleanup detail. As the time of sunset approaches we go with Father Antony and, most nights, with four or five of the other fraters, to a low hill just west of the skullhouse; there we perform the rite of drinking the sun's breath. This is done by assuming a peculiar and uncomfortable cross-legged squat—a combination of the lotus position and a sprinter's crouch—and gazing directly into the red globe of the descending sun. Just at the moment when we think we're beginning to burn holes in our retinas, we must close our eyes and meditate on the spectrum of colors flowing from the sun's disk to us. We are instructed to concentrate on bringing that spectrum into our bodies, entering through the eyelids and spreading by way of the sinuses and nasal passages into the throat and chest. Ultimately the solar radiance is supposed to settle in the heart and generate life-giving warmth and light. When we are true adepts, we're allegedly going to be able to shunt the indrawn radiance to any part of the body that happens to be in special need of invigoration—the kidneys, say, or the genitals, or the pancreas, or whatever. The fraters who squat beside us on the hilltop presumably are doing such shunting now. How much value this routine has is beyond my capacity to judge; I can't see how it can be worth a damn, scientifically, but as Eli kept insisting from the beginning there's more to life than what science says, and if the longevity techniques here rely on meta-phorical and symbolic reorientations of the metabolism, leading to empirical changes in body mechanism, then perhaps it's of major importance for us to drink the sun's breath. The fraters don't show us their birth certificates; we must take this entire operation, as we knew, purely on faith.

When the sun is down we repair to one of the larger public rooms to fulfill the last obligation of our day: the gymnastics session, with Frater Bernard. According to the Book of Skulls, keeping the body supple is essential to the prolongation of life. Well, that's not news, but of course a special mystical-cosmological aspect informs the Brotherhood's technique of keeping the body supple. We begin with breathing exercises, the significance of which Frater Bernard has explained to us in his usual laconic way; it has something to do with rearranging one's rela-tionship to the universe of phenomena so that the macrocosm is inside one and the microcosm is outside, I think, but I hope to get further clarifications of this as we go along. Also there is much esoteric stuff involving devel-opment of the "inner breath," but apparently it's not considered important for us to comprehend this yet. Any-way, we squat and vigorously hyperventilate, dumping all impurities out of our lungs and sucking in good clean spiritually approved night air; after an extended period of exhaling and inhaling, we move on to breath-retention drills that leave us giddy and exalted, and then to strange breath-transportation maneuvers, in which we must learn to direct our inhalations to various parts of our bodies much as we did previously with the sunlight. All this is hard work, but the hyperventilation produces a satisfactory euphoria: we become light-headed and optimistic and convince ourselves easily that we are well along the road to life eternal. Perhaps we are, if oxygen = life and carbon dioxide = death.

When Frater Bernard judges that we have breathed ourselves into a state of grace, we begin the reeling and writhing. The exercises have been different each night, as though he draws on a repertoire of infinite variety developed over a thousand centuries. Sit with legs crossed and heels on floor, clasp hands over head, touch elbows five times rapidly to floor. (Ouch!) Touch left hand to left knee, raise right hand over head, breathe deeply ten times. Repeat with right hand to right knee, left hand aloft. Now both hands high overhead, bob head vociferously until stars sparkle behind closed eyelids. Stand, put hands to hips, twist violently to the side until trunk is bent at a ninety-degree angle, first toward left, then toward right. Stand on one leg, clutch other knee to chin. Hop like madman. And so on, including many things we are not yet limber enough to do—foot wrapped around head, or arms flexed in inverted position, or rising and sitting with legs crossed, and so forth. We do our best, which is never quite good enough to satisfy Frater Bernard; wordlessly he reminds us, through the suppleness of his own movements, of the great goal toward which we strive. I'm prepared to learn, any day now, that in order to attain life eternal it will be absolutely necessary to master the art of sticking one's elbow in one's mouth; if you can't do it, it's tough, baby, but you're doomed to wither by the wayside.

Frater Bernard works us close to the point of exhaustion. He himself goes through every routine he demands of us, never missing a single bending or flexing, and showing no particular signs of strain as he cavorts. The best of us at these calisthenics is Oliver, the worst Eli; yet

Eli goes about them with a weird clumsy enthusiasm that must be admired.

Finally we are dismissed, usually after about ninety minutes of work. The rest of the evening is free time, but we take no advantage of our freedom; at that point we're ready to topple into bed, and do, for all too soon will come the dawn and Frater Franz's cheery rat-tat-tat on my door. And so to sleep. I've been sleeping soundly, more soundly than ever before.

Thus our daily routine. What does it all mean? Are we growing younger here? Are we growing older? Will the shining promise of the Book of Skulls be fulfilled for any of us? Does any of what we do each day make sense? The skulls on the walls give me no answers. The smiles of the fraters are impenetrable. We discuss nothing with one another. Pacing my ascetic room, I hear the paleolithic gong tolling in my own skull, clang, clang, clang, wait and see, wait and see, wait and see. And the Ninth Mystery hangs over us all like a dangling sword.

twenty-nine

timothy

This afternoon, while we were scraping up barrels of hen shit in ninety-degree heat, I decided that I'd had it. The joke had gone on long enough. Vacation was just about over, anyway; I wanted out. I had felt that way the first day we were here, of course, but for Eli's sake I suppressed my feelings. Now I couldn't keep it in any longer. I decided that I'd speak to him before dinner, during the rest period.

When we came in from the fields I took a quick bath and went down the hall to Eli's room. He was still in the tub; I heard the water running, heard him singing in his deep monotone voice. Eventually he came out, toweling himself. Life here was agreeing with him: he looked stronger, more muscular. He gave me a frosty look.

"Why are you here, Timothy?"

"Just a visit."

"It's the rest period. We're supposed to be alone."

"We're always supposed to be alone," I said, "except when we're with *them*. We never get a chance to talk privately to each other any more."

"That's evidently part of the ritual."

"Part of the game," I said, "part of the crappy game they're playing with us. Look, Eli, you're practically like a brother to me. There isn't anyone can tell me when I can talk to you and when I can't."

"My brother the *goy*," he said. Quick smile, on-off. "We've had plenty of time for talking. We're under instructions now to keep apart from one another. You ought to go, Timothy. Really, you ought to go, before the fraters catch you in here."

"What is this, a goddamn jail?"

"It's a monastery. A monastery has rules, and by coming here we've made ourselves subject to those rules." He sighed. "Will you please go, Timothy?"

"It's those rules that I want to talk about, Eli."

"I don't make them. I can't excuse you from any of them."

"Let me talk," I said. "You know, the clock keeps ticking while we stay here being a Receptacle. We'll be missed, soon. Our families will notice they haven't heard from us. Somebody'll discover we didn't go back to school after Easter."

"So?"

"How long are we going to stay here, Eli?"

"Until we have what we want."

"You believe all the crap they've been telling us?"

"You still think it's crap, Timothy?"

"I haven't seen or heard anything to make me change my original opinion."

"What about the fraters? How old do you think they are?"

I shrugged. "Sixty. Seventy. Some of them may be in their eighties. They lead a good life, plenty of fresh air and exercise, careful diets. So they keep themselves in shape."

"I believe Frater Antony is at least a thousand years old," Eli said. His tone was cold, aggressive, defiant: he was daring me to laugh at him, and I couldn't. "Possibly he's much older than that," Eli went on. "The same for Frater Miklos and Frater Franz. I don't think there's one of them who's less than a hundred fifty or so."

"Wonderful."

"What do you want, Timothy? Do you want to leave?"

"I've been considering it."

"By yourself or with us?"

"Preferably with you. By myself if necessary."

"Oliver and I aren't leaving, Timothy. And I don't think Ned is either."

"I guess that puts me on my own, then."

"Is that a threat?" he asked.

"It's an implication."

"You know what'll happen to the rest of us if you pull out."

"Are you seriously afraid that the fraters will enforce that oath?" I asked.

"We swore not to leave," Eli said. "They named the penalty and we agreed to abide by it. I wouldn't underestimate their ability to impose it if one of us gave them cause."

"Crap. They're just a bunch of little old men. If any of them came after me, I'd break them in half. With one hand."

"Perhaps you would. Perhaps we wouldn't. Do you want to be responsible for our deaths, Timothy?"

"Don't hand me that melodramatic garbage. I'm a

free agent. Look at it existentially, the way you're always asking us to do: we shape our own fates, Eli, we go our own paths. Why should I be bound to you three?"

"You took a voluntary oath."

"I can renounce it."

"All right," he said. "Renounce it. Pack up and clear out." He was lying sprawled out naked on his cot, staring me down; I had never see Eli look this determined, this formidable, before. Suddenly he was tremendously together. Or else he had a demon inside him. He said, "Well, Timothy? You're a free agent. Nobody's stopping you. You can be in Phoenix by sundown."

"I'm not in that much of a rush. I wanted to discuss this with the three of you, come to some kind of rational understanding, nobody bludgeoning anybody else but all of us agreeing that—"

"We agreed to come here," Eli said, "and we agreed to give it a chance. Further discussion's not necessary. You can pull out whenever you please, bearing in mind, of course, that by doing so you'll expose us to certain risks."

"That's blackmail."

"I know." His eyes flashed. "What are you afraid of, Timothy? The Ninth Mystery? Does that scare you? Or is it the possibility of really getting to live forever that you're worried about? Are you bowed down under existential terror, man? Seeing yourself going on and on through the centuries, tied to the wheel of karma, unable to get free? Which frightens you more, Timothy—living or dying?"

"You little cocksucker."

"Wrong room," he said. "Go out to the left, two doors up the hall, ask for Ned."

"I came in here with something serious on my mind. I didn't ask for jokes and I didn't ask for threats and I didn't ask for personal smears. I just want to know how long you and Oliver and Ned plan to stay here."

"We've only just arrived. It's too soon to talk about leaving. Will you excuse me now?"

I went out. I was getting nowhere, and we both

knew it. And Eli had stung me, a few times, in places where I hadn't realized I was so vulnerable.

At dinner, he acted as though I hadn't said a thing to him.

And now? Do I just sit and wait and wonder? Jesus, I can't put up with much more of this, honestly. I simply wasn't designed for the monastic life—completely leaving out of the question the matter of the Book of Skulls and all it may offer. You have to be bred for this sort of thing; you have to have renunciation in your genes, a touch of masochism. I've got to make them realize that, Eli and Oliver. The two madmen, the two immortality-crazed lunatics. They'd stay here ten or twenty years, pulling weeds, breaking their backs with these exercises, staring at the sun till they're half blind, breathing deep, eating peppered mush, and convincing themselves that this was the right way to get to live forever. Eli, who always struck me as freaky and neurotic but fundamentally pretty rational, seems definitely to have flipped. His eyes are strange now, glassy and fierce, like Oliver's: psychotic eyes, terrible eyes. Things are stirring inside Eli. He's gaining strength day by day, adding not just muscles but a sort of moral strength, a fervor, a dynamism: he's bound on his course and he lets you know that he isn't going to allow anything to come between him and what he wants. For Eli that's something brand new. Sometimes I think he's turning into Oliver—a short, dark, hairy Yiddish edition of Oliver. Oliver, of course, keeps his mouth shut and does enough chores for six and at exercise time bends himself into a pretzel trying to out-frater the frater. And even Ned is catching the faith. No wisecracks from him now, no little snotty quips. In the morning we sit there listening to Frater Miklos spin long driveling skeins of senile gibberish, with maybe one intelligible sentence out of every six, and there's Ned, like a six-year-old being told about Santa Claus, screwing up his face in excitement, sweating, chewing his nails, nodding, gulping it all down. Right on, Frater Miklos! Atlantis, yes, and Cro-magnon Man, sure, and the Aztecs, and all the rest, I believe, I believe! And then we eat our lunch, and then we meditate on the cold stone floor of our rooms, each by himself, and then we go out and sweat for the fraters in the fucking fields. Enough. I can't take very much more. I muffed my chance today, but I'll go back to Eli again in a day or two and see if I can't get him to be reasonable. Though I don't have much hope of that.

Eli frightens me a little, now.

And I wish he hadn't said that bit about what I'm afraid of, whether the Ninth Mystery or living forever. I very much wish he hadn't said that to me.

thirty

OLIVER

A small accident while we were working in the fields before breakfast. I was passing between two rows of chili-plants and I put my bare left foot down on a sharp slab of stone that somehow had worked its way up to the surface and was sticking out, edge-on. I felt the stone starting to cut into my sole, and I shifted weight quickly, too quickly. My other foot wasn't ready to take the burden. My right ankle began to buckle. There was nothing I could do but let myself fall, the way they teach you to fall on the basketball court when you've been faked badly out of position and are faced with a quick choice between toppling and tearing a bunch of ligaments. Down I went, catabloop, smack on my ass. I didn't hurt myself in any way, but this section of the fields had been heavily irrigated the night before and still was muddy; I landed in a sticky, soggy patch, and there was a squooshy sucking sound as I pulled myself up. My shorts were a mess—the whole seat mudstained and wet. Well, nothing serious about that, though I didn't like the feel of the damp dirt as it soaked through the fabric to my skin. Frater Franz came trotting over to see if I had hurt myself, and I showed him that I was all right, all except my shorts. I asked if I should go back to the house and change, but he grinned and shook his head and told me there wasn't any need of that. I could just take the shorts off and hang them on a tree and the sun would dry them in half an hour. Okay, why not? I'm not uptight about going around without clothes on, and anyway how much more privacy did I need than out here in the middle of the desert? So I wriggled out of the shorts and draped them on a branch and brushed the mud off my rump and began pulling weeds again.

It was only about twenty minutes since daybreak but the sun was already climbing fast and getting hot, and the temperature, which must have dipped into the forties or fifties during the night, was rapidly heading through the seventies toward the higher regions of the thermometer. I felt the warmth on my bare skin, the sweat beginning to burst from me in rivers, running down my back, my buttocks, my legs, and I told myself that this was the way it always ought to be when men went out to work in the fields on a hot day, that it was clean and good to be naked under the bright sun, that it made no sense at all to have to wrap a strip of rough dirty cloth around your middle when you could strip down all the way like this. The more I thought about it, the less sense it made to me to wear clothes at all: so long as the weather is warm and your body doesn't offend the eye, why must you cover yourself? Of course a lot of people aren't so pretty to look at; they're better off clothed, I guess, or at least we are if they are. But I was glad to be out of my muddy shorts. Out here among other men, what the hell.

And as I worked my way down the row of chili,

sweating the good sweat, my nakedness put me in mind of other times, years ago, when I was first discovering my body and the bodies of others. I suppose it was the heat that stirred a ferment of memory in me, images drifting freely in my head, a hazy easy formless cloud of recollection. Down by the creek, a scorching July afternoon, when I was—how old?—eleven, yes, eleven, it was the year my father died. I was with Jim and Karl, my friends, my only really close friends, Karl twelve, Jim my age, and we were looking for Karl's dog, the mutt, who ran away that morning. Following his spoor, we were, like Tarzan, trailing the dog upstream, finding a couple of turds here and a puddle of wet at the base of a treetrunk there, until we had gone a mile, two miles, out into nowhere, and the heat was on us and the sweat was drenching our clothes, and we hadn't found the dog at all, and we came to the deep part of the creek, beyond the Madden farm, where it's deep enough for swimming. Karl said, "Let's go swimming," and I said, "But we didn't bring our trunks," and they both laughed at me and started to take their clothes off. Well, of course, I had been naked in front of my father and my brothers, and I had even gone swimming naked now and then, but still I was so conventional, so tied to the right way of doing things, that the line about not having brought our trunks came out of me without thinking. But I stripped. We left our clothes on the bank and walked out on the wobbly flat rocks to the deep part of the stream, Karl first, then Jim, then me, and jumped in and splashed around for twenty minutes or so, and then when we came out we were wet, naturally, so we sat down on the bank to dry in the sun since we didn't have any towels. That part of it was new to me, just sitting around naked with naked people in the open, the water not hiding our bodies. And we looked at each other. Karl, a year older than Jim or me, had begun to develop already, his balls were bigger, he had a dark patch of hair down there—I had a little hair, too, but because I was blond, it didn't show—and he was proud of what he had, he lay belly up showing it off. I saw him looking at me, too, and I wondered what he was thinking.

Criticizing my cock, maybe, because it was too small, it was a little boy's cock and his was a man's? But it was good to be in the sun, anyway, the heat on my skin, drying me, tanning me around the middle where I was fishbelly white. And then suddenly Jim gave a sort of shriek and clapped his knees together with his hands over his groin, and I looked around and there was Sissy Madden, who I suppose must have been sixteen or seventeen years old. She was out giving her horse some exercise. The sight of her is printed on my mind: a plump teenage girl with long red hair, big freckles, tight brown shorts, a white polo shirt out of which her fat breasts were practically exploding, and she sat atop her swaybacked roan mare looking down at the three of us and laughing. We scrambled to our feet, Karl, me, Jim, one, two, three, and we started to run like wild men, zigzag, every which way, desperately trying to get someplace where Sissy Madden couldn't see our nakedness. I remember the urgency of it, the necessity of escaping that girl's gaze. There weren't any good places to hide, though. The only trees were behind us, down by the deep part of the creek where we had been swimming, but Sissy was there. Ahead lay only low shrubbery and tall grass, not tall enough. We couldn't think straight. I ran one, two hundred yards, getting my feet all cut up, running as hard as I could, my little cock flapping against my body—I hadn't ever run naked before, and I was discovering the inconveniences of it—and finally I just threw myself face down in the grass, huddling into myself, hiding like an ostrich. The shame was that intense. I must have stayed crouched there for fifteen minutes, and finally I heard voices and realized Karl and Jim were looking for me. Cautiously I stood up. They had their clothes on and Sissy was nowhere in sight. I had to walk all the way back to the creek naked for my clothes—it seemed I was walking miles, and I even felt ashamed being with them, the two of them with clothes and me stripped bare—and I turned my back on them to get dressed. Four days later at the movie house I saw Sissy Madden standing in the lobby talking to Joe Falkner, and she grinned at me and winked and I wanted to crawl into the guts of the earth. *Sissy Madden saw my thing,* I told myself, and those five words must have gone through my head a million times during the movie, so that I couldn't pay attention to the story.

But the shame I felt when I was eleven, that embarrassment over my half-formed manhood, soon disappeared. I filled out, I developed physically, I grew tall, and there was no reason after that for me to feel ashamed of my body. And so I remember a lot of swimming expeditions, and I never once came out with that line about bringing bathing suits. Sometimes there even were girls with us, a bunch of us skinnydipping, four girls and five fellows, maybe, politely getting out of our clothes behind different trees, girls here, guys there, but then everybody running down to the creek together in one mad rush, cocks and tits bouncing and jiggling. And in the water you could see everything pretty well, when they jumped around. And afterward sometimes we coupled off, when we got to be thirteen, fourteen years old, for our first fumbling experiments in screwing. I recall never quite getting over my amazement that the bodies of the girls looked the way they did, so blank at the crotch, so empty there. And their hips wider than ours, and their buttocks bigger and softer, like round pink cushions. All the skinnydipping I did in my middle teens made me look back on that time with Karl and Jim and Sissy Madden and laugh at my own stupid shyness. Especially the time once when Billie Madden came swimming with us; she was our age, but she looked just like her older sister, and somehow, standing there naked at the edge of the creek next to Billie, looking at the freckles running down into the valley between her fat breasts and the deep dimples puckering her big behind, I felt as if all the shame of that time with Sissy had now been canceled out, that the fact of Billie's nakedness evened the score between me and the Madden girls, that none of it mattered any longer in any important way.

Thinking of these things as I plucked weeds in the fraters' chili patch, my bare ass warmed by the climbing sun, I was aware also of other things floating in the deep places of my memory, old events, dark and unpleasant and half-forgotten, that I had no wish to remember. A whole curdled mass of memories. Myself naked on other days, with other people. Boyhood games, some of them not so innocent. Unwanted images came roaring like a spring flood out of my past. I stood still, swept by waves of fear. Muscle tensing against muscle, body gleaming with sweat. And something shameful happened to me. I felt a familiar throbbing down below, felt it starting to stiffen and rise, and I looked, and yes, yes, there it was, coming up hard. I could have died. I wanted to fling myself face down to the ground. It was like that time after Sissy Madden had seen us swimming, when I had had to walk naked back to the creek when Karl and Jim already had their clothes on, and I had experienced a real sense of what it is to be naked and ashamed among those who are clothed. Again, now: Ned and Eli and Timothy and the fraters all had their shorts on, and I was bare, and I hadn't cared a damn about it, until suddenly *this* had started to happen and now I felt as exposed as though I was on network television. They would all be staring at me, seeing me aroused, wondering what had turned me on, what nasty thoughts had passed through my mind.

Where could I hide? How could I cover myself? Were any of them watching me?

Actually no one seemed to be. Eli and the fraters were far up the row. Timothy, ambling lazily along, was almost out of sight behind me. The only one close to me was Ned, perhaps fifteen feet to my rear. Standing as I was with my back to him, my shame was screened. Already I could feel myself beginning to sag; in another moment I'd be back to normal and I could saunter down the row to the tree where my shorts were hanging. Yes. It was down, now. All clear. I turned.

Ned gave a guilty start, practically jumped as my eyes met his. His face went crimson. He looked away. And I understood. I didn't need to inspect the front of his shorts for bulges to know what was going on in his head. For fifteen or twenty minutes now he'd been treating himself to a little fantasy trip, studying my body, contemplating my buttocks, snatching little glimpses of other goodies now and then. Dreaming his tricksy homo dreams about me. Well, there's nothing surprising in that. Ned *is* a fag. Ned *has* always wanted me, even if he's never dared to make a pass. And I *was* on display right in front of him, all of me, a temptation, a provocation. Still, I was taken aback by that look of desire, so obvious on his face, so raw; that shook me. To be wanted like that by another man. To be the object of his yearnings. And he seemed so stunned and abashed as I walked past him to get my shorts. As if he'd been caught off guard, with his real intentions showing. And what, pray tell, what sort of intentions had *I* been showing? My intentions had been sticking out six inches in front of me. We're into something very deep here, deep and nasty and complicated. It frightens me. Were Ned's gay vibes getting into my head by some sort of telepathy and stirring old shames? It's strange, isn't it, that I would get hard just then. Christ. I thought I understood myself. But I keep finding out that I don't know a damned thing for certain. Not even who I am. What kind of person I want to be. An existential dilemma, right, Eli, right, right? To choose one's own destiny. We express our identities through our sexual selves, is that right? I don't think so. I don't want to think so. And yet I'm not sure. The sun was hot on my back. I was so stiff down there for a couple of minutes that it hurt. And Ned breathing hard behind me. And the past churning in me. Where's Sissy Madden now? Where's Jim? And Karl? Where's Oliver? *Where's Oliver?* Oh, Christ, I think Oliver's a very very sick boy.

thirty-one

eli

The meditation, I'm convinced, is the core of the process. Being able to turn inward. You absolutely have to do that if you hope to accomplish anything here. The rest—the gymnastics, the diet, the baths, the field-labor—all that is just a series of techniques for achieving self-discipline, for lifting the balky ego toward the degree of control on which real longevity depends. Of course, if you want to live a long time it helps to get plenty of exercise, keep your body in trim, avoid unhealthy foods, etc., etc. But I think it's a mistake to place much emphasis on those aspects of the Brotherhood's routine. Hygiene and gymnastics may be useful in extending the average lifespan to eighty or eighty-five, but something more transcendental is required if you want to live to eight hundred or eight hundred and fifty. (Or eighty-five hundred? Eighty-five thousand?) Complete control of bodily function is needed. And meditation's the key.

At this stage they're stressing the development of inner awareness. We're supposed to stare at the setting sun, say, and convey its heat and power to different parts of our bodies—the heart, first, then the testicles, the lungs, the spleen, and so forth. I maintain that it isn't the solar radiance they're interested in—that part is just metaphor, just symbol—but rather the idea of putting us in contact with heart, testicles, lungs, spleen, etc., so that in case of problems in those organs we can go to them with our minds and fix whatever has to be fixed. This whole business of skulls, around which so much of the meditation revolves: more metaphor, which I'm sure is intended solely to give us a convenient focus of attention. So that we can pick up off the image of the skull and use it as a spring-board for the inward leap. Any other symbol would have worked just as well, probably—a sunflower, a cluster of acorns, a four-leaf clover. Once invested with the proper psychic clout, the *mana,* anything could serve. The Brotherhood just happened to fasten on the symbology of skulls. Which was quite good enough, really; there's mystery in a skull, there's romance, there's wonder. So we sit and stare at Frater Antony's little jade skull-pendant, and we're told to perform various metaphorical absorp-tions and engulfments having to do with the relation of death to life, but what they really want us to do is learn how to focus all our mental energy on a single object. Having mastered concentration, we can apply our new skill to the tasks of perpetual self-repair. That's the whole secret. Longevity drugs, health foods, sunshine cults, prayer, and such things are peripheral; meditation is all. It's a king of yoga, I guess—mind over matter—although, if the Brotherhood is as ancient as Frater Miklos implies, perhaps it's more accurate to say that yoga is an offshoot of the skullhouse.

We have a long way to go. These are still the preliminary stages of the series of training routines that the Brothers term the Trial. What lies ahead, I suspect, is largely psychological or even psychoanalytic: a purging of excess baggage from the soul. The ugly business of the Ninth Mystery is part of that. I still don't know whether to interpret that passage of the Book of Skulls literally or metaphorically, but in either event I'm sure it deals with the banishing of bad vibes from the Receptacle; we kill one scapegoat, actually or otherwise, and the other scapegoat removes himself, actually or otherwise, and the net effect of this is to leave two fledgling fraters who are without the jangling death-jitters borne by the defective duo. Besides purging the group as a whole, we must purge our individual inner selves. Last night after dinner Frater Javier visited me in my room, and I assume visited each of the others; he told me that I must prepare myself for the confessional rites. I was asked to review my entire life, giving special attention to episodes of guilt and shame, and to be ready to discuss those episodes in depth when asked to do so. I suppose some kind of primordial encounter group will be organized shortly, with Frater Javier in charge. A formidable man, that one. Gray eyes, thin lips, chiseled face. As accessible as a slab of granite. When he moves through the halls I imagine that I hear an accompaniment of dark groaning music. Enter the Grand Inquisitor! Yes. Frater Javier: the Grand Inquisitor. Night and chill; fog and pain. When begins the Inquisition? What shall I say? Which of my guilts shall I place on the altar, which of my shames?

I gather that the purpose of this unburdening will be to simplify our souls through a yielding up of—what term shall I use?—neuroses, sins, mental blocks, hangups, engrams, deposits of bad karma? We must pare ourselves down, pare ourselves down. Bone and flesh, these we retain, but the spirit must be whittled. We must strive toward a kind of quietism, in which there are no conflicts, in which there is no stress. Avoid everything that goes against the grain, and, if necessary, redirect the grain. Effortless action, that's the key. No energy rip-offs allowed; struggles shorten lives. Well, we'll see. I'm carrying plenty of inner dross, and so are we all. A psychic enema might not be such a bad thing.

What shall I tell you, Frater Javier?

thirty-two

ned

Review your life, declares the mysterious and vaguely reptilian Frater Javier, entering my monastic cell unannounced, bringing with him the faint hissing rustle of scales against stone. Review your life, rehearse the sins of your past, make yourself ready for confession. Right on, cries Ned the depraved choirboy! Right on, Frater Javier, chortles the fallen Papist! This is up his well-greased alley. The ritual of the confessional is certainly something he comprehends: it is encoded in his very genes, it is imprinted in his bones and balls, it is utterly natural to him. *Mea culpa, mea culpa, mea maxima culpa.* Whereas those other three are strangers to the closet of truth, the uptight Israelite and the two Protestant bullocks. Oh, oh, I suppose the Episcopalians have the custom of the confessional too, crypto-Romans that they are, but they always tell lies to their priests. I have that on the authority of my mother, who feels that the flesh of Anglicans isn't fit to feed to pigs. But mother, I say, pigs don't eat meat. If they did, she says, they wouldn't touch the tripes of an Anglican! They break every commandment and lie to their priests, she says, and crosses herself, four vigorous thumps, *om mani padme hum!*

Ned is obedient. Ned is a good little fairy. Frater Javier gives him The Word, and Ned instantly commences reviewing his misspent past, so that he can gush it all forth at the appropriate occasion. What have been my sins? Where have I transgressed? Tell me, Neddy-boy, have you had any other gods before Him? No, sir, in truth I can't say that I have. Have you made unto yourself any graven images? Well, I've doodled a bit, I admit, but we don't apply that commandment so rigorously, do we, sir? We're not bloody Moslems, eh, sir? Thank you, sir. Next: have you taken the name of the Lord in vain? God help me, Father, would I do a thing like that? Very well, Ned, and have you remembered the Sabbath Day and kept it holy? Abashed, the honest boy replies that he has occasionally been guilty of dishonoring the Sabbath. Occasionally? Shit, he's polluted more Sundays than a Turk! A venial sin, though, a venial sin. *Ego absolvo te,* my child. And have you honored thy father and thy mother? I have indeed, sir, honored them in my way. Hast thou killed? I have not killed. Hast thou committed adultery? To the best of my knowledge, Father, I have not. Hast thou stolen? I have not stolen, at least, nothing important, sir. Nor have I borne false witness against my neighbor. And hast thou coveted thy neighbor's house, or thy neighbor's wife, or thy neighbor's manservant, or his maidservant, or his ox, or his ass, or anything that is thy neighbor's? Well, sir, there's that part about my neighbor's ass; I admit I'm on shaky grounds there, but otherwise—but otherwise—I do my best, sir, considering that I came into this world tainted, considering the odds against us all from the start, bearing in mind that in Adam's fall we sinned all, nevertheless I regard myself as relatively pure and good. Not perfect, of course. Tut, my child, what would you confess? Well, Father—*confiteor, confiteor,* the fist striking the boy's chest with admirable zeal, thump, thump, thump, thump, *Om! Mani! Padme! Hum!*—my fault, my most grievous fault—well, I did go one Sunday after mass with Sandy Dolan to spy on his sister changing her clothes, and I saw her bare breasts, Father, they were small and round with little pink tips, and at the base of her belly, Father, she had this hairy black mound, something I had never seen before, and then she turned her back to the window and I saw her ass, Father, the two most beautiful sweet plump white cheeks that I had ever seen, with these lovely deep dimples just at the top of them, and down the center this delicious shadowy cleft that—what's that, Father? I can go on to something else? All right, then, I confess that I did lead Sandy astray in other ways, that I engaged in sins of the body with him, sins against God and Nature, that when we were eleven years old and spending the night together in the same bed, his mother being occupied in childbirth and there being no one at his house to look after him, I did fetch from under my bed a bottle of Vaseline and did scoop from it a good-sized glob and wantonly apply it to his sexual organ, telling him not to be afraid, that God wasn't able to see us here in the dark with the covers over us, and then I—and then he—and then we—and then we—

And so, at Frater Javier's behest, I plumbed my degenerate past and dredged up much mucky detritus, the better to shine at the sessions of confessions that I assumed would be commencing. But the fraters are less linear-minded than that. A variation in our daily routine was about to be introduced, yes, but it involved neither Frater Javier nor any confessional aspects. That must lie still further in the future. The new rite is a sexual one, Buddha save me, a *hetero*sexual one. These fraters, I now realize, are Chinamen of some sort beneath their deceptive Caucasian skins, for they are instructing us now in nothing less than the *tao* of sex.

They don't call it that. They don't speak of *yin* and *yang*, either. But I know my Oriental erotica, and I know the ancient spiritual significances of these sexual exercises, which are close kin to the various gymnastic and contemplatory exercises we've been practicing. Control, control, control over every bodily function, that's the aim here.

The dark-haired women in short white robes who we've been seeing flitting about the skullhouse are, in fact, priestesses of sex, holy cunts, who serve the needs of the fraters and who, by playing the part of receptacles for the Receptacle, now indoctrinate us into the sacred vaginal mysteries. What used to be the rest period after afternoon chores has now become the hour of transcendental copulation. We were given no warning. The day it began, I had come back from the fields and had had my bath and was sprawled out on my cot when in the usual no-knock manner of this place my door opened and Frater Leon, the physician-frater, entered my room, followed by three of the girls in white. I was naked, but I figured it was no obligation of mine to conceal my vital organs from those who barged in on them, and quickly I was made to realize that there was no point whatever in covering myself.

The women arranged themselves against one of the walls. This was the first time I had ever had a chance to look closely at them. They could have been sisters: all of them short, slender, nicely stacked, with swarthy skins, prominent noses, large liquid dark eyes, full lips. In a way they reminded me of the girls in Minoan murals, although they might also have been American Indians; in any case they were definitely exotic. Midnight hair, heavy breasts. Anywhere between twenty and forty years in age. They stood like statues. Frater Leon delivered a brief oration. It is essential, he said, for candidates to learn the arts of mastering the sexual passions. To expend the seminal fluid is to die a little. Right on, Frater Leon! Old Elizabethan idiom: to come = to die. We must not, he continued, repress the sexual impulse, but rather we must dominate it and turn it to our service. Hence intercourse is praiseworthy but ejaculation is to be deplored. I recalled having encountered all this stuff before, and eventually I remembered where: it's pure Taoism, is what. Union of *yin* and *yang,* cunt and cock, is harmonious and necessary to the welfare of the universe, but expenditure of *ching,* semen, is self-destructive. One must strive to conserve the *ching,* to increase one's supply of it, and so forth. Funny, Frater Leon, you don't *look* Chinese! Who, I wonder, is stealing theories from whom? Or did the Taoists and the Brotherhood hit independently on the same principles?

Frater Leon finished his little prologue and said something to the girls in a language I didn't understand. (I checked with Eli afterward, but he couldn't identify it either. Aztec or Mayan, he supposed.) Instantly off came the short white robes, and three mother-naked mounds of

yin stood there at my service. Sniveling faggot that I am, I
was still capable of pronouncing esthetic judgment: they
were impressive girls. Heavy breasts with no more than a
moderate amount of sag, flat bellies, firm rumps, outstanding thighs. No scars of appendectomy, no traces of preg-
nancy. Frater Leon barked a quick unintelligible command
and the priestess closest to the door promptly stretched
out on the cold stone floor, knees flexed and slightly
parted. Turning now to me, Frater Leon allowed himself a
slight smile and gestured with the tips of the fingers of one
hand. Go to it, lad, he seemed to be saying. Angelic Ned
was nonplussed. He gaped and clutched for words. Here,
now is that it? You don't understand, Frater Leon, the
bitter truth is that I am what they call an urning, a fairy, a
fag, an invert, a deviate, a pansy, a queer; I am not
particularly attracted by cunt; my addiction, I must reveal,
is to buggery. But I said none of this, and Frater Leon
beckoned again, less amiably. What the devil, the truth is
that I have always been bisexual with gay leanings, and on
occasion I have been willing to fill the clerically approved
vacancy. Since life everlasting appears to depend on it, I
will undergo the ordeal. And I advanced toward the parted
thighs. With fraudulent hetero cockiness I sank my sword
into the waiting wench. What now? Conserve your *ching*, I
told myself, conserve your *ching*. I moved in slow stately
thrusts while Frater Leon coached me from the sidelines,
advising me that the rhythms of the universe demanded
that I bring my partner to orgasm although I myself should
endeavor not to get there. Very well. Admiring my own
performance every inch of the way, I induced the proper
spasms and grunts in my spiritual concubine, myself
remaining aloof, apart, wholly divorced from the adventures of my tool. When the divine moment was over, my
satisfied partner evicted me with a deft and expert flip of
her pelvis, and I discovered that priestess number two was
settling to the floor, assuming the receiving position. Very
well, the master stud will oblige. In. Out. In. Out. Gasp.
Grunt. Moan. With a surgeon's precision I coolly stitched
her off to ecstasy, Frater Leon providing an approving

commentary from a point above my left shoulder. Again the pelvic flip, again the change of partners; one more dark yawning *yoni* awaited my glistening rigid rod. God help me. I was beginning to feel like a rabbi whose doctor has told him that he'll drop dead unless he eats a pound of pork a day. But old devil-may-care Ned slammed home the bolt. This time, said Frater Leon, I could allow myself the self-indulgence of coming. By now I was very much pushed to my limits anyway, and it was with some relief that I relaxed my iron self-control.

And so our Trial moves into a new and raunchier phase. The priestesses call upon us every afternoon. I suppose for studs like Timothy and Oliver this is an unexpected bonus, an unalloyed delight, though perhaps not; what's being offered here is nothing so simple as the kind of good, hearty fucking they enjoy, but rather an arduous, highly demanding exercise in extreme self-control, which to them may seem to drain all the joy out of the act. That's their problem. Mine is different. Poor old Ned, he's had more heterosex this week than in the previous five years. Give him credit, though: he's doing all that they ask of him and nary a complaint. But it's a struggle. Mother of God, never in my bummest trips did I imagine that the road to immortality would take me through so many heaving female bellies!

thirty-three
eli

Last night in the dark small hours the thought came to me
for the first time that I should offer myself to fulfill the
suicide requirement of the Ninth Mystery. A quick moment of evanescent despair, here and gone, but worth
examination in bright light. Obviously it's the sexual thing
that's preying on me. My total failure to make a start at
mastering the techniques. Fiasco after fiasco; how can I
hold myself back? They give me beautiful women, they
tell me to plough two or three in a row—oh, *schmendrick,
schmendrick, schmendrick!* It's the Margo scene all over
again. I get inflamed, I get carried away—the opposite of
the proper Skullish attitude. I haven't once succeeded in
restraining myself long enough to handle all three. I don't
think it's humanly possible, at least for me. But of course
the kind of longevity we're talking about here isn't humanly possible either. It's necessary to transcend the merely
human, to become literally inhuman, nonhuman, if one
would defeat death. But if I can't even govern the treacher-
ous twitches of my cock, how can I hope to monitor my
metabolism, reverse organic decay through mental effort,
acquire the sort of cellular-level body control these fraters
must have? I can't. I see failure looming. Frater Leon and
Frater Bernard have said they'll give me special training,
they'll show me some useful techniques for sexual de-es-
calation, but I don't have much confidence in that. The
problem is rooted too deeply in my essential Eli-ness, and
it's too late to alter that; I am what I am. I mount these
wenches, these silent supple Aztec priestesses, and though
my mind is full of instructions about withholding my seed,
my body goes at full gallop, running away, and I explode
with passion, and passion is precisely what must be con-
quered if one is to survive the Trial. By failing this test, I

fail everything; I fall by the wayside, immortality lost; let me therefore destroy my unworthy self now, since someone must, and thus I will open the path for the others. So I thought last night in the dark small hours, at any rate. Thinking, also, that Timothy is another who must certainly fail, for he is unable or unwilling to achieve the necessary innerness; he is the prisoner of his scorns, so contemptuous of the Brotherhood and its rites that he can barely contain his impatience. Thus he can never attain even the basic disciplines. We meditate; he merely watches. There is a real danger that he will simply walk out, in the next few days, which would, of course wreck everything by unbalancing the Receptacle. I therefore privately nominate Timothy to fulfill the other part of the Ninth Mystery; he can't possibly win what the Brotherhood offers, so therefore let him lose, let him be slain for the others' sake. Last night, lying dismally awake, I thought I would bring matters immediately to their desired climax: steal a knife from the kitchen, nail Timothy as he sleeps, then skewer myself. The Ninth Mystery thereby would be obeyed, and Ned and Oliver would have their passports to eternity. I actually sat up. But at the critical moment I paused to ask myself whether this was the right time for what I planned to do. Perhaps there is an appointed place in the unfolding ritual for the Ninth Mystery, at some later stage in the process. Perhaps I would be spoiling things by doing it now, arbitrarily, without a signal from the fraters. If a premature sacrifice would be worthless, I had better not act. So I remained in bed, and the impulse fled. This morning, though I'm still depressed, I find I have no wish at all to take my own life. I have grave misgivings about myself, I'm deeply dismayed by my assorted glaring inadequacies, yes, but all the same I want to live as long as possible. The prospects for attaining the longevity of the fraters suddenly seem quite bleak, though. I don't think any of us going to make it. I think this Receptacle is falling to pieces.

thirty-four

oliver

At lunchtime, as we were coming from our session with Frater Miklos, Frater Javier intercepted us in the hall. "Please meet with me after lunch in the Room of Three Masks," he said, and went solemnly on about his business. There's something repellent about that man, something chilly; he's the only frater I prefer to avoid. Those zombie eyes, that zombie voice. Anyway, I assumed that the time had arrived for beginning the confession therapy that Frater Javier had told us about the week before. I was right, although the format wasn't what I'd been expecting. I anticipated something like an encounter group: Ned, Eli, Timothy, and me and maybe two or three fraters sitting around a circle, and each candidate in turn rising and baring his soul to the entire gathering, after which we'd comment on what we had heard, try to interpret it in terms of our own life experience, and so on. Not so. Frater Javier told us that we were to be each other's confessors, in a series of private one-to-one confrontations.

"This week past," he said, "you have been examining your lives, reviewing your darkest secrets. Each of you holds locked in his soul at least one episode that he is certain he could never admit to another person. It is on that one crucial episode, and no other, that our work must focus."

What he was asking of us was to identify and isolate the ugliest, most shameful incident of our lives—and then to reveal it, in order to purge ourselves of that kind of bad-vibes baggage. He put his pendant on the floor and spun it to determine who would confess to whom. Timothy to me; me to Eli; Eli to Ned; Ned to Timothy.

But the daisy chain was complete among the four of us, with no outsiders included. It wasn't Frater Javier's intention to turn our innermost horrors into common property. We were not supposed to tell him or anyone else about the things that we would learn from one another in these confessional sessions. Each member of the Receptacle was going to become the custodian of somebody else's secret, but what we confessed, said Frater Javier, was to go no further than one's own confessor. The purge was what counted, the unburdening, rather than the information revealed.

So that we wouldn't contaminate the pure atmosphere of the skullhouse by liberating too much negative emotion all at once, Frater Javier decreed that there would be only one confession per day. Again the spinning pendant decided the order of things. Tonight, just before bedtime, Ned would go to Timothy. Tomorrow Timothy would come to me; the day after that I would pay a call on Eli; and on the fourth day Eli would close the circuit by confessing to Ned.

That gave me almost two and a half days to decide what story I was going to tell Eli. Oh, of course I knew which one I *ought* to tell. That was obvious. But I threw up two or three feeble substitutes, screens for the real story, flimsy pretexts for hiding the one necessary choice. As fast as the possibilities arose, I shot them down. There was only one option open to me, only one true focus of shame and guilt. I didn't know how I was going to be able to face up to the pain of telling it, but that was what I had to tell, and I hoped that maybe in the moment of telling it the pain would go away, though I doubted that very much. I'll worry about that part of it, I told myself, when the time comes. And then I proceeded to banish the problem of the confession entirely from my mind. I suppose that's an example of repression. By evening I had managed to forget about Frater Javier's project altogether. But I woke, sweating, in the middle of the night, imagining that I had admitted everything to Eli.

thirty-five
timothy

Ned came prancing in, winking, smirking. He always puts on an exaggerated swish routine when he's really clutched about something. "Forgive me, Father, for I have sinned," he said in a singsong tone. Doing a little soft-shoe number. Twitching. Grinning. Rolling his eyes. He was turned on, and, I realized, what was turning him on was this business of confessing. After all this time the old Jesuit was coming to life in him. He wanted to spill his beans, and I would be the target of the spill. Suddenly the thought of having to sit here listening to some slippery pansy story of his made me feel sick. Why the hell should I have to accept his sweaty confidences? Who was I to hear Ned's confessions, anyway? I said, "Are you really going to tell me the big secret of your life?"

He looked surprised. "Of course I am."

"Do you have to?"

"Do I have to? Timothy, it's *expected* of us. And anyhow I want to." Yes, he certainly did want to. He was trembling, tingling, all flushed and charged up. "What's the matter with you, Timothy, don't you have any interest in my private life?"

"No."

"Tsk. Let nothing human be alien to you."

"I don't want it. I don't need it."

"Too bad, man. Because I have to tell it. Frater Javier says that unloading my guilts is necessary to the prolongation of my earthly stay, and so I'm going to ventilate, man. I'm going to *ventilate*."

"If you have to," I said, resigning myself.

"Make yourself comfortable, Timothy. Open wide the ears. You cannot choose but hear."

And hear I did. Ned's an exhibitionist at heart, like a lot of his kind. He wants to wallow in self-denunciation, in self-revelation. He told his story very professionally, sketching in the details like the short-story writer he claimed to be, underlining this, shading that. What he told me was about what I expected from him, something grimy, a fag fantasia. "This happened," he said, "before you ever met me, in the spring of our freshman year, when I was not quite eighteen. I had an apartment off campus, sharing it with two other men." Naturally, they were both queers. It was actually their apartment; Ned had moved in with them after midterm intersession. They were eight or ten years older than Ned, and they'd been living together a long time in a sort of gay equivalent of marriage. One of them was gruff and masculine and dominant, an assistant professor of French literature who was also a rugged athlete—his hobby was mountain climbing—and the other was more of a stereotyped fairy, delicate and ethereal, almost feminine, a wispy, retiring poet who stayed at home most of the time, took care of the housework, watered the potted plants, and I suppose did knitting and crocheting too.

Anyway there were these two gay lads happily keeping house, and they met Ned in some pansy bar and found that he didn't like the place where he was living, so they invited him to move in with them. The arrangement was supposed to be strictly a matter of accommodation; Ned would have his own room, he'd pay rent and a share of the grocery bill, and there wasn't to be any sexual involvement with either of the other two, who had quite a strong fidelity thing going. For a month or two the arrangement worked out. But fidelity among fags isn't any stronger, I guess, than it is among straights, and the presence of Ned in the household became a disturbing factor, the way the presence of a nicely stacked eighteen-year-old chick would disturb an ordinary marriage. "Consciously or otherwise," Ned said, "I fostered temptation. I walked around naked in the apartment, I flirted with them, I did a lot of casual fondling." Tensions rose, and the inevitable inevitably happened. One day the lovers quarreled about something—possibly about Ned, he wasn't sure—and the masculine one went storming out. The feminine one, all aflutter, came to Ned for consolation. He consoled "her" by taking "her" to bed. They both felt guilty afterward, but that didn't stop them from doing it again a few days later, and then from making a regular affair of it, Ned and this poet, whose name was Julian. Meanwhile the other one, Oliver—isn't that interesting, another Oliver?—who was apparently unaware of what was going on between Ned and Julian, started making passes at Ned and soon they were bedding down, too. So for a couple of weeks Ned carried on simultaneous independent affairs with both of them. "It was fun," he said, "in a nervous-making way—all the clandestine appointments, all the little lies, the fears of having the other one walk in on us." Trouble was bound to come. Both of the older queers fell in love with Ned. Each one decided that he wanted to break up with his original partner and live just with Ned. Tug of war. Ned got propositions from both sides. "I just didn't know how to handle the situation," Ned said. "By this time Oliver knew I was up to something with Julian, and Julian knew I was up to something with Oliver, but no one had made any open charges yet. If it came down to a choice between them, I inclined slightly toward Julian, but I didn't intend to be the one who made any of the critical decisions."

The image of himself that Ned was painting for me was that of a naive, innocent kid, caught up in a triangle not of his own making. Helpless, inexperienced, buffeted by the stormy passions of Oliver and Julian, etc., etc. But under the surface something else was coming through, conveyed to me not in words but in smirks, campy flicks of the eyebrows, and other nonverbal forms of commentary on the story. At any given time Ned functions on at least six levels, and whenever he starts telling you about how naive and innocent he is, you know he's putting you on. The under-the-surface story that I picked up showed me a sinister, scheming Ned, manipulating those two hapless fags for his own amusement—coming between them, tempting and seducing each in turn, forcing them toward a rivalry for his affections.

"The climax came one weekend in May," he said, "when Oliver invited me to go with him on a mountain climbing expedition in New Hampshire—leaving Julian behind. Oliver explained that there was much we needed to discuss, and the clear pure air of a mountaintop was the best place to discuss it." Ned agreed to go, which sent Julian into hysterics. "If you go," Julian sobbed, "I'll kill myself." Ned was turned off by that sort of emotional blackmail, and he simply told Julian to cool it—it was just for the weekend, it didn't matter all that much, he'd be back Sunday night. Julian continued to carry on, with much talk of suicide. Paying no attention, Ned and Oliver packed for the camping trip. "You'll never see me alive again," Julian shrieked. Ned, telling this to me, did a fine contemptuous imitation of Julian's panicky screeching. "I was afraid that Julian might be serious," he said. "On the other hand, I knew it was a mistake to play up to that kind of tantrum. And also—secretly, deep down—I was flattered by the thought that I was important enough for anybody to consider committing suicide over." Oliver told him not to worry about Julian—"She's just being melodramatic," he said—and that Friday they went off to New Hampshire.

By late Saturday afternoon they were four thousand feet up the side of some big mountain. Oliver chose this moment to make his pitch. Come live with me and be my love, he said, and we will all the pleasures prove. The time of dillydallying was over; he wanted an immediate and final decision. Choose between Julian and me, he told Ned, and choose fast. "I had decided by this time that I didn't really care much for Oliver, who tended to be blustery and bullying a lot of the time, coming on as a sort of fag Hemingway," Ned said. "And though I found Julian attractive, I also thought that 'she' was much too dependent and weak, a clinging vine. Besides, no matter which one of them I picked, I was certain to get all sorts of static from the other—flamboyant scenes, threats, fistfights, whatnot." So, Ned went on, he declared politely that he didn't want to be the cause of the breakup of Oliver and Julian, whose thing he respected in the utmost, and that rather than make any such impossible choice he'd simply move out of their apartment. Oliver then began to accuse Ned of preferring Julian, of conspiring secretly with Julian to oust him. The discussion got loud and irrational, with all sorts of shouted recriminations and denials, and finally Oliver said, "There's no way I can go on living without you, Ned. Promise you'll take me over Julian, promise me right now, or I'm going to jump."

As he came to this part of his story, Ned's eyes took on a freaky glow, a devilish kind of gleam. He was thoroughly enjoying himself. Spellbound by his own eloquence. In a way, so was I. He said, "I was tired of being whipsawed by these suicide threats. It was a drag, having every move dictated by somebody's insistence that he'd kill himself if I didn't cooperate. 'Oh, shit,' I said to Oliver, 'are you going to pull that number too? Well, fuck you. Go ahead and jump, then. I don't give a damn what you do.' I assumed Oliver was bluffing, the way people usually are when they say things like that. Oliver wasn't bluffing. He didn't answer me, he didn't even stop to think, he just stepped off the ledge. I saw him hanging in midair for what seemed like ten seconds, looking at me, his face very calm, peaceful. Then he fell two thousand feet, hit an outcropping, bounced like a dropped doll, and fell the rest of the way to the ground. It had all happened so quickly that I couldn't begin to comprehend it—the threat, my peevish, snappy response, the jump—one two three. Then it started to sink in. I began to shiver all over. I was screaming like a madman." For a few minutes, Ned said, he seriously considered jumping also. Then he got himself together some and headed down the mountain path, having a rough time of the descent without Oliver to help him. It took him hours to get down, and by the time he reached

ground night had fallen. He had no idea where Oliver's
body was, and there were no state troopers around or
telephones or anything, so he hiked a mile and a half out
to the main highway and started hitching his way back to
school. (Because he didn't know how to drive then, he had
to leave Oliver's car parked at the foot of the mountain.)
"I was in a state of total panic all the way back," he said.
"The people who gave me rides thought I was sick, and
one of them wanted to take me to a hospital. The only
thing running through my mind was a feeling of guilt,
guilt, guilt, guilt for having killed Oliver. I felt as responsible for his death as if I had pushed him." As before, Ned's
words told me one thing and his expressions were telling
me another. "Guilt," he said out loud, and telepathically I
was picking up *satisfaction.* "Responsible for Oliver's
death," he said, and underneath he was saying, *thrilled
that someone would kill himself for love of me.* "Panic,"
he said, and silently he was boasting, *delighted at my
success in manipulating people.* He went on, "I tried to
persuade myself that it hadn't been my fault, that there
wasn't any reason to have thought Oliver was speaking
seriously. But that didn't work. Oliver was gay, and gay
people are by definition unstable, right? Right. And if
Oliver said he'd jump, I shouldn't have virtually dared him
to do it, because that was all he needed to make him go
over the edge." On the verbal level Ned was saying, "I was
innocent and foolish," and below that I received: *I was a
murderous bitch.* He said, "And then I wondered what I
was going to tell Julian. Here I had come into their
household, I had flirted with them until I had what I
wanted, I got between them, and now I had in effect
caused Oliver's death. And here was Julian left all alone,
and what was I supposed to do? Offer myself as Oliver's
substitute? Take care of poor Julian forever? Oh, it was a
mess, a fearful mess. I got back to the apartment about
four in the morning and my hand was shaking so much I
could hardly get my key in the lock. I had rehearsed about
eight different speeches to deliver to Julian, all kinds of

explanations, self-justifications. But as it turned out I didn't need any of them."

"Julian had run away with the janitor," I suggested.

"Julian had cut his wrists right after we left on Friday," Ned said. "I found him in the bathtub. He'd been dead at least half a day. You see, Timothy, I killed them both? Do you see? They loved me and I destroyed them. And I've carried the guilt with me ever since."

"You feel guilty for not having taken them seriously enough when they threatened to commit suicide?"

"I feel guilty for getting such a charge out of it when they did," he said.

thirty-six

OLIVER

Timothy showed up as I was getting ready to go to sleep. He came slouching in, looking surly and sullen, and for an instant I didn't understand why he was there. "Okay," he said, flopping down against the wall. "Let's get it over with fast, huh?"

"You look angry."

"I am. I'm angry about this whole fucking pile of crap I've been forced to wallow in."

"Don't take it out on me," I said.

"Am I?"

"That's not exactly a friendly expression on your face."

"I don't exactly feel friendly, Oliver. I feel like getting the hell out of this place right after breakfast. How long have we been here, anyway? Two weeks, three weeks? Too fucking long, however long it is. Too fucking long."

"You knew it was going to take time when you agreed to go into it," I said. "There was no way that the Trial could have been a quickie deal, four days, in, out. If you pull out of it now you spoil it for the rest of us. And don't forget that we swore—"

"We swore, we swore, we swore, we swore! Oh, Christ, Oliver, you're starting to sound just like Eli now! Scolding me. Nagging me. Reminding me that I swore to something. Oh, Jesus, do I hate this whole crappy routine! It's like the three of you are holding me prisoner in a boobyhatch."

"So you *are* angry at me."

He shrugged. "I'm angry at everyone and everything. Most of all I'm angry at myself, I guess. For getting myself into this. For not having had the sense to tell you to count me out, right at the start. I thought it would be amusing, so I went along for the ride. *Amusing!* Sheesh!"

"You still believe it's nothing but a waste of time?"

"Don't you?"

"I don't think so," I told him. "I can feel myself changing day by day. Deepening my control over my body. Extending my range of perceptions. I'm tuning in on something big, Timothy, and Eli and Ned are, too, and there's no reason why you can't be doing it also."

"Lunatics. Three lunatics."

"If you'd try to be a little less uptight about it and actually do some of the meditations and spiritual exercises—"

"There you go. Nagging me again."

"I'm sorry. Forget it, Timothy. Forget the whole bit." I took a deep breath. Timothy was perhaps my

closest friend, maybe my only friend, and yet suddenly I
was sick of him, sick of his big beefy face, sick of his
close-chopped hair, sick of his arrogance, sick of his
money, sick of his ancestors, sick of his contempt for
anything beyond the reach of understanding. I said, keeping my voice flat and frosty, "Look, if you don't like it
here, go. Just go. I don't want you to think I'm the one
who's holding you. You go, if that's what you want. And
don't worry about me, about the oath, any of that stuff. I
can look after myself."

"I don't know what I want to do," he muttered,
and for an instant the cranky scowl left his face. The
expression that replaced it was one I couldn't easily as-
sociate with Timothy: a look of confusion, a look of
vulnerability. It vanished and he gave me the scowl once
more. "Another thing," he said, sounding cranky again.
"Why the crap do I have to tell secrets to anybody?"

"You don't have to."

"Frater Javier said we should."

"What's that to you? If you don't want to spill
anything, don't spill it."

"It's part of the ritual," said Timothy.

"But you don't believe in the ritual. Anyway, if
you're leaving here tomorrow, Timothy, you don't need to
do anything Frater Javier says you should do."

"Did I say I was leaving?"

"You said you wanted to."

"I said I *felt like* leaving. I didn't say I *was going* to
leave. That's not the same thing. I haven't made up my
mind."

"Stay or not, as you please. Confess or not, as you
please. But if you aren't going to do what Frater Javier
sent you here to do, I wish you'd go away and let me get
some sleep."

"Don't hassle me, Oliver. Don't start pushing. I
can't move as fast as you want me to."

"You've had all day to decide whether you're
going to tell me anything or not."

He nodded. He bent forward until his head was between his knees and sat like that, silent, for a very long time. My annoyance faded. I could see he was in trouble. This was a whole new Timothy to me. He wanted to unbend, he wanted to get into the skullhouse thing, and yet he despised it all so much that he couldn't. So I didn't push him. I let him sit there, and finally he looked up and said, "If I tell you what I have to tell you, what assurance do I have that you won't repeat it?"

"Frater Javier instructed us not to repeat anything we hear in these confessions."

"Sure, but will you really keep quiet about it?"

"Don't you trust me, Timothy?"

"I don't trust anybody with this. This could destroy me. The frater wasn't kidding when he said that each of us must have something locked inside him that he doesn't dare let out. I've done a lot of crappy things, yes indeed, but there's one thing so crappy that it's almost holy, almost a sacred sin, it's so monstrous. People would despise me if they knew about it. You'll probably despise me." His face was gray with strain. "I don't know if I want to talk about it."

"If you don't then don't."

"I'm supposed to let it out."

"Only if you're committed to the disciplines of the Book of Skulls. And you aren't."

"If I wanted to be, though, I'd have to do as Frater Javier says. I don't know. I don't know. You absolutely wouldn't tell this to Eli or Ned? Or anybody else?"

"I absolutely wouldn't," I said.

"I wish I could really believe that."

"I can't help you on that score, Timothy. It's like Eli says: some things you have to take on faith."

"Maybe we could make a deal," he said, sweating, looking desperate. "I'll tell you my story, and then you tell me your story, and that way we'll each have leverage. We'll have something to hold against each other by way of guaranteeing that there'll be no gossiping."

"The person I'm supposed to confess to," I said, "is Eli. Not you. Eli."

"No deal, then?"

"No deal."

He was silent again. An even longer time. At last he looked up. His eyes frightened me. He moistened his lips and moved his jaws, but no words came out. He seemed to be on the edge of panic, and some of his terror was bleeding through to me; I felt tense and jumpy, itchy, uncomfortably aware of the blanket of close, clinging heat. Eventually he forced a few words out. "You've met my kid sister," he said.

Yes, I had met his sister, several times, when I had gone home with Timothy for Christmas holidays. She was two or three years younger than Timothy, a leggy blonde, quite goodlooking but not especially bright: Margo without Margo's personality, in fact. Timothy's sister was a Wellesley girl, your stereotyped debutante-Junior League-charity tea kind of girl, your tennis-golf-horseback-riding kind of girl. She had a fine body, but otherwise I hadn't found her attractive at all, because I was turned off by her smugness, her moneyedness, her air of don't-touch-me virginity. I don't think virgins are terribly interesting. This one gave a definite impression of being far above such coarse, vulgar things as sex. I could imagine her drawling to her fiance, as the poor freak tried to get his hand into her blouse, "Oh, darling, don't be so crude!" I doubt that she cared for me very much more than I did for her: my Kansas background marked me as a clodhopper, and my daddy hadn't belonged to the right clubs and I wasn't a member of the right church. My total lack of upper-class credentials dumped me into that very large class of male human beings whom girls of that sort simply don't consider as potential escorts, lovers, or husbands. For her I was just part of the furniture, like a gardener or a stable boy. "Yes," I said, "I've met your kid sister."

Timothy studied me for an endless moment.

"When I was in my last year at prep school," he

said in a voice as hollow and as rusty as an abandoned tomb, "I raped her, Oliver. I raped her."

I think he expected the heavens to open and lightning to descend when he made his big confession. I think that at the very least he expected me to recoil, covering my eyes, and cry out that I was shattered by his shocking words. Actually I was a little surprised, both that Timothy should have bothered with any such grubby business and that he had managed to put it to her without any immediate consequences, such as getting horsewhipped when her screams brought the rest of the family running. And I had to rearrange my image of her, knowing now as I did that her supercilious thighs had been furrowed by her brother's cock. But otherwise I wasn't exactly astounded. Where I come from the sheer weight of boredom is always driving the young 'uns to incest and much worse; and though I hadn't ever balled my sister, I knew plenty of fellows who had had theirs. It was lack of inclination, not tribal taboo, that led me to keep my sticky hands off Sis. Still, this was clearly a serious business to Timothy, and I maintained a respectful silence, looking grave and disturbed, as he told me his story.

He spoke haltingly at first, in obvious embarrassment, sweating and stumbling and stammering, like Lyndon Johnson beginning to explain his Vietnam policy to a war-crimes tribunal. But before long the words were flowing freely, as though this was a story Timothy had told many times in the privacy of his own head, rehearsing it so often that by now the telling of it was automatic once the first awkwardness of speaking was behind him. It had happened, he said, exactly four years ago this month, when he was home for Easter recess from Andover and his sister was in from the girls' academy in Pennsylvania that she attended. (At that time my own first meeting with Timothy was still five months in the future.) He was 18 and his sister about 15½. They didn't get along well, never had; she was the sort of kid whose relationship with her older brother had always been conducted on the sticking-her-tongue-out-at-him level. He thought she was impossibly snotty and snobbish and she thought he was impossibly rude and brutish. During the previous Christmas holiday he had laid his sister's closest friend and classmate, which the sister had found out about, and that had placed an extra strain on their relationship.

It was a difficult season in Timothy's life. At Andover he was a powerful and universally admired leader, a football hero, president of his class, a famed symbol of virility and *savoir faire;* but in a couple of months he'd be graduating and all that accumulated prestige would count for zip as he moved on to become just another freshman in a large, world-famous university. That was traumatic for him. He had also been conducting a strenuous and expensive long-distance love affair with a girl from Radcliffe who was a year or two his senior; he didn't love her, it was just a status thing for him to be able to say he was fucking a college girl, but he was pretty sure she was in love with *him.* Just before Easter he had accidentally learned from a third party that in fact she regarded him as an amusing pet, a sort of prep-school trophy to display to her innumerable suave Harvard boyfriends; her attitude to him, in short, was even more cynical than his to her. So he came home to the family acres that spring feeling pretty crushed, which was a novelty for Timothy. Immediately he was into a new source of uptightness. In his home town there was a girl he loved, really *loved.* I'm not sure what Timothy means by "love," but I think it's a term he applies to any girl who fits his criteria of looks, money, and birth, and who won't let him sleep with her; that makes her unattainable, that puts her up on a pedestal, and so he tells himself he "loves" her. The Don Quixote number, in a way. This girl was seventeen and had just been accepted by Bennington, came from a family with nearly as much bread as Timothy's, was an Olympic-quality equestrienne, and, to hear him tell it, had a body that was strictly Playmate-of-the-Year category. He and she belonged to the same country-club set, and he had been golfing, dancing, and

playing tennis with her since before puberty, but his occa-
sional attempts to achieve a deeper friendship had been
expertly turned aside. He was obsessed by her to the point
where he even thought of marrying her eventually, and he
deluded himself into thinking that she had already picked
him as her eventual husband; therefore, he reasoned, she
wasn't letting him get his hands on her because she knew
he was a double-standard man at heart and was afraid he'd
regard her as unmarriageable if he got into her this early.

The first few days he was home he phoned her
every afternoon. Polite, friendly, distant conversation. She
didn't seem to be available for solo dating—dating apparently wasn't much of a custom in their group—but she
said she'd see him at the country-club dance on Saturday
night. High hopes building. The dance was one of those
formal deals with constantly changing partners, inter-
rupted by interludes of necking in various approved recesses of the club. He succeeded in getting her into one of
those recesses by mid-evening, and, though he didn't even
come close to entering *her* recesses, he did manage to get
further with her than ever before: tongue in the mouth,
hands under the bra. And he thought he saw a certain
glitter in her eye. The next time he danced with her he
invited her to take a stroll with him—also part of the
country-club ritual. They paraded the grounds. He suggested that they go down to the boathouse. In that set, a
trip to the boathouse was code for fucking. They went to
the boathouse. His fingers slithered eagerly along her cool
thighs. Her palpitating body throbbed to his caresses. Her
passionate palm rubbed the swollen front of his trousers.
Like a maddened bull he seized her with the intention of
plonking her right then and there, and with the skill of an
Olympic virginity champion she gave him a maidenly knee
in the balls, escaping certain rape at the very last minute.
After delivering some choice remarks on his bestial habits
she stormed out, leaving him numb and dazed in the chilly
boathouse. There was a fierce ache in his groin and there
was blind rage in his head. What would any redblooded

American youth have done in such a situation? What Timothy did was to stagger back to the clubhouse, grab a half-full bottle of bourbon from the bar, and go lurching out into the night, feeling furious and very sorry for himself. After gulping half the bourbon he jumped into his sleek little Mercedes sports car and drove home at eighty miles an hour; then he sat in the garage finishing off the bourbon; then, blind drunk and raging mad, he went upstairs, invaded his virginal young sister's bedroom, and flung himself on top of her. She struggled. She implored. She whimpered. But his strength was as the strength of ten and nothing could swerve him from his chosen course, not with that giant hard-on doing his thinking for him. She was a girl; she was a bitch; he was going to use her. He didn't currently see any difference between the luscious cock-teaser in the boathouse and this uppity sister of his; they were both bitches, they were *all* bitches, and he was going to get even with the whole tribe of women at once. He held her down with his knees and elbows. "If you yell," he told her, "I'll break your neck," and he meant it, because just then he was out of his head, and she knew it, too. Down came his trembling sister's pajama bottoms. Cruelly the snorting stallion of a brother battered at her tender gate. "I don't even think she was a virgin," he told me morosely. "I went right in, easy." It was all over in two minutes. Then he rolled free of her, and they were both shivering, she from shock and he from release, and he pointed out to her that it wouldn't do her any good to complain to their parents about this, since they probably wouldn't believe her, and if they called in a doctor to check the story there would certainly be a scandal, whispers, insinuations, and once that began to get around town it would ruin her chances of getting married, *ever*, to anyone worth marrying. She glared at him. He had never seen such hate in anyone's eyes.

He made his way to his own room, falling down a couple of times. When he woke, sober and aghast, it was late the next afternoon and he expected to find the police waiting for him downstairs. But there was no one there but his father and his stepmother and the servants. Nobody acted as if anything unusual had happened. His father smiled, asked him how the dance had gone. His sister was out with friends. She didn't return until dinnertime, and when she came in she behaved as though everything was as it should be, giving Timothy a cool, distant, customary nod as a greeting. That evening she called him aside and said in a menacing, terrifying voice, "If you ever try anything like that again, you'll get a knife in the balls, I promise you." But that was the last reference she ever made to what he had done. In four years she hadn't spoken of it once, at least not to him and probably not to anyone; she apparently had sealed the episode into some stony compartment of her mind, filing it away as a night's unpleasantness, like an attack of the trots. I could testify that she maintained a perfect icy surface, playing the role of the eternal virgin no matter who or what had been into her.

That was all. That was the whole thing. When he was finished, Timothy looked up, drained, empty, gray-faced, a million and a half years old. "I can't tell you how crappy I've always felt about doing something like that," he said. "How much goddamned guilt I've had."

"You feel better now?" I asked.

"No."

I wasn't surprised. I've never believed that opening your soul brings you surcease from sorrow. It just spreads the sorrow around some. What Timothy had told me was a dumb story, a sordid story, a downer, a bummer. A tale of the idle rich, mind-fucking each other in the usual fashion, worrying about virginity and propriety, creating little melodramatic operas starring themselves and their friends, with snobbishness and frustration spinning the plot. I almost felt sorry for Timothy, big hulking good-natured upper-crust Timothy, as much victim as criminal, simply looking for a little action at the country club and getting kneed in the groin instead. So he got drunk and raped his sister because he thought it would make him feel better, or because he wasn't thinking at all. And that was his great secret, that was his terrible sin. I felt soiled by the story. It was such a shabby thing, such a pitiful thing; and now I would have to carry it around in my head forever. I couldn't say a word to him. After what seemed like ten silent minutes he got heavily to his feet and shambled toward the door.

"All right," he said. "I did what Frater Javier wanted me to do. Now I feel like a load of shit. How do you feel, Oliver?" He laughed. "And tomorrow it's your turn."

He went out.

Yes. Tomorrow it's my turn.

thirty-seven

eli

Oliver said, "There was this day in early September when my friend Karl and I went hunting, just the two of us, chasing doves or partridges all morning through the scrubby woods north of town, catching nothing but dust. Then we came out of the trees and saw a lake before us, a pond, really, and we were hot and sweaty, for summer wasn't entirely over yet. So we put down our guns and got out of our clothes and took a swim, and afterward we sat naked on a big flat rock, drying ourselves and hoping some birds would fly by, so we could pot them—*pow*—without even getting up. Karl was fifteen then and I was fourteen, and I was finally bigger than he was, because I had reached my full growth and passed him in the spring. Karl had seemed so mature and big a few years before, but now he looked thin and flimsy next to me. We didn't speak for a long time, and then, just as I was thinking of suggesting that we get dressed and move along, Karl turned toward me with a peculiar look in his eyes, and I saw he was studying my body, my groin. And he said something about girls, how stupid girls are, what stupid noises they make while you're laying them, how tired he was of having to make love talk with them before they'd let him get into them, how bored he was with their dumb floppy tits, their makeup, their giggling, how much he hated buying them sodas and listening to their chatter, and so on. He said a lot of stuff along those lines. I laughed and said, Well, girls may have their flaws, but it's the only game in town, isn't it? And Karl said, No it isn't.

"Now I was sure he was putting me on, and I told him, I never went much for fucking cows or sheep, Karl. Or maybe it's ducks you've been going with lately. He shook his head. He looked annoyed. I'm not talking about fucking animals, he said, in the sort of tone you'd use in speaking to a small child. That kind of shit is for morons, Oliver. I'm just trying to tell you, he said, that there's a way you can get yourself off, a good way, a clean way, it doesn't involve girls, you don't have to sell yourself out to girls and do all the shit they want you to do for them, you know what I mean? It's simple and it's honest and it's clear-cut, all the cards on the table, and I want to tell you something, he said, don't knock it till you've tried it. I still wasn't sure what he meant, partly because I was naive and partly because I didn't want to believe that he meant what I thought he might mean, and I made a noncommittal grunt which Karl must have mistaken for a go-ahead, because he reached over and put his hand on me, high up on my thigh. Hey, wait, I said, and he said, Don't knock it till you've tried it, Oliver. He went on talking in a low intense voice, words tumbling out of him, explaining to me that women were nothing but animals and he was going to keep clear of them for life, that even if he got married he wasn't going to touch his wife except to make kids, but otherwise, so far as his pleasures went, he hoped to keep them on a strictly man-to-man basis because that was the only decent and honest way. You hunt with other men, you play cards with other men, you get drunk with other men, you talk with men the way you'd never talk with women, really opening yourself up, and so why not go the whole route, why not get your sex kicks from men, too?

"And as he was explaining this to me, speaking very fast, never once letting me get a word in edgewise, making everything sound almost rational and logical, he had his hand on me, putting it there in a very casual way, on my thigh, the way you might put your hand on some-body's shoulder while you're saying something to him, meaning nothing particular by it, and Karl was rubbing this hand up and down, up and down, still talking a streak, moving the hand closer and closer to my crotch all the time. And he was getting hard, Eli, and so was I, that's what amazed me so much, so was I. I was getting hard. With an empty blue sky above us and not another human being within five miles. I was afraid to look down at myself, ashamed of what I knew was happening to me. That was a revelation to me, that another fellow could arouse me like that. Just this once, he said, just once, Oliver, and if you don't like it I'll never mention the subject to you again, but you mustn't knock it till you've tried it, you hear? I didn't know how to answer him and I didn't know how to get his hand off me. And then the hand moved farther up, up to here, and even higher, and—look, Eli, I mean, I don't want to get too graphic. If this is embarrassing you, just tell me and I'll try to describe it in general terms—"

"Say it however you need to say it, Oliver."

"Reaching his hand up and up, until his hand was

clasped tight around my—around my cock, Eli, he was holding my penis, holding me there just like a girl might, the two of us naked by that little lake where we'd just been swimming, at the edge of the woods, and his words pouring through my head, telling me how we could do it with each other, how men managed it. I know all about it, he said, I learned it from my brother-in-law. You know, he hates my sister, they've been married only three years and he can't stand her, the way she smells, the way she files her nails all the time, everything about her, and one night he said, Let me show you some fun, Karl, and he was right, it was fun. So let me show you some fun, Oliver. And afterward you tell me who gave you a better time, me or Christa Henrichs, me or Judy Beecher."

The bitter odor of sweat was strong in the room. Oliver's voice was hard-edged and sharp; every syllable came forth with the force of a dart. His eyes were glazed and his face was flushed. He seemed to be in some sort of trance. If it hadn't been Oliver, I would have thought he was stoned. This confession was costing him some tremendous inner price; that had been plain from the moment he walked in, jaws rigid, lips clamped, looking weirdly uptight as I had seen him only a few times previously, and began his rambling, hesitant tale of a late-summer day in the Kansas woods when he was a boy. As the story unwound I had been trying to anticipate its route and guess its payoff. Obviously he had betrayed Karl in some way, I supposed. Had he cheated Karl in the division of the day's catch? Had he stolen ammunition from Karl when his friend's back was turned? Had he shot Karl dead in some sudden quarrel and told the sheriff it was an accident? None of those possibilities persuaded me; but I was unprepared for the actual turn in the narrative, the wandering hand, the skillful seduction. The rural background—guns and wild game and woods—had misled me; my simpleminded image of Growing Up In Kansas left no room for homosexual adventures and other manifestations of what to me was a purely urban species of decadence. Yet here was Karl, the virile huntsman, groping innocent young Oliver, and here was an older Oliver crouching before me pulling the reluctant words from his bowels. The words became less reluctant; Oliver was caught up in the rhythms of his tale, now, and, though his anguish seemed no less, his flow of description became more copious, as if he took some masochistic pride in baring this episode to me: it was not so much a confession as an act of abasement. The story rolled inexorably on, liberally embellished with telling detail. Oliver portraying his maidenly shyness and uneasiness, his gradual succumbing to Karl's earnest sophistries, the critical moment when his uncertain hand at last sought Karl's body. Oliver spared me nothing. Karl had not been circumcised, I learned, and in case I might not be familiar with the anatomical implications of that fact Oliver carefully explained to me the appearance of an uncircumcised member, both flaccid and erect. He told me also of the manual caresses and of his indoctrination into the oral joys, and finally he painted the picture of the two sinewy young male bodies writhing in elaborate copulation beside the pond. There was Bible Belt fervor in his words: he had committed an abomination, he had dabbled in the sins of Sodom, he had fouled himself unto the seventh generation, all in that one afternoon of boyish fun. "All right," I wanted to say, "all right, Oliver, so you made out with your pal, why stretch it into such a big *megillah?* You're still basically hetero, aren't you? Everyone fools around with other boys when he's a kid, and Kinsey told us a long time ago that at least one male adolescent out of three goes to the point of climax with—" But I said not a word. This was Oliver's big moment and I didn't want to put him down. This was his shaping trauma, this was the fiery-eyed demon that rode him, and he was letting it all hang out for my inspection. He had awesome momentum now. He swept me grandly along to the final orgasmic spurt, and then sat back, spent, dazed, face going slack, eyes going dull. Waiting for my verdict, I guess. What could I say? How could I pass judgment on him? I said nothing.

"What happened afterward?" I asked at last.

"We took a swim and cleaned ourselves up and got dressed and went and shot some wild ducks."

"No, I mean *afterward*. Between Karl and you. The effect on your friendship."

"On our way back to town," Oliver said, "I told Karl that if he ever went near me again I'd blow his fucking head off."

"And?"

"He never went near me again. A year later he lied about his age and joined the marines and got killed in Vietnam." Oliver looked at me challengingly, evidently awaiting another question, something he was sure I must inevitably ask, but I had no more questions; the sheer inconsequentiality, the irrelevance, of Karl's death had broken the narrative thread for me. There was a long pause. I felt foolish and inarticulate. Then Oliver said, "That was the only time in my life I ever had any sort of gay experience. Absolutely the only time. You believe me, don't you, Eli?"

"Of course I do."

"You better. Because it's true. There was that once with Karl, when I was fourteen, and that was all. You know, one reason I agreed to have a gay roommate was as a sort of a test, to see whether I could be tempted, to learn where my natural inclinations lay, to find out whether what I did that day with Karl was a one-shot, a fluke, or if it would happen again if there was the opportunity. Well, there was the opportunity, all right. But I'm sure you know I've never made it with Ned. You know that, don't you? The question of a physical relationship just hasn't ever come up between Ned and me."

"Of course."

His eyes were on me, fierce again. Still waiting, Oliver? For what?

He said, "There's just one thing else I have to say."

"Go on, Oliver."

"Just one thing. A little footnote, but it carries the

whole point of the story, because it isolates the guilt for me. Where the guilt lives, Eli, isn't in what I did. It's in how I *felt* about what I did." A nervous chuckle. Another pause. He was having trouble getting his one last thing said. He looked away from me. I think he was wishing he had left well enough alone and had ended his confession five minutes before. At length he said, "I'll tell you. I enjoyed it, Eli. With Karl. I got a real thrill out of it. My whole body seemed to be erupting. It may have been the biggest kick of my life. I never went back for a second time, because I knew that kind of thing was wrong. But I wanted to. I still want to. I've always wanted to." He was shaking. "I've had to fight it, every minute of my life, and I never realized until just a short while ago how hard I actually was fighting. That's all. That's the whole thing, Eli, right there. That's all I have to say."

thirty-eight

ned

Enter Eli, somber, shuffling, mantled in rabbinical gloom, a stoop-shouldered personification of the Wailing Wall, two thousand years of sorrow on his back. He is down. Very far down. I had noticed, we all had noticed, how well Eli was responding to life in the House of Skulls; he had been up since the day we got here, far up and cresting, as up as I had ever seen him. Not any more. For the past week he'd been heading downward. And these few confessional days seemed to have thrust him into the uttermost abyss. Sad eyes, drooping mouth. The quirky grimace of self-doubt, self-contempt. He radiates a chill. He is *veh-is-mir* made flesh. What buggest thou, beloved Eli?

We rapped a bit. I felt free and loose, pretty far up myself, as I had been for three days, since dumping the tale of Julian and The Other Oliver onto Timothy. Frater Javier knows his business; ventilating all that garbage was exactly what I needed. Getting it into the open, analyzing it, discovering which part of the episode was the part that was hurting me. So now with Eli I was relaxed and expansive, my usual mild maliciousness altogether absent; I had no wish to needle him, but simply sat waiting, the coolest kind of cat I had ever been, ready to receive his pain and ease him of it. I expected him to blurt out his confession in a soul-clearing hurry, but no, not yet, indirection is Eli's hallmark; he wanted to talk of other things. How, he wondered, did I evaluate our chances in the Trial? I shrugged and told him that I rarely thought about such things and simply went through our daily round of weeding and meditating and exercising and screwing, telling myself that every day in every way I was getting closer and closer to the goal. Eli shook his head. A sense of impending failure obsessed him. He had been confident at first that our Trial would have a successful outcome, and the last vestiges of skepticism had dropped from him; he believed implicitly in the truth of the Book of Skulls and believed also that its bounty would be extended to us. Now his faith in the Book was unshaken but his self-confidence was shattered. He was convinced that a crisis was approaching that would doom our hopes. The problem, he said, was Timothy. Eli felt certain that Timothy's tolerance for the skullhouse was virtually at its end and that in another couple of days he'd take off, leaving us stranded in an incomplete Receptacle.

"I think so, too," I said.

"What can we do about it?"

"Not much. We can't force him to stay."

"If he goes, what happens to us?"

"How do I know, Eli? I guess we'll be in trouble with the fraters."

"I won't let him leave," Eli said with sudden vehemence.

"You won't? How do you propose to stop him?"

"I haven't worked it out yet. But I won't let him leave." His face contorted into a tragic mask. "Oh, Jesus, Ned, don't you see, it's all coming apart?"

"I actually thought we were getting it together," I said.

"For a while. For a while. Not any longer. We never had any real hold on Timothy, and now he doesn't even bother to hide his impatience, his contempt—" Eli pulled his head into his shoulders, turtlewise. "And this priestess thing. The afternoon orgies. I'm bungling them, Ned. I'm not gaining control over myself. It's great to have all that easy tail, sure, but I'm not learning the erotic disciplines I'm supposed to be mastering."

"You're giving up on yourself too early."

"I don't see any progress. I haven't been able to last for all three women yet. Two of them, a couple of times. Three, no."

"It's a matter of practice," I said.

"Are *you* managing?"

"Pretty well."

"Of course," he said. "That's because you don't give a damn for women in the first place. It's just a physical exercise for you, like swinging on a trapeze. But I *relate* to those girls, Ned, I see them as sexual objects, what I do with them has enormous significance for me, and so—and so—oh, Christ, Ned, if I don't master this part of it, what's the good of working so hard on all the rest of it?"

He disappeared into a chasm of self-pity. I made properly encouraging noises: don't give up, lad, don't sell yourself short. Then I reminded him that he was supposed to be making confession to me. He nodded. For a minute or more he sat in silence, distant, rocking back and forth. At last he said, suddenly, with startling irrelevance, "Ned, are you aware that Oliver is gay?"

"It must have taken me all of five minutes to discover it."

"You *knew?*"

"It takes one to tell one, haven't you ever heard that line? I saw it in his face the first time I met him. I said, this man is gay whether he knows it or not, he's one of us, it's obvious. The glassy eyes, the tight jaw, the look of repressed longing, that barely concealed ferocity of a soul that's trussed up tight, that's in pain because it's not allowed to do what it desperately wants to do. Everything about Oliver advertises it—the self-punishing academic load, the way he goes about his athletic commitments, even his compulsive studding. He's a classic case of latent homosexuality, all right."

"Not latent," Eli said.

"What?"

"He's not just *potentially* gay. He's had a homosexual experience. Only one, true, but it made a profound impression on him, and it's colored all of his attitudes since he was fourteen years old. Why do you think he asked you to room with him? It was to test his self-control—it's been an exercise in stoicism for him, all these years when he hasn't let himself touch you—but you're what he wants, Ned, did you realize that? It's not just latent. It's conscious, it's just below the surface."

I looked strangely at Eli. What he was saying was something I might perhaps turn to my own great advantage; and aside from the hope of personal gain from Eli's revelation, I was fascinated and astonished by it, as one always is by intimate gossip of that sort. But it gave me a queasy feeling. I was reminded of something that had happened during my summer in Southampton, at a drunken, bitchy party where two men who had been living together for about twenty years got into an exceptionally vicious quarrel, and one of them suddenly ripped the terrycloth robe from the other, showing him naked to all of us, revealing a fat jiggling belly and an almost hairless crotch and the undeveloped genitals of a ten-year-old boy, and screaming that this was what he'd had to put up with all those years. That moment of exposure, that catastrophic unmasking, had been a source of delicious cocktail-party chatter for weeks afterward, but it left me sickened, because I and everyone else in that room had been made involuntary witness to someone else's private agony, and I knew that what had been stripped bare that day was not merely someone's body. I had not needed to know what I learned then. Now Eli had told me something that might be useful to me in one way but which in another had transformed me without my bidding into an intruder in another man's soul.

I said, "Where'd you find all this out?"

"Oliver told me the other night."

"In his confes—"

"In his confession, yes. It happened back in Kansas. He went hunting in the woods with a friend of his, a kid a year older than he was, and they stopped for a swim, and when they came out of the water the other fellow seduced him, and it turned Oliver on. And he's never forgotten it, the intensity of the situation, the sheer physical delight, although he's taken care never to repeat the experience. So you're absolutely correct when you say that it's possible to explain a lot of Oliver's rigidity, his obsessive character, in terms of his constant efforts to repress his—"

"Eli?"

"Yes, Ned?"

"Eli, these confessions are supposed to be confidential."

He nibbled his lower lip. "I know."

"You're violating Oliver's privacy by telling me all this. Me, of all people."

"I know I am."

"Then why are you doing it?"

"I thought you'd be interested."

"No, Eli, I won't buy that. A man of your moral perception, of your general existential awareness—balls, man, you don't just have gossip-peddling on your mind. You came in here intending to betray Oliver to me. Why? Are you trying to get something started between Oliver and me?"

"Not really."

"Then why'd you tell me about him?"

"Because I knew it was wrong."

"What kind of half-assed reason is that?"

He gave me a funny chuckle and an embarrassed grin. "It provides me with something to confess," Eli said. "I regard this breach of confidence as the most odious thing I've ever done. To reveal Oliver's secret to the one person most capable of taking advantage of his vulnerability. Okay, I've done it, and now I formally confess that I've done it. *Mea culpa, mea culpa, mea maxima culpa.* The sin has been committed right before your eyes, and give me absolution, will you?" He rattled the words out so fast that for an instant I couldn't follow the Byzantine convolutions of his reasoning. Even after I understood, I wasn't able to believe that he was serious.

Finally I said, "That's a cop-out, Eli!"

"Is it?"

"It's cynical shit that wouldn't even be worthy of Timothy. It violates the spirit and maybe the letter of Frater Javier's instructions. Frater Javier didn't intend us to commit sins on the spot and then instantly repent of them. You have to confess something real, something out of your past, something that's been burning your guts for years, something deep and poisonous."

"What if I have nothing of that kind to confess?"

"Nothing, Eli?"

"Nothing."

"You never wished your grandmother would drop dead because she made you put on a clean suit? You never peeked into the girls' shower room? You never pulled the wings off a fly? Can you honestly say you have no buried guilts at all, Eli?"

"None that matter."

"Can you be the judge of that?"

"Who else?" He was fidgeting now. "Look, I would have told you something else if I had anything to tell. But I don't. What's the use of making a big scene out of pulling the wings off flies? I've led a piddling little life full of piddling little sins that I wouldn't dream of boring you with. I didn't see any way I could possibly fulfill Frater Javier's instructions. Then at the last moment I thought of this business of violating Oliver's confidence, which I've now done. I think that's sufficient. If you don't mind I'd like to leave now."

He moved toward the door.

"Wait," I said. "I reject your confession, Eli. You're trying to make me go along with an *ad hoc* sin, with willed guilt. Nothing doing. I want something real."

"What I told you about Oliver is real."

"You know what I mean."

"I have nothing to give you."

"This isn't for me, Eli. It's for you, your own rite of purification. I've been through it, Oliver has, even Timothy, and here you stand, putting down your own sins, pretending that nothing you've ever done is worth feeling guilty about—" I shrugged. "All right. It's your own immortality you're screwing up, not mine. Go on. Go. Go."

He threw me a terrible look, a look of fear and resentment and anguish, and hurried from the room. I realized, after he was gone, that my nerves were stretched taut: my hands were shaking and a muscle in my left thigh was jumping. What had strung me out this way? Eli's cowardly self-concealment or his revelation of Oliver's availability? Both, I decided. Both. But the second more than the first. I wondered what would happen if I went to Oliver now. Staring straight into those icy blue eyes of his.

I know the truth about you, I'd say in a calm voice, a quiet voice. I know all about how you were seduced by your pal when you were fourteen. Only don't try to tell me it was a seduction, Ol, because I don't believe in seductions, and I have some knowledge of the subject. Being seduced isn't what brings you out, if you're gay. You come out *because you want to,* isn't that so? It's in you from the start, it's programed into your genes, your bones, your balls, it's just waiting for the right occasion to show itself, and some-body gives you that occasion and that's when you come out. All right, Ol, you got your chance, and you loved it, and then you spent seven years fighting against it, and now you're going to do it with me. Not because my wiles are irresistible. Not because I've stupefied you with drugs or booze. It won't be a seduction. No, you'll do it because you want to, Ol, because you've always wanted to. You haven't had the courage to let yourself do it. Well, I'd tell him, here's your chance. Here I am. And I'd go to him, and I'd touch him, and he'd shake his head and make a rattling, coughing noise deep in his throat, still fighting it, and then something would snap in him, a seven-year tension would break, and he'd stop fighting. He'd surrender, and we'd make it at last. And afterward we'd lie close together in an exhausted sweaty heap, but his fervor would cool as it always does just afterward, and the guilt and shame would rise up in him, and—I could see it so vividly!—he would beat me to death, clubbing me down, smashing me against the stone floor, staining it with my blood. He'd stand above me while I twitched in pain, and he'd howl at me in rage because I had shown him to himself, face to face, and he couldn't bear the knowledge of what he had seen in his own eyes. All right, Ol, if you have to destroy me, then destroy me. That's cool, because I love you, and so what-ever you do to me is cool. And it fulfills the Ninth Mystery, doesn't it? I came here to have you and die, and I've had you, and now at the proper mystic moment I'm going to die, and it's cool, beloved Ol, everything's cool. And his tremendous fists crush my bones. And my broken frame twists and writhes. And is finally still. And the ecstatic voice of Frater Antony is heard on high, intoning the text of the Ninth Mystery as an invisible bell tolls, dong, dong, dong, Ned is dead, Ned is dead, Ned is dead.

The fantasy was so intensely real that I began to shiver and quake; I could feel the force of that vision in every molecule of my body. It seemed to me that I had already been to Oliver, had already grappled with him in passion, had already perished beneath his flaming wrath. Thus there was no need for me to do these things now. They were over, accomplished, encapsulated in the sealed past. I savored my memories of him. The touch of his smooth skin against me. The granite of his muscles unyielding to my probing fingertips. The taste of him on my lips. The flavor of my own blood, trickling into my mouth as he began to pummel me. The sense of surrendering my body. The ecstasy. The bells. The voice on high. The fraters singing a requiem for me. I lost myself in visionary revery.

Then I became aware that someone had entered my room. The door, opening, closing. Footsteps. This, too, I accepted as part of the fantasy. Without looking around, I decided that Oliver must have come to me, and in a dreamy acid-high way I became convinced that it *was* Oliver, it necessarily *had* to be Oliver, so that I was thrown into confusion for an instant when eventually I turned and saw Eli. He was sitting quietly against the far wall. He had merely appeared depressed on his earlier visit, but now—ten minutes later? half an hour?—he seemed utterly disintegrated. Downcast eyes, slumping shoulders. "I don't understand," he said hollowly, "how this confessional thing can have any value, real, symbolic, metaphorical, or otherwise. I thought I understood it when Frater Javier first spoke to us, but now I can't dig it. Is this what we must do in order to deliver ourselves from death? Why? Why?"

"Because they ask it," I said.

"What of that?"

"It's a matter of obedience. Out of obedience grows discipline, out of discipline grows control, out of control grows the power to conquer the forces of decay. Obedience is anti-entropic. Entropy is our enemy."

"How glib you are," he said.

"Glibness isn't a sin."

He laughed and made no reply. I could see that he was on the thin edge, walking the razor-sharp line between sanity and madness, and I, who had teetered on that edge all my life, was not going to be the one to nudge him. Time passed. My vision of myself and Oliver receded and became unreal. I bore no grudge against Eli for that; this night belonged to him. Ultimately he started to tell me about an essay he had written when he was sixteen, in his senior year in high school, an essay on the moral collapse of the Western Roman Empire as reflected in the degeneration of Latin into the various Romance languages. He remembered a good deal of what he had written even now, quoting lengthy chunks of it, and I listened with half an ear, giving him the polite pretense of attention but nothing more, for although the essay sounded brilliant to me, a remarkable performance for a scholar of any age and certainly astonishing for a boy of sixteen to have written, I did not at that particular moment have any vast desire to hear about the subtle ethical implications to be found in the patterns of evolution of French, Spanish, and Italian. But gradually I comprehended Eli's motives for telling me this story and paid closer heed: he was, in fact, making confession to me. For he had written that essay for submission to a contest sponsored by some prestigious learned society and had won, receiving thereby a valuable scholarship that had underwritten his college tuition. Indeed, he had built his entire academic career on that piece, for it had been reprinted in a major philological journal and had made him a celebrity in that small scholastic realm. Though only a freshman, he was mentioned admiringly in the footnotes of other scholars; the gates of all libraries were open to him; he would not have had the opportunity to find the very manuscript that had led us to the House of Skulls had he not written the masterly essay on which his fame depended. And—so he told me in the same expressionless tone with which, moments before, he had been expounding on irregular verbs—the essential concept of that thesis had not been his own work. He had stolen it.

Aha! The sin of Eli Steinfeld! No trifling sexual peccadillo, no boyhood adventure in buggery or mutual masturbation, no incestuous snuggling with his mildly protesting mother, but rather an intellectual crime, the most damning of all. Little wonder he had held back from admitting it. Now, though, he poured forth the incriminating truth. His father, he said, lunching one afternoon in an Automat on Sixth Avenue, had happened to notice a small, gray, faded man sitting by himself, exploring a thick, unwieldy book. It was an arcane volume on linguistic analysis, Sommerfelt's *Diachronic and Synchronic Aspects of Language,* a title that would have meant nothing whatever to the elder Steinfeld had he not just a short while before forked out $16.50, no trivial sum in that family, to buy a copy for Eli, who felt he could not live much longer without it. The shock of recognition, then, at the sight of that bulky quarto. Upwelling of parental pride: my son the philologist. An introduction follows. Conversation. Immediate rapport; one middle-aged refugee in an Automat has nothing to fear from another. "My son," says Mr. Steinfeld, "he's reading that same book!" Expressions of delight. The other is a native of Rumania, formerly professor of linguistics at the University of Cluj; he had fled that land in 1939, hoping to enter Palestine but arriving instead, by a roundabout route through the Dominican Republic, Mexico, and Canada, in the United States. Unable to secure an academic appointment anywhere, he lives in quiet poverty on Manhattan's Upper West Side, holding whatever jobs he can find: dishwasher in a Chinese restaurant, proofreader for a short-lived Rumanian newspaper, mimeograph operator for a displaced-persons information service, and so on. All the

while he is diligently preparing his life's work, a structural
and philosophical analysis of the decay of Latin in early
medieval times. The manuscript now is virtually complete
in Rumanian, he tells Eli's father, and he has begun the
necessary translation into English, but the work goes very
slowly for him, since even now he is not at home in
English, his head being so thoroughly stuffed with other
languages. He dreams of finishing the book, finding a
publisher for it, and retiring to Israel on the proceeds. "I
should like to meet your boy," the Rumanian says abruptly. Instant emanations of suspicion from Eli's father. Is
this some kind of pervert? A molester, a fondler? No! This
is a decent Jewish man, a scholar, a *melamed,* a member of
the international fellowship of victims; how could he mean
any harm to Eli? Telephone numbers are exchanged. A
meeting is negotiated. Eli goes to the Rumanian's apartment: one tiny room, crammed with books, manuscripts,
learned periodicals in a dozen languages. Here, read this,
the worthy man says, this and this and this, my essays, my
theories; and he thrusts papers into Eli's hands, onionskin
sheets closely typed, single spaced, no margins. Eli goes
home, he reads, his mind expands. Far out! This little old
man has it all together! Inflamed, Eli vows to learn
Rumanian, to be his new friend's amanuensis, to help him
translate his masterwork as quickly as possible. Feverishly
the two, the boy and the old man, plan collaborations.
They build castles in Rumania. Eli, out of his own money,
has the manuscripts Xeroxed, so that some *goy* in the next
apartment, falling asleep over a cigarette, does not wipe
out this lifetime of scholarship in a mindless conflagration.
Every day after school Eli hurries to the little cluttered
room. Then one afternoon no one answers his knock.
Calamity! The janitor is summoned, grumbling, whiskey-
breathed; he uses his master key to open the door; within
lies the Rumanian, yellow-faced, stiff. A society of refugees
pays for the funeral. A nephew, mysteriously unmentioned
previously, materializes and carts off every book, every
manuscript, to a fate unknown. Eli is left with the

Xeroxes. What now? How can he be the vehicle through which this work is made known to mankind? Ah! The essay contest for the scholarship! He sits possessed at his typewriter, hour after hour. The distinction in his own mind between himself and his departed acquaintance becomes uncertain. They are collaborators now; through me, Eli thinks, this great man speaks from the grave. The essay is finished and there is no doubt in Eli's mind of its worth; it is plainly a masterpiece. Moreover he has the special pleasure of knowing that he has salvaged the life's work of an unjustly neglected scholar. He submits the required six copies to the contest committee; in the spring the registered letter comes, notifying him he has won; he is summoned into marble halls to receive a scroll, a check for more money than he can imagine, and the excited congratulations of a panel of distinguished academics. Shortly afterward comes the first request from a professional journal for a contribution. His career is launched. Only later does Eli realize that in his triumphant essay he has, somehow, forgotten entirely to credit the author of the work on which his ideas are based. Not an acknowledgment, not a footnote, not a single citation anywhere.

This error of omission abashes him, but he feels it is too late to remedy the oversight, nor does the giving of proper credit become any easier for him as the months pass, as his essay gets into print, as the scholarly discussion of it begins. He lives in terror of the moment when some elderly Rumanian will arise, clutching a parcel of obscure journals published in prewar Bucharest, and cry out that this impudent young man has shamelessly rifled the thought of his late and distinguished colleague, the unfortunate Dr. Nicolescu. But no accusing Rumanian arises. Years have gone by; the essay is universally accepted as Eli's own; as the end of his undergraduate days approaches, several major universities vie for the honor of having him do advanced study on their faculty.

And this sordid episode, Eli said in conclusion, could serve as metaphor of his whole intellectual life—all of it fake, no depth, the key ideas borrowed. He had gone a long way on a knack for making synthesis masquerade as originality, plus a certain undeniable skill in assimilating the syntax of archaic languages, but he had made no real contribution to mankind's store of knowledge, none, which at his age would be pardonable had he not fraudulently gained a premature reputation as the most penetrating thinker to enter the field of linguistics since Benjamin Whorf. And what was he, in truth? A golem, a construct, a walking Potemkin Village of philology. Miracles of insight now were expected of him, and what could he give? He had nothing left to offer, he told me bitterly. He had long ago used up the last of the Rumanian's manuscripts.

A monstrous silence descended. I could not bear to look at him. This had been more than a confession; it had been hara-kiri. Eli had destroyed himself in front of me. I had always been a little suspicious, yes, of Eli's supposed profundity, for though he undoubtedly had a fine mind his perceptions all struck me in an odd way as having come to him at second hand; yet I had never imagined this of him, this theft, this imposture. What could I say to him now? Cluck my tongue, priestlike, and tell him, Yes, my child, you have sinned grievously? He knew that. Tell him that God would forgive him, for God is love? I didn't believe that myself. Perhaps I might try a dose of Goethe, saying, Redemption from sin through good works is still available, Eli, go forth and drain marshes and build hospitals and write some brilliant essays that aren't stolen and all will be well for you. He sat there, waiting for absolution, waiting for The Word that would lift the yoke from him. His face was blank, his eyes devastated. I wished he had confessed some meaningless fleshly sin. Oliver had plugged his playmate, nothing more, a sin that to me was no sin at all, only jolly good fun; Oliver's anguish thus was unreal, a product of the conflict between his body's natural desires and the conditioning society had imposed. In the Athens of Pericles he would have had nothing to confess. Timothy's sin, whatever it was, had surely been something equally shallow, sprouting not from moral absolutes but from local tribal taboos: perhaps he had slept with a serving wench, perhaps he had spied on his parents' copulations. My own was a more complex transgression, for I had taken joy in the doom of others, I perhaps had even engineered the doom of others, but even that was a subtle Jamesian sort of thing, in the last analysis fairly insubstantial. Not this. If plagiarism lay at the core of Eli's glittering scholastic attainments, then nothing lay at the core of Eli: he was hollow, he was empty, and what absolution could anyone offer him for that? Well, Eli had had his cop-out earlier in the evening, and now I had mine. I rose, I went to him, I took his hands in mine and lifted him to his feet, and I said magic words to him: *contrition, atonement, forgiveness, redemption.* Strive ever toward the light, Eli. No soul is damned for all eternity. Work hard, apply yourself, persevere, seek self-understanding, and there will be divine mercy for you, because your weakness comes from Him and He will not chastise you for it if you show Him you are able to transcend it. He nodded remotely and left me. I thought of the Ninth Mystery and wondered if I would ever see him again.

I paced my room a long while, brooding. Then Satan inflamed me and I went to call on Oliver.

thirty-nine

OLIVER

"I know the story," Ned said. "I know the whole bit." Smiling shyly at me. Soft eyes, cow eyes, looking into mine. "You don't need to be afraid of being what you are, Oliver. You mustn't ever be afraid of what you are. Can't you see how important it is to get to know yourself, to get into your head as far as you can go, and then *to act on what you find in there?* But instead so many people set up dumb walls between themselves and themselves, walls made out of useless abstractions. A lot of Thou Shalt Nots and Thou Dost Not Dares. Why? What good is any of that?" His face was glowing. A tempter, a devil. Eli must have told him everything. Karl and me, me and Karl. I wanted to smash Eli's head for him. Ned circled around me, grinning, moving like a cat, like a wrestler about to spring. He kept his voice low, almost a crooning tone. "Come on, Ol. Loosen up. LuAnn won't find out. I don't play kiss and tell. Let's go, Ol, let's do it, let's *do it.* We're not strangers. We've kept apart long enough. This is you, Oliver, this is the real you in there who wants to get out, and this is the moment for you to let him come out. Will you, Ol? Will you? Now? Here's your chance. Here I am." And he came close to me. Looked up at me. Short little Ned, chest-high to me. His fingers lightly running along my forearm. "No," I said, shaking my head. "Don't touch me, Ned." He continued to smile. To stroke me. "Don't refuse me," he whispered. "Don't deny me. Because if you do, you'll be denying yourself, you'll be refusing to accept the reality of your own existence, and you can't do that,

Oliver, can you? Not if you want to live forever. I'm a station you've got to pass through on your journey. We've both known that for years, down deep. Now it surfaces, Ol. Now everything surfaces, everything converges, all time runs to now, Ol, this place, this room, this night. Yes? Yes? Say yes. Oliver. Say yes!"

forty

eli

I no longer knew who I was or where I was. I was in a trance, a daze, a coma. Like my own ghost I haunted the halls of the House of Skulls, drifting through the chilly night-darkened corridors. The stone images of skulls looked out from the walls, grinning at me. I grinned at them. I winked, I blew them kisses. I stared at the row of massive oaken doors receding toward infinity, every door tightly shut, and mysterious names crossed my consciousness: this is Timothy's room, this is Ned's, this is Oliver's. Who are they? And this is the room of Eli Steinfeld. Who? *Eli Steinfeld.* Who? E. Li. Stein. Feld. A series of incomprehensible sounds. An agglomeration of dead syllables. E. Li. Stein. Feld. Let us proceed. This room belongs to Frater Antony, and in here one may find Frater Bernard, and here Frater Javier, and here Frater Claude, and Frater Miklos, and Frater Maurice, and Frater Leon, and Frater This and Frater That, and who are these fraters, what do

their names mean? Here are more doors. The women must
sleep here. I opened a door at random. Four cots, four
fleshy women, naked, sprawling in a tangle of rumpled
sheets. Nothing hidden. Thighs, buttocks, breasts, loins.
The slack-mouthed faces of sleepers. I could go to them, I
could enter their bodies, I could possess them, all four of
them, each in turn. But no. Onward, to a place where there
is no roof, where the glistening stars shine through the bare
beams. Colder, here. Skulls on the walls. A fountain,
bubbling. I passed through the public rooms. Here we take
instruction in the Eighteen Mysteries. Here we perform the
sacred gymnastics. This is where we eat our special foods.
And here—this opening in the floor, this *omphalos,* the
navel of the universe is here, the gateway to the Pit. I must
go down. Down, then. A musty smell. No light here. The
angle of descent flattens; this is no abyss, but only a
tunnel, and I remember it. I have been through here
before, coming the other way. A barrier now, a stone slab.
It yields, it yields! The tunnel continues. Forward, forward, forward. Trombones and basset horns, a chorus of
basses, the words of the Requiem trembling in the air: *Rex
tremendae majestatis, qui salvandos salvas gratis, salva me,
fons pietatis.* Out! I emerged into the clearing through
which I had first entered the House of Skulls. Before me,
barren wastes, a prickly desert. Behind me, the House of
Skulls. Above me the stars, the full moon, the vault of the
heavens. What now? I made my way uncertainly across the
clearing, past the row of basketball-sized stone skulls that
bordered it, and down the narrow path running into the
desert. I had no goal in mind. My feet took me. I walked
for hours or days or weeks. Then, on my right, I saw a
huge chunky boulder, coarse in texture, dark in color, the
road marker, the giant stone skull. By moonlight the
deep-set features were stark and sharp, black recesses holding pools of night. Brothers, let us meditate here. Let us
contemplate the skull beneath the face. And so I knelt.
And so, using the techniques taught me by the pious
Frater Antony, I sent forth my soul and engulfed the great

stone skull, and purged myself of all vulnerability to death. Skull, I know you! Skull, I fear you not! Skull, I carry your brother behind my skin! And I laughed at the skull, and I amused myself by transforming it, first into a smooth white egg, then into a globe of pink alabaster streaked and veined with yellow, then into a crystal sphere, the depths of which I explored. The sphere showed me the golden towers of lost Atlantis. It showed me shaggy men in woolly furs, capering by torchlight before painted bulls on the walls of a smoky cave. It showed me Oliver lying numb and exhausted in Ned's arms. I transformed the sphere into a rough skull rudely carved of black rock, and, satisfied, went back up the thorny path toward the House of Skulls. I did not enter the subterranean passage but instead walked around the side of the building and along the face of the lengthy wing in which we took instruction from the fraters, until I came to the building's end, where the path began that gave access to the cultivated fields. By moonlight I searched for weeds and found none. I caressed the little pepper plants. I blessed the berries and the roots. This is the holy food, this is the pure food, this is the food of life eternal. I knelt between the rows, on the cold wet muddy ground, and prayed that forgiveness be extended to me for my sins. I went next to the hillock west of the skullhouse. I ascended it and removed my shorts and, naked to the night, performed the sacred breathing exercises, squatting, sucking in the darkness, mingling it with the inner breath, drawing power from it, diverting that power to my vital organs. My body dissolved. I was without mass or weight. I floated, dancing, on a column of air. I held my breath for centuries. I soared for eons. I approached the true state of grace. Now it was proper to perform the rite of the gymnastics, which I then did, moving with grace and an agility I had never attained before. I bent, I pivoted, I twisted, I leaped. I flung myself aloft; I clapped hands; I tested every muscle. I tested myself to my limits.

The dawn was coming now.

The first gleam of sunlight tumbled upon me out of the eastern hills. I assumed the sunset squat and stared at that point of rosy light growing on the horizon, and I drank the sun's breath. My eyes were twin conduits; the holy flame leaped through them and into the labyrinth of my body. I was in total control, directing that wondrous blaze at will, shunting the warmth as I pleased into my left lung, into my spleen, into my liver, into my right kneecap. The sun broke the line of the horizon and sailed into full view, a perfect globe, dawn's red swiftly declining into morning's gold, and I took my fill of its radiance.

At length, ecstatic, I returned to the House of Skulls. As I neared the entrance a figure emerged from the tunnel: Timothy. He had found his city clothes somehow. His face was harsh and tense, jaws clamped, eyes tormented. When he saw me he scowled and spat. Acknowledging my presence in no other way, he walked quickly on, across the clearing, toward the desert path.

"Timothy?"

He did not halt.

"Timothy, where are you going? Answer me, Timothy."

He turned. Giving me a look of frosty contempt, he said, "I'm splitting, man. Why the crap do you have to be skulking around this early in the morning?"

"You can't go."

"I can't?"

"It'll shatter the Receptacle," I said.

"Fuck the Receptacle. You think I'm going to spend the rest of my life in this castle for idiots?" He shook his head. Then his expression softened, and he said less coarsely, "Eli, look, come to your senses, will you? You're trying to live a fantasy. It won't work. We've got to get back to the real world."

"No."

"Those two are hopeless, but you still can think rationally, maybe. We can have breakfast in Phoenix and make the first plane for New York."

"No."

"Last chance."

"No, Timothy."

He shrugged and turned away from me. "All right. Stay with your crazy friends, then. I've had it, man! I've had it."

I stood frozen as he crossed the clearing, stepped between two of the small stone skulls set in the sand, and approached the beginning of the path. There was no way I could convince him to stay. This moment had been inevitable from the beginning; Timothy was not like us, he lacked our traumas and our motives, he could never have been made to submit to the full course of the Trial. Through a long instant I considered my options and sought communion with the forces guiding the destiny of this Receptacle. I asked whether the right time had come, and I was told, Yes, the time has come. And I ran after him. As I came to the row of skulls I knelt briefly and scooped one of them from the ground—I needed both hands to carry it, and I suppose it weighed twenty or thirty pounds—and, running again, I came up behind Timothy just at the place where the path began. In a single graceful motion I lifted the stone skull and brought it forward against the back of his head with all my strength, and there was transmitted by my fingers through that basalt sphere the sensation of collapsing bone. He fell without a cry. The stone skull was bloody; I dropped it and it remained where it landed. Timothy's golden hair was tinged with red, and that red stain spread with surprising swiftness. It is necessary for me now to secure witnesses, I told myself, and to request the appropriate rites. I looked back toward the skullhouse. My witnesses were already there. Ned, naked, and Frater Antony, in his faded blue shorts, stood before the facade of the building. I went to them. Ned nodded; he had seen the whole thing. I dropped to my knees in front of Frater Antony, and he put his cool hand to my fevered forehead and said gently, "The Ninth Mystery is this: that the price of a life must always be a life. Know, O Nobly-Born, that eternities must be balanced by extinctions." And he said, "As by living we daily die, so then by dying we shall forever live."

forty-one

ned

I tried to get Oliver to help with the task of burying Timothy, but he sulked in his room like Achilles in his tent, so the job fell entirely to Eli and me. Oliver wouldn't open his door, he wouldn't even acknowledge my knock with a surly grunt from within. I left him and rejoined the group outside the building. Eli, standing beside fallen Timothy, wore a seraphic, transfigured look; he glowed. His face was flushed and his body glistened with a coating of sweat in the morning light. Surrounding him were four of the fraters, the four Keepers, Fraters Antony, Miklos, Javier, and Franz. They were calm and seemed gratified by what had occurred. Frater Franz had brought gravediggers' tools, picks and shovels. The burying ground, said Frater Antony, was a short distance into the desert.

Perhaps for reasons of ritual purity, the fraters would not touch the corpse. I doubted that Eli and I could carry Timothy as much as ten yards by ourselves, but Eli was not at all daunted. Kneeling, he knotted Timothy's feet around each other and put his shoulder under Timothy's calves, signaling to me to grab Timothy by the middle. Hup! and we heaved and hauled and lifted that inert 200-pound hulk from the ground, staggering a little. With Frater Antony leading us, Eli and I marched toward the burying ground, the other fraters somewhere to the rear. Though dawn was not far behind us, the sun was already remorseless, and the effort of bearing that terrible burden through the shimmering heat haze of the desert cast me into a quasi-hallucinatory state; my pores opened, my knees swayed, my eyes lost focus, I felt an invisible hand clutching my throat. I entered an instant-replay trip, seeing again the flashback shots of Eli's great moment in slow motion, the camera stopping at the critical intervals. I saw Eli running, Eli bending to snatch that heavy basalt globe, Eli in pursuit of Timothy again, Eli catching him, Eli winding up like a shot-putter, the muscles of his right side standing out in startling relief, Eli slowly extending his arm in a wonderfully fluid way, reaching forward as though he meant to rap Timothy on the back but instead gently and smoothly driving the stone skull against Timothy's more fragile one, Timothy crumpling, dropping, lying still. Again. Again. Again. The chase, the assault, the impact, in a magic newsreel of the mind. Intersecting these pictures came other familiar images of mortality, drifting like phantom overlays of gauze: the astonished face of Lee Harvey Oswald as Jack Ruby approaches him, the rumpled form of Bobby Kennedy on the kitchen floor, the severed heads of Mishima and his companion neatly resting back of the general's desk, the Roman soldier prodding the figure on the Cross with his spear, the gaudy mushroom unfolding over Hiroshima. And again Eli, again the trajectory of the antique blunt object, again the impact. Stop-time. The poetry of termination. I stumbled and nearly fell, and the beauty of those images sustained me, flooding my cracking joints and bursting muscles with new strength, so that I remained upright, a plodding diligent pallbearer, lurching over the crumbling alkaline earth. As by living we daily die, so then by dying we shall forever live.

"We have reached the place," said Frater Antony.

Was this a graveyard? I saw no tombstones, no markers of any kind. The low leathery-leaved gray plants of the thirsty wasteland grew in random splotches on an empty field. I looked more closely then, perceiving things with the strange tripped-out intensity of exhaustion, and noticed certain irregularities in the terrain, a patch here that seemed sunken by a few inches, a patch there that looked to be elevated above the rest, as though there had indeed been some disturbances of the surface. Carefully we lowered Timothy. When we put him down my body, relieved, seemed to float; I thought actually I would leave the ground. My limbs trembled and my arms, of their own accord, rose shoulder-high. It was a short respite. Frater Franz handed us the tools and we began to dig the grave. He alone assisted us; the other three Keepers stood apart, like votive statues, motionless, aloof. The soil was coarse and soft, perhaps having had all the cohesion baked out of it by ten million years of Arizona sun. We dug like slaves, like ants, like machines, thrust and heave, thrust and heave, thrust and heave, each of us making his own little pit and then joining the three pits. Occasionally we intruded on someone else's work area; once Eli nearly speared my bare foot with his pick. But we got the job done. At length a rough trench, perhaps seven feet long, three feet wide, four feet deep, lay open before us. "It is sufficient," said Frater Franz. Gasping, sweat-shiny, dizzied, we threw down our tools and stepped back. I was at the edge of exhaustion and could barely remain standing. An attack of dry heaves threatened me; I fought it and converted it, absurdly, into hiccups. Frater Antony said, "Place the dead man in the ground." Just like that? No coffin, no covering at all? Dirt in the face? Dust to dust? It seemed that way. We found a final reservoir of energy and lifted Timothy, swung him out over our excavation, eased him down. He lay on his back, the ruined head cradled on soft earth, the eyes—did they show a look of surprise?— staring up at us. Eli reached in, closed the eyes, turned Timothy's head slightly to the side, a position more like that of sleep, a more comfortable way to spend one's eternal rest. The four Keepers now took up stations at the four corners of the grave. Fraters Miklos, Franz, and Javier put their hands to their pendants and bowed their heads. Frater Antony, staring straight ahead, recited a brief service in that liquid, unintelligible language that the fraters use when talking to the priestesses (Aztec? Atlantean? The Cro-Magnon *muttersprach?*), and, switching to Latin for the final phrases, spoke something which Eli told me later, confirming my own guess, was the text of the Ninth Mystery. Then he gestured to Eli and me to fill the grave. We seized our shovels and flung dirt. Farewell, Timothy! Golden scion of the Wasps, heir to eight generations of careful breeding! Who will have your trust funds, who will carry the family name onward? Dust to dust. A thin layer of Arizona sand now covering the burly frame. Like robots we toil, Timothy, and you disappear from view. As it was ordained in the beginning. As it was written in the Book of Skulls ten thousand years ago.

"All regular activities are canceled this day," said Frater Antony when the grave was filled and the earth had been tamped down. "We will spend today in meditation, taking no meals, devoting ourselves to a contemplation of the Mysteries." But there was more work for us before our contemplations could begin. We returned to the House of Skulls, intending first of all to bathe, and discovered Frater Leon and Frater Bernard in the hall outside Oliver's room. Their faces were masks. They pointed within. Oliver lay sprawled face-up across his cot. Evidently he had borrowed a kitchen knife, and, surgeon that he never lived to be, he had done an extraordinary job on himself with it, belly and throat, nor had he spared even the traitor between his thighs. The incisions were deep and had been cut by a steady hand: disciplined to the end, rigid Oliver had slaughtered himself with a characteristic adherence to methodology. I could no more have endured finishing such a project, once I had begun it, than I could walk on moonbeams, but Oliver always had had unusual powers of concentration. We studied the results in a curiously dispassionate way. I have many squeamish attitudes, and so does Eli, but on this day of the Ninth Mystery's fulfillment all such weaknesses were purged from me. "There is one among thee," said Frater Antony, "who has relinquished eternity for his brothers of the four-sided figure, so that they may come to comprehend the meaning of self-denial." Yes. And so we staggered to the burial place a second time. And afterward, for my sins, I scrubbed the thick clotted stains from the room that had been Oliver's. And finally I bathed, and sat alone in my room, examining in my mind the Mysteries of the Skull.

forty-two

eli

Summer lies heavy on the land. The sky throbs with stupefying heat. All seems predetermined and properly ordered. Timothy sleeps. Oliver sleeps. Ned and I remain. In these months we have grown quite strong and our skins are dark from the sun. We live in a kind of waking dream, floating placidly through our daily round of chores and rites. We are not quite full-fledged fraters yet, but our time of Trial is nearing its end. Two weeks after that day of gravedigging I mastered the ritual of the three women and since then I have had no difficulties in absorbing any lesson the fraters would teach me.

The days flow together. We stand outside time here. Was it April when we came first to the fraters? Of what year, and what year is this? A waking dream, a waking dream. I feel sometimes that Oliver and Timothy are figures in another dream, one that I had long ago. I have begun to forget the details of their faces. Blond hair, blue eyes, yes, but then what? How were their noses shaped, how prominent were their chins? Their faces fade. Timothy and Oliver are gone, and Ned and I remain. I still remember Timothy's voice, a warm supple bass, well controlled, beautifully modulated, with faintly nasal aristocratic inflections. And Oliver's, a strong clear tenor, the tones hard-edged and firm, the accent neutral, the accentless American of the prairies. To them my gratitude. They died for me.

This morning my faith wavered, only for an instant, but it was a frightening instant; an abyss of uncertainty opened beneath me after so many months of wholehearted assurance, and I saw devils with pitchforks and heard the shrill laughter of Satan. I was coming in from the fields, and I happened to look far across the flat scrubby land to the place where Timothy and Oliver lie, and unexpectedly a thin scratchy voice in my head asked me, *Do you think you've gained anything here? How can you be sure? How certain are you that it's possible to have the thing that you seek?* I knew a moment of awful fear, in which I imagined I stared with red-rimmed eyes into an icy future, seeing myself wither and shrivel and turn to dust in an empty, blasted world. The moment of doubt then left me, as suddenly as it had come. Perhaps it was just a vagrant gust of unfocused discontent, blowing idly across the continent toward the Pacific, that had paused briefly to unsettle me. I was shaken by what I had undergone, and I ran to the house, meaning to find Ned and tell him about it, but by the time I neared his room the episode seemed too ridiculous to share with him. *Do you think you've gained anything here?* How could I have doubted at all? A strange backsliding, Eli.

His door was open. I looked in and saw him sitting slumped, his head in his hands. Somehow he sensed my presence; he looked up quickly, rearranging his face, replacing a transient look of despair or dejection with a carefully bland expression. But his eyes were bright with strain and I thought I saw the glitter of incipient tears.

"You felt it too, then?" I asked.

"Felt what?" Almost defiantly.

"Nothing. Nothing." An airy shrug. *How can you be sure?* We were playing games with one another, pretending. But doubt was general that morning. An infection running through both of us. *How certain are you that it's possible to have the thing that you seek?* I felt a wall rising between him and me, preventing me from telling him of the fears I had felt, or from asking him why he had seemed so distraught. I left him and went to my room to bathe, and afterward to breakfast. Ned and I sat together but said little. Our morning session with Frater Antony was due to follow, but I felt somehow that I should not go, and when I had eaten I returned instead to my room. *Do you think you've gained anything here?* In confusion I knelt before the great mosaic-work skull-mask on my wall, staring at it with unblinking eyes, letting myself absorb it, compelling the myriad tiny bits of obsidian and turquoise, of jade and shell, to melt and flow and change, until that skull put on flesh for me and I saw a face over the gaunt bones, another face, another, a whole series of faces, a flickering, ever-shifting array of faces. Now I saw Timothy, and now the mask put on the finer features of Oliver, and now I saw my father, who swiftly was transformed into my mother. *How can you be sure?* Frater Antony looked down from the wall, speaking to me in an unknown tongue, and became Frater Miklos, murmuring of lost continents and forgotten caves. *How certain are you that it's possible to have the thing that you seek?* Now I saw the slender, timid, big-nosed girl I had loved momentarily in New York, and I had to grope for her name—Mickey? Mickey Bernstein?—and I said, "Hello, I went to Arizona, just as I told you," but she made no reply; I think she had forgotten who I was. She vanished and in her place came the sullen girl in the Oklahoma motel, and then the heavy-breasted succubus who had floated past me that night in Chicago. I heard the shrill laughter again, rising from the abyss, and wondered if I would have another of those moments of devastating doubt. *Do you think you've gained anything here?* Suddenly Dr. Nicolescu peered down at me, grayfaced, sad-eyed, shaking his head, accusing me in his mild self-deprecatory way of having treated him unkindly. I made no denials, but neither did I wince nor look away, for my guilt had been taken from me. I kept my weary eyelids open, staring at him until he was gone. *How certain are you that it's possible to have the thing that you seek?* Ned's face came. Timothy's, again. Oliver's. And then my own, the face of Eli himself, the prime instigator of the journey, the feckless leader of the Receptacle. *Do you think you've gained anything here?* I studied my face, deplored its flaws, seized control of it, retrogressed it to plump pasty-faced boyhood—then brought it forward in time again to the present, to the new and unfamiliar Eli of the House of Skulls, and went beyond that Eli to another I had never seen before, an Eli to come, timeless, stolid, phlegmatic, an Eli-turned-frater, a face of fine leather, a face of stone. As I examined that Eli I heard the Adversary insistently asking His question: *How can you be sure? How can you be sure? How can you be sure?* He asked it over and over, hammering me with it, until all echoes blurred into a single formless rumbling boom, and I was without answer for Him and found myself alone on a dark polar plateau, clawing at a universe whose gods had fled, thinking, I have shed the blood of my friends, and for what? And for what? For *this?* But then strength returned to me, and I shouted my answer into His booming derisions, crying out that I fell back upon my faith, I was sure because I was sure. "I believe! I believe! I deny You Your victory!" And showed myself my own image striding through the shining streets of distant tomorrows, treading the sands of alien worlds, an eternal Eli embracing the torrent of years. And I laughed, and He laughed also, and His laughter drowned mine, but my faith would not waver and at last He fell still, allowing me to laugh last.

Then I found myself sitting, hoarse-throated and trembling, before the familiar mosaic mask. There were no more metamorphoses. The time of visions was over. I gave the mask a wary glance but it remained as it was. Very well. I searched my soul and found no residue of doubt in it; that final conflagration had burned all those late-lingering impurities away. Very well. Rising, I left my room and walked quickly down the hall, into that part of the building where bare beams alone stand forth against the open sky. Looking up, I saw a huge hawk circling far above me, dark against the fierce blank blueness. Hawk, you will die, and I will live. Of this I have no doubt. I turned the corner and came to the room where our meetings with Frater Antony are held. The frater and Ned were already there, but evidently they had waited for me; for the frater's pendant still hung around his neck. Ned smiled at me and Frater Antony nodded. *I understand,* they appeared to be saying. *I understand. These storms will come.* I knelt beside Ned. Frater Antony removed his pendant and placed the tiny jade skull on the floor before us. *Life eternal we offer thee.* "Let us turn the interior vision upon the symbol we see here," said Frater Antony gently. Yes. Yes. Joyously, expectantly, undoubtingly, I gave myself anew to the Skull and its Keepers.

Robert Silverberg was born in 1935. He began to write while studying for his BA. By 1956 he was publishing prolifically and he was given the Hugo Award for Most Promising New Author in that year. For the next three years Silverberg turned out short stories under numerous pseudonyms for *Amazing Stories, Fantastic, Science Fiction Adventures* and *Super-Science Fiction.* While continuing a prodigious output of SF novels (usually re-written short stories), Silverberg branched out into non fiction during the 60's with such titles as *The Golden Dream* (1967) and *Mound-Builders of Ancient America* (1968). In the late 60's Silverberg started writing more stylized and intense work, such as *Thorns* (1967), *The Man in the Maze* (1969). *A Time of Changes* (1971) won the Nebula Award, as did several of his novellas. He was awarded a Hugo in 1969 for the novella 'Nightwings' which was later expanded into a novel of the same name. Having written solidly for so long, Silverberg quit for four years after *Shadrach in the Furnace* (1976), disenchanted and exhausted. He resumed his work with *Lord Valentine's Castle* (1980) and has continued to write ever since. Throughout his career he has also contributed to the field of SF with the many original anthologies he has compiled. The most highly regarded of these was *New Dimensions*, which ran to 12 volumes, finally finishing in 1981.